searching for justice

redwood coast rescue, book 3

Tonya Burrows

part one
hate

From the deepest desires often come the deadliest hate.
— Socrates

chapter **one**

"SO, I'VE BEEN THINKING…"

Elbow deep in suds, Rose Galasso lifted her gaze from the sink where she had been washing beer steins and watched her slightly tipsy aunt slide onto one of the bar stools. Rainbow Rodriguez met her girlfriends for drinks at the Mad Dog Pub every Tuesday night, and she always drank too much, then hung out until her partner, Rose's chef, Marcel Dupont, closed the kitchen. But the kitchen had closed an hour ago, and Marcel had left alone, so the pair were either fighting or Rainbow was up to something.

Going by her speculative tone, it was the latter. "Scheming is more like it."

"Me, scheme? Never!" Rainbow was as colorful as her name suggested, with big dark eyes and an explosion of dyed red hair that spiraled out from her head in tight corkscrews. She often adorned her curls with beads and feathers and wore so many bracelets it was impossible for her to move quietly.

And, yes, Rainbow was her given name. They were from a long line of proud granola-crunching hippies, and while Rose had shied away from that lifestyle as a teenager, both her aunt and mom had embraced it. It was how she ended up with a name like Ambrosia Wildflower Galasso. She'd always hated it and, as soon as she entered middle school, started insisting she be called simply Rose.

She dried her hands and turned to face the woman who had raised her through those awful, angsty teenage years. "You're always scheming, Auntie. It's one thing I love about you."

"Well, not this time." Rainbow propped her elbows on the bar, her many bracelets clinking as she leaned over. "I've just had this thought that won't leave my head. What if that Jane Doe uncovered by the wildfire last fall is your mom? You should go to the sheriff's office and offer a DNA sample for comparison. I could go do it, but I read the results are more accurate with a sample from a child than a sibling."

Rose sighed. She supposed she should've seen this coming. Since the discovery of the unknown woman's remains, the town's rumor mill had been churning double-time about her identity. Some people said she must have been a lost hiker, while others claimed her death was drug-related because she was found on Murder Mountain. The conspiracy theorists posited she was a victim of The Shadow Stalker—the urban legend serial killer that children had been scaring each other with for decades, who was about as real as the Hookman or Sasquatch.

But whoever the woman was, Rose doubted she was Harmony Galasso.

"The sheriff won't reopen Mom's case. As far as the state of California is concerned, they got her killer: my dad."

Her aunt's cupid-bow lips dipped into a frown. "Have you seen him recently?"

"It's been a couple of weeks. The pub was slammed last week, and I couldn't get away to visit, but he called yesterday. I plan to go out tomorrow."

"How's he doing?"

She raised a shoulder. "You know, it's prison. Same old, same old. They do have him working in the library, though, which means he's in his happy place. Surrounded by books."

Rainbow exhaled a pent-up breath. "Oh, I should go visit."

"He'd like that."

"I know, but it just ... it makes me so sad to see Pete in there. He loved your mother, despite all of her many faults. He would've killed himself a thousand times over before harming a hair on her head. But they convicted him without a body, so if we can prove the Jane Doe is Harmony, Sheriff Rawlings will have no choice but to reopen the case, and maybe your dad will win an appeal."

Rose shook her head. "Even if we proved it, there's no guarantee the sheriff will listen. And even if he does, the chances of Dad getting an appeal are slim to none. He's been in there for thirteen years."

Rainbow's expression softened. "I know it's a long shot, but we have to try. We can't just give up on finding out what happened to Harmony or getting justice for Pete."

"I just don't know if I can handle the disappointment if it doesn't pan out again."

"Hey, I understand," Rainbow said, placing a comforting hand on her arm. "And you need to focus on taking care of yourself. You've been so caught up in work, you're neglecting your own well-being. This place doesn't have to be your life."

Rose scanned her pub with its eclectic mix of booths and high-top tables. Vintage dog posters decorated the walls, along with framed photos of many of her patrons' dogs. The brick fireplace was quiet and cold now but had been crackling merrily earlier in the evening to ward off the damp February chill. She'd made some updates since taking over five years ago, but the deep burgundy upholstery on the chairs was showing wear from their many years of use. She couldn't bear to change them, though. Her dad had chosen those chairs back when he owned the pub. Back when her mom was alive, and their lives were still perfect.

She looked at her aunt. "But I love this place."

"Of course you do, but you also need to find balance in your life. Take a day off, go for a hike, and do something that makes you happy."

Her gaze landed on a picture of her dad. Back then, Pete had a full head of dark hair that he wore in a long tail down his back. He wore his favorite tie-dye Grateful Dead t-shirt, shorts, and his ever-present flip-flops as he held her up on his shoulders while he slung drinks to his customers. He'd been happiest behind this bar. At one time, so had she, but lately, it felt more and more like work.

"Well ... maybe I do need a break. A hike isn't a bad idea."

"Good. It's supposed to be beautiful tomorrow. Don't open and instead go soak up some nature vibes." Rainbow gave one decisive nod, then grinned sloppily. "And who knows? Maybe on that hike, you'll stumble onto a clue that will help crack your mom's case wide open."

Rose laughed. "You really are optimistically delusional, aren't you?"

"Hey, it's better than being pessimistically realistic."

Rose turned to put away the clean beer steins and tried to ignore the anxiety swirling in her stomach. The possibility of finding her mother's remains after all these years was both exhilarating and terrifying. She had been searching for answers since she was a teenager. What would she do when she finally had them? Could her dad get a new trial? But what if the Jane Doe wasn't Mom? She didn't want to get her hopes up. Or, worse, what if she was Mom and the evidence only proved that Dad was guilty?

Throat suddenly dry, Rose grabbed a bottle of water from the mini-fridge under the bar and twisted off the cap. The cool liquid soothed the heat of her nerves. Maybe Rainbow was right about more than her needing a day off. Maybe it was time to confront the past and try to find some sort of closure.

"Okay, I'll do it," she said, setting down her water with a decisive thunk. "I'll give a DNA sample."

Rainbow beamed at her. "That's my girl. We'll go to the sheriff's office after your hike tomorrow and sort this out once and for all."

Rose scoffed. "I doubt that. Our esteemed sheriff is a fuckwit."

"Well, even fuckwits can surprise you sometimes. And at least he's dedicated to his job, unlike that lazy-ass Jerry Tennison. Janine Roberts—remember her? She's the sheriff's secretary and says he has case files stacked this high on his desk." She lifted her hand up over her head, obviously exaggerating the height. The movement threw off her equilibrium, and she nearly fell off her stool. She righted herself with a giggle. "Who knows, maybe he'll even find a chill pill buried in there somewhere. If not, I can always recommend the best indica strains for stress relief."

Rose chuckled, shaking her head at the ridiculous mental image of the sheriff smoking a joint. "Could you imagine Ash Rawlings stoned? I'd pay to see that just once."

"I don't have to imagine. I saw it plenty when he was a teenager. He was quite the hell-raiser back in his day with Zak Hendricks and Donovan Scott. The Terrible Trio. They were my biggest customers for a while, and that was before cannabis was legal for recreational use."

Rainbow had a legal marijuana farm on Mt. Humboldt and ran the town's only dispensary, but Rose couldn't picture the sheriff as one of her customers. It was like imagining Hitler as a baby—just wrong.

"Okay, now Zak and Donovan, I believe. Those two are still hell-raisers. But you're telling me uptight, by-the-book

Sheriff Ashley Rawlings the Third didn't always have a stick up his ass?"

"That's exactly what I'm telling you." Rainbow grinned and laced her fingers together under her chin. She was in her gossip queen element right now. "He was the worst of them because he was spoiled rotten as the heir to the Rawlings empire. He could've gotten away with murder back then and nobody would've batted an eye."

Rose didn't think it was possible, but she disliked the man even more now. "What a hypocrite."

A thoughtful expression crossed Rainbow's face. "I think something happened that scared him straight." She held up a hand to stop Rose's next question. "And before you ask, I don't know what it was. Which is crazy, yes, because I always know what's going on around this town. But right around the time he turned twenty, he stopped the hell-raising and joined the Sheriff's Department. Shocked the ever-loving hell out of everyone, even his parents. Lee—his dad, the second Ashley Rawlings—wanted him to take over the ranch, but he was adamant about becoming a cop. Maybe it was that whole mess with Donovan being accused of murder? That happened around the same time." She finished her drink and nudged it across the bar. "I just don't know. Wish I did. Whatever happened, bet it's juicy."

"Refill?"

"Isn't it closing time?"

Rose scanned the mostly empty bar. The kitchen had closed when Marcel left, but one guy still sat in the back corner, picking at a cold plate of fries while he scrolled on his phone. He had barely touched his beer. Whatever he was doing on that phone must be very important or extremely fascinating because nobody could resist Marcel's parmesan fries, and her prize-winning Mad Dog Ale brought people in from all over the state.

She walked over to the end of the bar and rang the bell hanging there for last call. The man didn't even look up. She shrugged and returned to her aunt. "One more?"

Rainbow squinted one eye at her, then groaned. "The room's tilting. I'd better take water."

"Coming up. You're not driving, are you?"

"No, I'm walking to Marcel's."

"Ah, so you just stayed behind to ambush me about the DNA."

"I don't ambush."

"Uh-huh." As she took the empty glass and filled a fresh one with water, Rainbow leaned in and lowered her voice conspiratorially.

"Speaking of Marcel, have I told you about the hot new guy that's been coming into my store?"

"Another ambush. Two in one night. You're on a roll."

"I don't ambush! I..." She rolled her hand in the air, searching for the right words, and her bangles clinked together. "Nudge you gently in the right direction."

"Well, that gentle nudge was a sloppy segue, Auntie. Marcel is a big teddy bear, but he isn't hot. He's too hairy."

"Says you. I like my men looking like Sasquatch. I love running my hands through all that chest hair after we—"

"Ew. No, I don't want to hear it."

Rainbow grinned wickedly. "Then let me tell you about the hot new guy coming into my store."

Rose rolled her eyes, but a smile tugged at her lips. "Are you trying to set me up again?"

"What? No, of course not." The mischievous glint in Rainbow's eyes belied her words. "When have I ever tried to set you up?"

"Carlos. John. Warren. Jason. Mike." She ticked them each off on her fingers. "And what about Wesley, the convicted felon? Remember him?"

Rainbow winced. "I'll admit I misjudged Wesley's character."

"No offense, Auntie, but other than Marcel, you have horrible taste in men. And, honestly, the guys who frequent your store are not my type."

"Okay, so I was mistaken all those other times, but this guy is totally your type. He's a horror writer. He's not a pothead—he only comes in for CBD oil to help with an old injury. And did I mention he's hot? Like..." She fanned herself. "Hot, hot. He's asked about you, too. I guess he's been in here before and was bowled over by your beauty."

"Oh, please."

"He asked if you were single."

"Of course he did." Rose wasn't unaware of her beauty or that most men found her sexy. She heard it from drunk tourists every night during the summer months, and during the slower winter months, she still got it from the dumb local kids who frequented the pub on weekends. And she was not above weaponizing her looks, wearing tight clothes that showed off her figure and applying careful makeup every night to enhance her best features—the bright blue eyes she inherited from her dad, the sharp cheekbones she inherited from a Yurok great-grandmother on her mom's side, and the full, pouty lips she got from who knew where. She learned from the moment she stepped behind a bar, the sexier she looked, the better the tips. It was always startling when a night passed without a man attempting to sweep her away to his bed.

Though having one of those guys approach her aunt outside the pub was a first. She had to admit that intrigued her. "And what did you tell him?"

"I said that was none of his business," Rainbow replied, grinning. "But then he said he knows I'm your aunt and asked my permission to ask you out."

"How very Victorian of him."

"I may have said yes."

Rose groaned. "I'm not in the mood for dating right now."

"Understandable," Rainbow said with a nod. "But just keep it in mind. He's a nice guy. It doesn't have to be anything serious. I don't even think he's here long term. He's renting the Hendricks family's old cabin on Bluff Road while he finishes his next book, so he'll probably be gone by the end of summer. It couldn't hurt to get out and have some fun. Like I said, you spend entirely too much time in this bar." She pushed up from her stool. "Do you need help closing up?"

Rose glanced toward the man in the corner booth again. The weirdo still hadn't looked up from his phone. "No, you go on home. I have it covered."

Rainbow gave her a long hug and a kiss on the cheek. "You sure?"

"Yeah, I'll be fine. Go home and get some rest. Drink some more water. You're going to regret all of that sangria in the morning."

"Oh, don't I know it. Call me if you need anything, okay?"

"I will. Thanks, Auntie."

Rainbow grabbed her bag and headed to the door, giving one last wave before disappearing into the night. Thankfully, Marcel only lived a few blocks away. She'd give it ten minutes, then call him to make sure Rainbow got there safely.

She took a deep breath and returned to the bar, assessing what needed to be done. A few empty glasses scattered the tables and the other end of the long, u-shaped bar. She grabbed a bus bin and collected them, wiping down surfaces as she went. As she made her way to the back corner, she noticed the man was still on his phone, but now he was muttering to himself.

"Excuse me?" she said.

He didn't move. Didn't acknowledge her.

Weird.

Maybe he was wearing headphones she couldn't see under his beanie cap.

She waved a hand in front of him, trying to get his attention. "Sir? We're closed."

The man gazed up, his eyes bloodshot and unfocused.

Rose backed up a subtle step, not liking the look of him. A chill raised goosebumps on her arms. "Are you okay?"

"Are you Ambrosia Galasso?"

Her heart rate spiked. No one had called her by her full name in years. "Who's asking?"

The man's face twisted in anger. "Answer the damn question. Are you Ambrosia Galasso? Yes or no?"

"I don't see how that's any of your business," she replied, keeping her voice cool and steady despite her thundering heart. "We're closed. You need to leave."

The man stood. He was rail thin but towered over her. "Answer me!"

Dammit, she shouldn't have let Rainbow leave. There was power in numbers, and this guy had obviously been biding his time until she was alone.

Stupid.

She took another step back. She kept the baseball bat behind the bar for when her clientele got too rowdy, but it was on the other side of the room. "Yes, I'm Ambrosia Galasso. Now leave, or I'll call the police."

The man's lips twisted into a sneer. He pulled out a knife, the blade glinting in the dim light. "Someone wants to meet you." He motioned toward the door. "Let's go."

Like hell.

She took another step back toward the bar. "I'm not going anywhere with you."

The man lunged forward, the knife coming too close to her face for comfort. "Don't make this difficult."

Okay, she was done with subtlety. She turned and sprinted for the bar. Grabbed the baseball bat and swung with all her strength as he gave chase, hitting him in the shoulder. He crashed into the shelves, sending bottles of booze shattering to the floor. He dropped the knife and cursed, clutching at his arm. She grabbed her phone and dialed 911, keeping her eyes on the man.

"911, what's your emergency?" The operator's voice was calm and professional.

"There's a man with—" Something hit her upside the head and shattered, raining glass and alcohol down on her. She stumbled and fell to the ground. Her vision swam as she watched the Johnnie Walker King George V bottle fall to the floor in pieces. Blood drizzled down her face, but she didn't know if she was seeing red because of it or the rage that exploded inside her.

This fucker came in here, threatened her with a knife, busted up hundreds of dollars of liquor, and then broke a special edition, five hundred dollar bottle of scotch...

Over. Her. Head.

She grabbed the bat with both hands and, with a shout of pure rage, surged to her feet, swinging again, aiming for his head. He ducked and lunged at her middle, shoving her into the bar. Pain flared through her side as her ribs cracked against the bar rail, but she ignored it and kicked out, hitting him in the shin and causing him to stumble.

It was the distraction she needed.

She broke free from his grasp and made a run for the door, her head throbbing with each step. Bile surged up her throat, but she couldn't take the time to be sick. She had to get outside. She was at the edge of town but close enough that someone had to be awake nearby to hear her screams for help. The man cursed behind her, but she didn't dare look back to see if he was giving chase.

She burst out into the cool night air and saw a car idling at the curb, its headlights glaring. For one hopeful moment, she thought she was safe. It had to be Marcel picking up Rainbow, or maybe some passerby who heard the ruckus in the bar...

She shielded her eyes against the headlights with one hand and waved at the shadows inside the car with her other. "Help!"

A man climbed out of the driver's seat and stared impassively over the door.

No, this wasn't someone here to help. This was the person the skinny man inside wanted her to "meet."

The skinny man caught up. He blocked her path and grabbed her by the arm, propelling her forward. "Get in the damn car."

She swung the bat at him again, but a powerful hand caught it and ripped it from her grasp. Through the stream of blood clouding her vision, she saw the man from the car, and he was wearing a mask with a white skull painted over his nose and mouth. He raised the bat.

She lifted her arms to cover her head. "If you want money, take whatever's in the register. It's yours. I don't care."

His lips curled into a smile under the mask as he swung. Pain burst in a white explosion behind her eyes, and she collapsed to the ground, losing the fight to keep her dinner down. She retched until her ribs ached and her head spun, and she heard him laughing softly as he approached her. She tried to crawl away, but her limbs weren't cooperating. He shoved her over with his boot and stared down with cold eyes.

"Please... don't..."

The last thing she remembered before the darkness claimed her was the man's hand closing around her throat.

chapter
two

"YOU HAVE A SERIAL KILLER, SHERIFF RAWLINGS."

Ash Rawlings looked up from his computer as Alexis Summers burst into his office with his flustered secretary, Janine, hot on her heels. He closed his eyes for a moment against his nearly constant headache and pinched the bridge of his nose.

"I'm so sorry, Ash," Janine said. "I tried to—"

He sighed and waved his secretary away. "It's fine." He'd put off the true crime podcaster for months, but it was time to deal with her meddling. "Hello, Ms. Summers. I didn't know you were back in town."

"I'm staying until I get some answers." Alexis drew a thick binder from the oversized bag on her shoulder and slapped it down on his desk, which was already overflowing with old cases he'd pulled for review. A stack of the files fell to the floor. He watched it happen, watched them slide and scatter, but couldn't find the energy to care. He'd been working eighty-plus hours a week and pulling all-nighters almost every night for months.

He shifted his gaze back to the podcaster. "What answers?"

"You have a serial killer who has been using your county as his hunting grounds for over twenty-five years," she said point-blank.

He groaned inwardly. Of course she'd latch on to that urban legend. A serial killer on the loose would make for an interesting podcast and better ratings. Forget that he was already inundated with "boring" crimes to solve, and his department was still dealing with the aftermath of the wildfire that had ripped through the county last fall. "Do you have proof?"

She pointed to the binder. "Thirty-three women, all murdered or missing since 1998. That's too many for a county of less than one hundred thousand people."

"Ms. Summers, we're a big county with a small population and lots of places to hide. Many people come here for the sole purpose of disappearing." When she opened her mouth, no doubt to protest, he held up a hand. "Yes, I'll readily admit we have a problem with murder, but that doesn't mean they're all connected."

Alexis leaned forward, her eyes fixed on his. "I've been investigating this for months, Sheriff. Talked to families, friends, witnesses. I've looked at crime scene photos, medical examiner reports, and police reports. There's a pattern here, a clear one. These women fit a specific profile: young, vulnerable, and alone. They were runaways, drug addicts, or sex workers. And all of them were last seen in this county before they disappeared. Including the Jane Doe uncovered on the mountain in the fire debris. I believe she might have been the first victim."

Ash rubbed his eyes. He couldn't just drop everything and chase after a theory, no matter how compelling. He had a department to run and fifteen years' worth of cases to review since the previous sheriff had turned out to be a corrupt asshole. "What exactly do you expect me to do with this information?"

"Investigate," she said with exasperation. "You honestly don't think it's weird that so many people—so many *women*—have disappeared here?"

She was right, dammit. Probably not about there being a serial killer at work, but the number of people going missing around here was an enormous problem. He'd been so focused on putting out fires for the last six months—literally and figuratively—that he'd let too many other cases fall through the cracks. He'd let down too many victims and their families. He was supposed to protect his people, and he was failing. It was unacceptable. And that knowledge fucking hurt.

But he wasn't about to let the podcaster know that.

He kept his face impassive and gave her his standard press conference spiel. "We are investigating all open cases, Ms. Summers. We're also reviewing all the closed and cold cases from the previous administration to ensure those investigations were handled correctly. If you go on your podcast and start talking about a serial killer—"

She huffed out a breath that fluttered her honey-blond hair. "Look, Sheriff. I know what you think of me, but I'm not looking to make headlines here. I don't want to get famous over other people's misfortune. My only goal is to give voice to victims who can't speak for themselves."

He stared at her for a stony beat. "Like Darcy Cantrell?"

She pressed her lips into a grim line. "That was ... unfortunate. But Darcy's case wouldn't have been solved at all without my podcast drawing your attention to the problems with the initial investigation."

"You accused my friend of murder."

"No, I never once accused Donovan Scott of anything. The former sheriff did that, and I simply stated the facts of the investigation as I understood them. But if you had listened to any of the episodes, you'd know I also pointed out inconsistencies and inaccuracies whenever I saw them. I always made sure to mention that Mr. Scott had faced no charges, and that you didn't consider him a suspect."

"You almost ruined his life. He was innocent, but people were signing petitions to have him tossed in jail. They called here nonstop, clogging up the phone lines, demanding I arrest him. They threatened me, my deputies, Donovan, and anyone close to him. All because of your podcast."

"I'm—" Her voice broke, and she glanced away. It was only for a second, but he saw the deep regret in the movement and softened a little toward her. After all, she was just doing her job, same as him. He didn't like her job or agree with it, but he couldn't fault her for wanting to do it to the best of her abilities, and the evidence, as flimsy as it was, had all pointed at Donovan.

"I'm sorry about that," she said finally. "I truly am. That was never my intention. I simply wanted Darcy found—just like I want these other women found. You have to admit, thirty-three women in twenty-five years is a lot for one rural county. Something else is going on here, and I want to find out what it is."

"Why? You're not from here. You have no ties to this community or even this state. So, why do you care so much?"

She blinked in surprise. "Because..." She seemed to search for the right words. "Nobody else cares."

Her words hit a nerve. Frustration and guilt twisted into a knot in his chest. "Accusing me of not caring about what happens in my community isn't the way to get my help."

"I-I didn't mean you specifically, Sheriff. Just—"

"Listen to me closely, Ms. Summers." Ash planted his hands on his desk and slowly rose to his feet. "You are not a law enforcement officer. You will not investigate these disappearances, and if you try, I will arrest you for obstruction of justice. If you're right and there is someone in my county killing women, it's too dangerous for you to go poking around. I'd rather see you in a jail cell than up on my case board, understand?"

She stayed silent.

"Do. You. Understand?"

She growled softly in frustration. "Okay, fine. I won't investigate—as long as *you* will. You can have all of my research." She slid the binder toward him, her expression intense but sincere. "This is your chance to bring justice to families who have been waiting for years. And to stop this serial killer from taking any more lives."

He stared at her. "You can't keep going around saying there's a serial killer. People will get scared and then angry. It will cause chaos."

She didn't squirm, didn't flinch. She just stared back, her chin jutting mulishly.

Jesus. She reminded him of his sister. Anna got that same expression when she wanted something. And if Alexis Summers was anything like his twin, he would not win this battle.

Finally, he exhaled hard and rubbed a hand over his beard before reaching for the binder. "Okay. I'll look at your research, Ms. Summers. But I can't promise anything."

She nodded, satisfaction glimmering in her eyes. "That's all I ask, Sheriff. Just don't dismiss this outright. Lives are at stake."

With that, she walked out of his office, leaving Janine, who was still hovering in the hallway outside the door, to scurry in her wake.

Great.

Janine was an excellent administrative assistant, but she was also one of the town's biggest gossips. Rumors of a serial killer in town would hit Roger's Market within an hour and The Grove by dinnertime.

This was going to be a clusterfuck.

"I don't want to hear a word about this on your podcast," he called.

Alexis Summers didn't respond. He hadn't expected her to, but fully expected her to ignore the command.

Ash stared at the binder on his desk for a long moment, then pulled up Jane Doe's case file on his computer. The fire had badly damaged the remains, but a forensic anthropologist in San Francisco determined the skeleton belonged to a female in her mid-to-late twenties who had given birth at least once and had Hispanic and/or Native American ancestry. Jane Doe had a surgical plate placed to fix a break in her wrist prior to her death, but corrosion had eroded the serial number. Radio-carbon dating suggested she likely died ten to twenty years ago, and there was no obvious cause of death. Her hyoid bone was fractured, possibly indicating strangulation, but it was impossible to say whether that happened at the time of death or if it was damaged later. A partial DNA profile was obtained but matched nothing on file.

He opened Alexis Summers' binder to the first victim she had listed: a twenty-two-year-old Native American woman named Maria Ayunli Socktish, who disappeared in June 1998. The age, timeline, and ancestry all aligned with his Jane Doe. Maria had a four-year-old son, but he was taken away from her in 1997 because of her struggles with substance abuse. At the time of her disappearance, she was trying to get him back. She was reported missing when she didn't show up for a custody hearing. So, another similarity—Jane Doe was likely also a mother. Nothing indicated Maria had ever broken her wrist, but she could have been treated at a reservation clinic, where medical records were often lost or incomplete. He'd have to check on that.

A sense of dread settled heavily in Ash's stomach. He couldn't ignore this, even if he wanted to. He had a responsibility to the people of his county to keep them safe, and that meant looking into every lead, no matter how far-fetched it might seem. And if there was even a slight chance that a serial killer was snatching women, he needed to find out who it was and stop them before anyone else got hurt.

He took a deep breath and flipped through the binder. Alexis was thorough. He had to give her that. She had pages and pages of detailed notes, witness statements, and even crime scene photos.

"Fuck," he whispered and gazed up at the county map on his wall. Binder in hand, he grabbed a box of pushpins from his desk drawer and walked over to the map, marking the locations of each disappearance. They scattered the county, but there was a heavy concentration around Mt. Humboldt to the northeast—right where they had found Jane Doe in the fire debris.

In the middle of the Emerald Triangle, locals called Mt. Humboldt "Murder Mountain"—a moniker he'd always thought was tongue-in-cheek because it was a place of outlaws and backwoods justice. While many people went missing up there, it was usually because they wanted to disappear. There was an untold number of marijuana farms on the mountain and in the surrounding hills, both legal and illegal, and the outfits often hired transient workers— "trimmigrants"—to trim the buds. Most of the people reported missing eventually came off the mountain and returned to their lives.

But these thirty-three women had stayed gone. They ranged from age sixteen to twenty-four, were all Native American or Hispanic, or looked like they could be with brown skin and long, dark hair. Alexis Summers was right—these weren't just random disappearances. He couldn't deny the pattern. It was there, in black and white, staring him in the face. This was someone preying on vulnerable women, someone who knew the area well and who knew how to stay hidden.

Lost County had a fucking serial killer.

He picked up his phone and dialed his chief deputy sheriff. "Hey, Wright. Get me a list of every single sex offender in the county and their whereabouts for the last twenty-five years. I want it on my desk by the end of the day."

"Yes, sir," Wright replied.

"I'm headed out to the old gas station on Route 10—"

"Why? Did something happen out there? Do you need backup?"

"No. I'm just reviewing an old case and want to see the crime scene in person. I should be back within the hour, but if I'm not, just leave the list on my desk."

"Sure thing, boss."

chapter
three

ASH HUNG UP THE PHONE, tucked the binder under one arm, and grabbed his jacket. He needed to get out from behind the desk before his ass started growing roots in the chair, so he might as well check Alexis' research. He stopped in the records office and put in a request for Maria Socktish's case file. It was before the former sheriff's time, so he hadn't pulled it for review—Tennison was only a deputy in '98—but now he wanted a look. Had Tennison been involved in this case, too? If so, did Ash have to pull everything the man touched during his nearly forty-year law enforcement career rather than just the cases he handled as sheriff?

The idea was daunting. His desk was already piled chest-deep with cases for review.

Since Ash hadn't found the Socktish case in the computer's database, her file must still be on paper. The department was digitizing old cases, but the process was laborious. Hopefully, records would get it back to him faster than their usual sloth pace.

That done, he drove north to the last place Maria Socktish had been seen alive. The area was a desolate stretch of highway, too deep into the redwoods to attract tourists. A lone gas station sagged on the side of the road, its two pumps long since dry. Before the state built the highway, this road had been a major trucking route, and this gas station was often used for drug deals and prostitution because it was easy to access but remote enough not to draw unwanted attention. It was a badly kept secret that the owner was always willing to keep his mouth shut for a price. That guy had died years ago, and although the station shut down after the highway opened and rerouted traffic, it was still a hotbed for drugs. The nearby transient camp meant his deputies responded to drug overdose calls out here multiple times a month.

Ash parked his Tahoe and got out, his boots crunching on the gravel. He checked his phone—no signal. He looked around and imagined what it would have been like for Maria to be out here, alone and vulnerable. Trapped by poverty and desperate choices. It made his blood boil.

Had she come out here to buy drugs? Or was she in such a bad situation she'd needed to sell herself to survive?

According to Alexis's research, a couple from Seattle on a road trip stopped at the station to fill their RV on June 12, 1998, and saw Maria talking to a man in a black San Francisco 49ers baseball cap. The couple went inside to use the bathroom and buy some snacks, and when they returned, Maria and the man were nowhere to be seen.

Had the man taken her? Or had she gone willingly?

Ash glanced up and down the road, bringing up a mental map of his county. If someone hiked through the forest from the gas station, it was only a few miles to where Jane Doe's remains had been found.

Could Jane Doe actually be Maria Socktish?

A chill clawed down his spine and raised goosebumps on his arms. The air was cold and damp today and even cooler under the canopy of trees, but with his lined Lost County

Sheriff parka zipped up to his neck, it couldn't account for the chill.

Someone was here, watching him from the cover of the thick forest.

He inched his hand toward the holster at his hip and released his gun. The weight of it was a comfort as he turned toward the gas station.

Movement.

Something big darted through the deepening shadows of evening. Not an animal. It was too early in the year for bears, and deer didn't run on two legs.

Human.

"Sheriff's Office," he called. "Come out with your hands up!"

The person—man? —wasn't even trying to be quiet anymore. He crashed through the underbrush, getting further away with every second Ash hesitated. Way out here, people only ran from the police if they were up to no good. He should know. He, Donovan, and Zak had been on the other side of this equation often enough as teens, with the sheriff hot on their heels due to some act of criminal mischief or another. So, even though whoever was crashing through the trees now probably had nothing to do with Maria Socktish, they also weren't just out for a leisurely hike.

Fuck.

Ash took a step to give chase, but a noise from inside the gas station drew his attention. It sounded like a groan or a soft cry of pain. Was someone injured in there? He edged around the corner of the building, heart pounding as he peeked through the boarded-up window.

There was a lump on the floor under a green fleece blanket. It shifted, and the blanket fell away, exposing a slim, tattooed arm and a hand with bright red nails.

A woman.

"Sheriff's Office!"

No response.

He flattened his palm against the door, surprised when it opened easily. He stepped inside and approached the woman slowly, gun at the ready. She lay with her back to him, unmoving. He knelt beside her and checked for a pulse. Weak, but it was there. He gently shook her shoulder.

"Ma'am? Can you hear me?"

Still no response.

He moved around her to get a better look. Her wrists and ankles were both bound with tape. She was dressed in jeans and a tight black crop top featuring a sneering dog in a fedora. The thorny stem of a rose tattoo stretched across her ribs and peeked out from under the edge of the shirt, and his heart nosedived into his stomach.

He knew that tattoo.

That shirt.

Those dagger-like nails.

Rose Galasso, owner of the Mad Dog Pub, and a massive pain in his ass. She was loud, obnoxious, disdained law enforcement, and always glowered at him like he was a lump of dog shit on the bottom of her high-heeled boots. The feeling was mutual. He couldn't stand her most of the time, but that didn't mean he wanted to see her hurt.

"Rose?" He pushed her black hair back from her face with a hand that trembled ever so slightly, and her head lolled to the side. Her usually golden complexion was too pale, and the red lipstick she always wore was smeared in a ghoulish slash across her faintly blue lips, but she was breathing. He set down his gun and clasped her face in his hands, running his thumbs over her high cheekbones, willing her to open her eyes. Dried blood clumped her hair together in thick, tangled strands. His fingers brushed a fresh wound on the side of her head.

"Rose, can you hear me? C'mon, open your eyes. Wake up and tell me what a bastard I am."

She didn't move.

Swearing under his breath, he let go of her long enough to grab his phone and check the screen again—still no signal.

The forest outside was silent except for the rustling of leaves in the wind. He had to go back to his Tahoe and use the radio to call for help, but he didn't dare leave her alone. As he sat there on his knees, debating, something crashed at the back of the building.

He grabbed his gun and spun toward the sound. A tall figure in a hooded jacket stood at the gas station's back door, his face shrouded in shadow. He had a strange energy about him that had Ash's skin prickling with a warning.

"Hands up," Ash demanded.

The man melted farther back into the shadows.

"Stop moving! Put your hands up!"

The man didn't comply. He just stood there, watching with an eerie calm. That stillness triggered something in his memory, and he lowered his gun a fraction. "Shane?"

Suddenly, the man smiled. He could only see the barest hint of it, a flash of white in the shadows, but it made his blood run cold. It wasn't a friendly smile. It was a smile that screamed of danger and violence.

No, this wasn't Shane Trevisano, the reclusive former SEAL who lived off the land out here. Shane was a weird guy, but he never made Ash's hair stand up on his arms like this.

The man lunged forward, his gloved hand wrapping around Ash's wrist, forcing his gun hand up. Their eyes locked for an instant as each man tried to force the other away. Ash was fast and strong, but his attacker was, too. The man struck out with his elbow, and Ash saw stars as it made contact under his eye.

The man twisted his arm behind his back and shoved him

face-first into the wall. He grunted in pain as his abused cheek-bone scraped the rough surface, and he felt hot breath on his ear as the man leaned close.

"You're not welcome here, Sheriff." The voice was low and menacing. He didn't recognize it. "Better run back to town before you get hurt."

The grip on Ash's arms tightened, and he grunted in pain. The way this guy moved with such fluidity screamed of someone who was trained in combat. He was outnumbered and outmatched, with no backup and no way to call for help. And Rose still lay bound and unconscious on the floor.

He needed a plan, and he needed one fast.

"Who are you?" he asked, trying to buy time.

The man chuckled darkly. "Someone who's been watching you. Watching all of you. And let me tell you, Sheriff, you and your little band of dog lovers are in over your head."

Did he mean Redwood Coast Rescue? Or Anna, Zak, and their girls? "Leave my family out of this."

"Your family?" The words dripped with hatred and bitterness. "Before we're done, I'll rip your fucking family apart, you sanctimonious prick."

The grip on him tightened and anger, hot and bright, overtook his momentary panic. Didn't this fucker know he was in control? He was always in control, even now. He kicked his leg back and made hard contact with the man's shin. Heard a satisfying crack, and the man stumbled back, releasing his grip.

Ash turned around, ready to face the bastard head-on, but the man was already running toward the gas station's exit. His first instinct was to give chase, but he couldn't leave Rose alone. Instead, he rushed to her side, carefully removing the tape that bound her wrists and ankles. She stirred slightly, and he breathed a sigh of relief. She was still alive. He scooped her up in his arms. She was lighter than he expected. She wasn't a big woman, but she was always so formidable during their verbal sparring matches, always larger than life. It seemed wrong for her to be so small and fragile in his arms.

He carried her to his Tahoe, gently laying her across the back seat. He shut the door and jogged to the driver's side, his heart pounding in his chest. He needed to get out of there and call for backup. As he turned the key in the ignition, the man in the hooded jacket stepped out from behind the gas station. Ash gunned the engine and peeled out of the parking lot, his eyes locked on the man in the rearview mirror.

Who the hell was this guy? And why did he have Rose? Was he working alone, or was there a larger threat waiting down the road?

Ash grabbed his radio and filled dispatch in on what happened, then checked his phone again, relieved to see a strong signal. He tapped his sister's name. When she answered, the surge of relief left him lightheaded. Or maybe that was the blow he'd taken to the head. Jesus, his face throbbed.

"Anna, are you with Zak?"

"Uh, no, he's out with Donovan—"

Panic took him in a stranglehold. Zak was combat trained and could protect Anna and the girls if anyone tried for them, but if he wasn't there...

Fuck.

"AJ, go to my office, lock yourself in with the girls, and don't leave until either Zak or I get there."

"Uh, okay." She sounded confused, but at least she wasn't protesting. "Where are you?"

He lifted his gaze to the rearview mirror, checking on Rose in the backseat. "On the way to the hospital. Rose Galasso was attacked."

Anna's voice turned sharp. "What? Is she okay?"

"Unconscious but breathing. I need you and the girls safe

until I get there. And if you see anything suspicious, call 911 and stay inside. Got it?"

"Got it. I'll call Zak and have him come home. You be safe, too, big brother. And keep us updated," Anna added before hanging up.

Ash shoved his phone in his pocket and focused on the road, his grip on the steering wheel white-knuckled. He couldn't shake the feeling that he was being watched, that danger lurked behind every tree, around every bend. He glanced in the rearview mirror again, half-expecting to see the man in the hooded jacket tailing him.

The road was empty.

He gritted his teeth, his grip on the steering wheel tightening until his hands ached. Fuck with him, fine. He could take it. But you didn't mess with his family.

He made it to the hospital in record time, screeching to a stop in front of the emergency entrance. Nurses rushed out with a gurney, and Ash helped them lift Rose onto it. One nurse tried to shoo him away, but he refused to leave. His stomach twisted into a weird knot at the idea that she might not be okay. Who would bitch at him every time he walked into the Mad Dog Pub if she wasn't there? He could admit, if only to himself, that he enjoyed their verbal sparring matches. He always came away from them feeling exhilarated, buzzing with adrenaline like he'd shotgunned multiple energy drinks.

Ash paced the waiting room, guilt eating him alive for not being able to protect Rose. As sheriff, it was his job to maintain safety and order, and he had failed. He let her down and he couldn't stand it.

He called back to his office and found that Zak had arrived to take Anna and the girls home. Zak was pissed. He wanted answers, and Ash had none to give. He'd have to call them later, but for now, he asked Janine to transfer him to his chief deputy, Walter Wright.

"Hey, boss," Wright said. "I put that list of sex offenders on your desk."

Shit.

Had Rose been raped?

The air left his lungs like someone had punched him, and he stopped pacing. Her attacker had been fully dressed, and so had she, but that didn't necessarily mean anything. His hand tightened on his phone until it creaked a protest.

Jesus. He needed to breathe and loosen his grip before he busted the damn thing. And he needed to answer his chief deputy. With considerable effort, he unlocked his jaw. "Yeah. Thanks. Uh, I need deputies and a crime scene unit out at the old gas station on Route 10."

"What happened?" Wright asked. "You okay?"

His face throbbed. He probed his sore left eye and sucked in a sharp breath through his teeth.

Yeah, maybe he shouldn't touch it.

"I'm fine. Rose Galasso was attacked. I found her out there, bound and gagged, and confronted her attacker, but he got away. I'm waiting at the hospital to see if I can get a statement from her. I'll send you a description of the guy. Check local cameras, see if anyone saw him. And send someone to watch my family. I don't want them alone."

"Got it. I'll call you back as soon as I find something."

Ash hung up and sank into a chair, taking deep, even breaths to calm himself. Everyone always thought his sister was the Rawlings with a temper, but that was only because he'd made it his mission to keep a tight lid on his. But right now, he was dangerously close to an eruption. If Rose had been raped, he didn't know how he'd cope with that news. If he was unable to keep the people in his personal orbit safe, he didn't deserve the sheriff's badge.

After what felt like an eternity, the doctor emerged from the ER, her face grave.

Ash's heart sank and his voice came out weirdly hoarse. "Is she okay?"

The doctor sighed. "She's in rough shape."

"What are her injuries?" Before the doctor could throw some bullshit about HIPAA at him, he held up a hand. "You don't have to go into specifics. An overview is all I need to know for the investigation."

The doctor hesitated for several seconds, then relented. "She suffered a concussion from a blow to the head. I pulled shards of glass from the wound, which makes me think the weapon was a bottle of some kind."

"Did you save the shards?"

She nodded.

"I'll need them for testing."

"All right. The patient also sustained a beating on her face and body. She has contusions all over and at least one broken rib. She was heavily drugged with an opiate, almost to the point of overdosing, but we gave her Naloxone and she's breathing on her own now. We'll need to monitor her closely for the next twenty-four hours."

"Rape?"

"No evidence of it, as far as I can tell."

Ash exhaled, surprised at the strength of the relief flooding through him. "Can I see her?"

The doctor nodded. "But only briefly. And Sheriff?" She tapped her cheek below her left eye with one finger. "After you see her, I want to take a look at that."

He waved her off. "It's nothing."

"Your eye is swelling shut."

Huh. That explained why his depth perception was off. "Later."

She led the way to Rose's room, and Ash's heart pounded uncomfortably in his chest as he followed. Rose lay on the bed, her face swollen and bruised, her chest rising and falling with each shallow breath. It was wrong. She should be snapping at him for not doing his job right. Needling him for not paying attention to his town. Snarling at him for looking at her wrong or breathing in her direction or whatever other heinous crime she thought he had committed that day.

He pulled up a chair and sat down beside her, taking her cold hand in his. "Who did this to you?"

WHEN THE DOCTORS assured Ash that Rose would not wake until morning, he reluctantly gave up on sitting there watching her breathe and drove to his office. He sank into his chair and shut his eyes, soaking in the silence.

But his reprieve was short-lived.

His sister burst into his office with her husband close on her heels.

Anna gasped when she saw him. "Oh my God, Ash! Are you okay? Why aren't you at the hospital?" She picked up the compress the doctor had given him and tried to press it to his eye. "Why aren't you using this?"

"I'm fine." He waved her away. "It's just a black eye. Stop fussing, AJ."

"Fussing is what she does best," Zak Hendricks said and propped a shoulder against the door frame. He eyed Ash up and down. "You look like hell."

Ash took the compress Anna kept shoving at him and, to make her happy, pressed it to his eye. "Thanks, man."

Zak glanced at his wife and then straightened. "Nah, I mean it. When was the last time you slept?"

"I've been busy."

"That's it," Anna declared, hands on her hips. "You're taking Dante."

Ash sighed heavily and set the compress down. "We talked about this. I'm not taking in one of your lost causes."

"Dante is not a lost cause. He's a trained police K9. Yes," she admitted, holding up a hand to stop any further protest, "he had some anxiety issues after his previous handler was killed, but we've worked through them, and he's ready to work again. He needs to work again, and you need someone to protect you."

"I don't need—"

In typical Anna fashion, she steamrolled over his protest. "You've been saying you want to invest in K9s for the sheriff's office, so you don't have to keep asking the state police to borrow theirs. So start with Dante. Give it a trial run. What could it hurt?"

Ash looked at his brother-in-law for help, but Zak only shrugged.

"We both know you won't win this argument with her. Or *any* argument," he added under his breath with an eye roll.

Anna jabbed her husband in the stomach with her elbow. "Behave."

"Why are you always poking me with that boney elbow of yours, woman?" He rubbed his stomach. "I'm just stating facts."

Ash eyed the pair of them. "Trouble in paradise?" He hoped not. He didn't have the energy to beat the hell out of Zak today, but if they were fighting, he'd be morally obligated as Anna's fifteen minutes older big brother.

"Nope," Anna said cheerfully. "He's just annoyed because he was being an ass this morning, and I told him so."

"Very colorfully," Zak muttered.

She ignored him and poked a finger at Ash's nose. "And now I'm telling you so. You're being a stubborn ass. Take

Dante. You'll like him. He's exactly like you." She softened her voice and folded her hands under her chin, giving him the pleading puppy eyes he could never resist. "Please. If only to make me feel better. I want to know you're never going into another situation like today without backup."

Shit. How could he say no to that? "Fine."

He already had a constant throbbing headache. What would it matter if he added on one more?

Anna's face lit up, and she clapped her hands together. "Thank you! You won't regret it."

"Yeah, yeah. We'll see. I'll come over later and pick him up."

"You don't have to. He's in the car. I'll go get him and fill you in on everything you need to know." She hurried out.

Ash groaned softly and stared up at the ceiling. "Of course he's in the car because she knew I wouldn't say no."

"Did you really expect anything else?" Zak slapped him on the back. "Good luck with this one, brother. He's an escape artist like my Ranger, but with a worse attitude."

"Are you fucking with me? Ranger almost bit off my arm once."

Zak merely grinned and trailed his wife out.

As he waited for them to return with the dog, he couldn't help but feel a twinge of jealousy at how easy their relationship seemed. Even when they were arguing, they were always so in sync, finishing each other's sentences and laughing at inside jokes that he wasn't privy to. Except for his twin, he'd never had someone like that in his life. Someone who knew him inside and out and accepted him for who he was, flaws and all. He didn't begrudge Anna's hard-won happiness with Zak, but he kind of missed the days when it was just the Rawlings twins against the world.

Anna returned with Dante on a leash, and— Jesus, the German Shepherd was massive and muscular, with sleek black fur and an intense gaze that seemed to pierce through him. He'd never admit it out loud, but the dog was intimating as hell.

Dante was well-trained, though, and immediately sat at attention beside Anna, awaiting further orders. His gaze darted around the room, assessing his surroundings, before finally landing on Ash. If he wasn't mistaken, that was the look of a predator zeroing in on prey.

"Here he is," Anna said with a grin, holding up the leash. "Meet Dante."

"Yeah, we've met." He knelt and offered his hand. "Hey, boy. Remember me?" He had saved the dog from a burning barn during the wildfire last fall when Redwood Coast Rescue's facilities got overwhelmed. Dante had seemed smaller then, cowered by fear. Now he sniffed Ash's outstretched hand with the suspicious thoroughness of a cop patting down a suspect. His gaze returned to Ash's face, and his lack of trust was obvious. His ears flattened in displeasure as Anna gave a brief rundown of his training, habits, and commands.

Yeah, this animal wasn't a lost cause at all. Sure.

He should know better than to believe his sister when she pulled her puppy dog eyes out of the arsenal to get her way. "I'm sure he'll be an asset to the sheriff's office."

"He will," Anna agreed. "And he'll keep you safe for me. Just remember to give him plenty of exercise and attention, and you'll have a loyal companion for life."

"Great." He tried to keep his tone casual even as the weight of this additional responsibility settled heavily on his shoulders. He had enough on his plate without having to worry about a dog. But he'd agreed to this, so Dante was his problem now.

He watched Anna and Zak leave before turning to face the dog sitting at his feet. Dante eyed him with suspicion and a hint of hostility.

"My sister could get away with murder, you know that?"

Dante only tilted his head to the side and let out a grumbling woof.

"Man of few words. I like that." Ash sighed and sat behind his desk, picking up the compress again and wincing as he pressed it to his eye. Maybe a little extra protection wouldn't hurt. He just hoped he didn't regret this decision.

chapter
five

I'M ALIVE!

Rose opened her eyes and stared up at the white ceiling above her bed. She instantly knew that she was in a hospital. Her head throbbed in time with her heart and the rest of her ... she didn't know where the pain was coming from. She felt like every cell in her body had taken a beating, and she wouldn't be surprised if her skin was now one enormous bruise.

How am I alive?

Tears leaked from the corners of her eyes, and she squeezed them shut to keep more from flowing.

Skinny man.

Knife.

Struggle.

Blood.

Masked man.

The images came in rapid-fire succession, playing out on the backs of her eyelids. She sucked in a sharp breath that had pain singing through her ribs and fisted her hands in the blanket.

Somehow, she survived. Whatever vile things the masked

man had planned for her, he hadn't accomplished them. She was alive and safe and—

Not alone.

Panic blazed through her at the sudden awareness of another presence in the room. Maybe she was wrong. Maybe she wasn't safe, and this was part of his twisted plan. Maybe—

But she was in the hospital.

And the other presence didn't feel threatening.

She turned her head on the pillow and blinked until the hulking figure backlit by the windows came into focus.

Sheriff Ash Rawlings.

What?

He was the absolute last person she expected to see at her bedside, but there he was, sitting at a small table by the windows, surrounded by paperwork. He glared at the documents, looking characteristically grumpy and uncharacteristically mussed.

Rose tried to speak, but her throat was dry and raw. She cleared it and tried again. "Sheriff," she croaked out.

Ash jerked, clearly startled. He looked up from his work and met her gaze. For a moment, his stormy blue eyes flickered with a range of powerful emotions before he schooled his expression into blankness.

"Rose," he said, his voice gruff.

She couldn't make sense of it. Why would Sheriff Rawlings be in her hospital room? Did he know what happened to her? Was he here to arrest her for something?

She tried to sit up, but the pain in her ribs made her gasp and fall back on the pillow.

Ash was on his feet in an instant, moving to help her. She leaned into his strength as he lifted her gently and stuffed pillows behind her back to prop her up.

"What are you doing here?" Her voice was a little stronger this time, but still barely audible.

His expression darkened. "You were attacked, and I need to get your statement."

"So you're working from my hospital room?"

He glanced over at the files. "I, uh..." He cleared his throat and shuffled the stack into a neat pile that he stuffed into a banged-up leather briefcase. "I'm on my lunch break."

Rose studied him for a moment, taking in the dark circles under his eyes and the wildness of his usually well-kept beard. He looked like he hadn't slept in days, and she didn't believe his bullshit excuse. Ash Rawlings wasn't the type to take lunch breaks, especially not during an investigation.

"Do you remember anything at all?" he asked, pulling a notepad from the back pocket of his jeans. She recognized that notebook—the one he'd carried as a new deputy thirteen years ago, though the dark green leather cover looked considerably more worn now.

Rose closed her eyes and took a deep breath, trying to steady her nerves. The memories were fuzzy, disjointed, but she did her best to piece them together.

"There was a man in the back booth of the pub all night," she said finally. "I told him I was closing, but he wouldn't leave. He was really skinny, and I think he was high on something. He had a knife. We struggled..." She trailed off.

"Do you remember anything else about him? Any other physical traits?"

She started to shake her head, but stopped when the room spun around her. She lifted a hand to her temple and found her head bandaged. "I don't remember."

"Was anyone else there before you closed? Did anyone else see him?"

"My aunt."

"Rainbow Rodriguez?"

"She left a few minutes before, but she was very tipsy. I doubt she remembers him."

He didn't seem happy at this news. Then again, that was nothing new. She'd never seen the sheriff happy. "Do you remember anything else about the guy?"

"No, but there was a second man waiting outside."

"Can you describe him?"

"He wore a mask."

"Did he say anything to you?"

"I... I don't think so. I told him he could have the money in the register. He hit me and..." Her fingers touched her neck. The skin there felt tender. "I think he tried to strangle me." She dropped her hand and looked at Ash. "Did you stop him?"

His expression gave nothing of his thoughts away. "You said this happened at closing time on Tuesday? Around two a.m.?"

God, the way he stressed the day of the week made her think she was unconscious a lot longer than she realized. "What day is it now?"

"Friday morning."

She'd lost days. Why couldn't she remember anything from that time? It was just a black hole.

"Rose?" he prompted.

"Uh... yes. Sorry. But it was midnight. The place was dead, so I was going to close early."

Ash scribbled something in his notepad before pocketing it. "All right. If you remember anything else, let me know."

He turned to leave, but Rose's hand shot out and grabbed his wrist. The contact sent a jolt of electricity up her arm, and her heart thumped against her abused ribs as she looked up at him.

"Wait," she said, voice still too hoarse. "How did I escape?"

He was silent for a long time. It seemed like he was wrestling with himself, like he didn't want to tell her the truth. When he finally spoke, his voice was tight. "I found you at the old gas station on Route 10 on Wednesday evening."

"So I didn't escape?" Her stomach churned at the news. "He had me for over a day?" What had he done to her during that time?

Ash turned back, his eyes narrowed. "Why do you say he?"

Uncomprehending, she stared up at him through a sheen of tears. "What?"

"You just said he not they, but earlier you told me there were two abductors."

"I... don't know why I said that." But even as she spoke, she knew it wasn't true. "I guess the first guy just seemed like a lackey. He wasn't in charge."

"You got the impression he answered to the second man, the one in the mask?"

"Yes."

"Do you know why the masked man would take you out to the old gas station?"

She closed her eyes and tried to think. Everything was so fuzzy, her head stuffed with cobwebs that muffled her thoughts. "I'm sorry. I don't."

He stared at her for a stony second. "Do you have a problem with substances, Ms. Galasso?"

"A problem with... what?"

His gaze dropped to her bare arms, and dread filled her belly. Despite the pain it caused, she lifted her arms and stared at the fresh track marks in the soft flesh there. "I've never..." The tears she'd been trying so hard to hold back flooded her vision and spilled over. "What did he do to me?"

His blue eyes hardened, a fire of simmering rage sparking to life in his irises. His hands remained still at his sides, but the intensity of his stare was enough to make her tremble. Just as suddenly as it had come, the emotion disappeared, and he stepped forward, cupping his hand around her shoulder in gentle support.

"I don't know yet," he said, and his usually indifferent voice was now filled with warmth. "But I give you my word—I will find out."

She stuffed her arm under the sheet. She couldn't look at those marks any longer. "Your word doesn't mean a damn thing to me, Sheriff."

"Be that as it may, I don't break my promises."

"You already broke one. Years ago. Remember?"

A muscle ticked in his jaw. "I'll need to interview you again soon." Once again, he turned away as if to leave.

Dammit, she was being an ungrateful bitch. She was angry and turning it on him, but he didn't deserve it—this time, at least. He'd been nothing but kind to her today. If he could table their shared animosity for the moment, she should, too.

"Wait." She swallowed hard, trying to maintain her composure while emotions ran wild inside her chest. "Thank you."

He nodded once and grabbed his briefcase. "I need your permission to review your medical records," he said, back in cold cop mode. "I need to know exactly what they did to you."

"Okay."

The thick muscle in his jaw tensed as he pulled open the door, his broad shoulders rigid with tension. "I'll call your aunt, let her know you're awake." She expected him to leave after that, but then he paused and looked back at her with an expression so soft she hardly recognized him. "The bastard will pay for hurting you."

chapter
six

WHY DID EVERYTHING HURT?

Rose surfaced to consciousness in a confused daze, her body covered in cold sweat, her heart beating like it was trying to drill out of her chest.

Where was she?

Why did it feel like her skeleton wanted to jump out of her skin?

Slowly, memories came back in jagged pieces. The men—skinny, twitchy guy and the cold man in the mask. Beating her. Dumping her on an old mattress. Injecting her, filling her veins with poison.

Oh, God.

That jittery, jumpy feeling was withdrawal.

The craving crawled under her skin, an insatiable itch ached all the way down to her bones and begged to be scratched. Sweat beaded on her forehead as her legs twitched uncontrollably, as if they had a mind of their own.

Tears welled up in her eyes, and she clenched her fists in frustration. She felt trapped in her own body, a prisoner of the torment she never asked for.

She shuddered and attempted to sit up, but a wave of

nausea hit her, and her stomach churned. Even the slightest movement feel like a monumental task.

She had to move. She had to leave. She had to do... something... anything... to make it stop.

She struggled to get out of bed, but her legs wouldn't cooperate, like they weren't even connected to her brain anymore. One second, she was standing, trying to shuffle toward the door, and the next, she collapsed. The sudden impact sent a sharp pain shooting through her abused body, and she cried out.

"Rose!" The door burst open, and Ash stood there, his enormous shoulders blocking out the hallway lights, his gun in hand. When he spotted her on the floor, he holstered the weapon and knelt in front of her. "What happened?"

She tried to speak, but all that came out was a weak groan. If she didn't feel so awful and her thoughts weren't so chaotic, she'd probably have been embarrassed about Ash seeing her like this, so weak and vulnerable. As it was, she was just grateful for his strong arms banding around her, pulling her upright. He leaned her against the side of the bed. The room spun like a carnival ride around her, and she groaned softly.

Ash's expression darkened with concern. "I'll get the nurse."

"I'm fine. Just a little dizzy." A blatant lie. The only thing holding her upright was her one shaky arm looped around the bed rail. "Let me get back in bed." She slowly stood and tried to take a step forward, but her legs gave out, and she crumpled again.

Ash caught her this time, holding her close as she trembled against him. Was that his hand stroking down her hair? She leaned into him like a cat seeking a cuddle. She shouldn't let him touch her like this. She shouldn't find his touch so soothing. This was Ash Rawlings, after all. The man she'd spent her entire adult life hating with the fire of a thousand suns.

"You're okay." His tone was gruff, but somehow also soothing. He didn't say more, but it didn't matter. His arms were strong and safe, and she needed to feel safe right now.

She closed her eyes and took a deep breath. "I can do this."

"Do what?"

She shook her head. "Nothing. Help me back to bed."

He grumbled low in his throat, but lifted her gently to the bed. As he set her down, she caught a whiff of him—outdoorsy, a little like rain on wood, like a man who enjoyed spending time in the forest. Not cologne. It was too subtle for that. Just his natural scent with a fresh hint of soap. For a moment, she forgot about the withdrawal and just breathed him in, wanting to stay close forever.

But then the withdrawal symptoms returned with a vengeance, and Rose squeezed her eyes shut, dropping her head back to the pillow. A whimper escaped her throat.

Ash stepped back, giving her space. She appreciated the gesture, but also felt an odd pang of sadness at the loss of his warmth.

"What can I do?" he asked.

"Just ... stay here. I need you here." The words came without her thinking, surprising her. But there was truth in them. The thought of being alone right now terrified her.

Ash hesitated, but then took a seat in the chair next to her bed, his eyes fixed on her like he thought she might die if he looked away for even a second.

The way she felt, maybe she would.

They sat in silence for a while, Rose fighting with her body and Ash watching her intently. The cravings ebbed and flowed, like waves crashing on the shore. Each time they hit, she dug her nails into her palms and tried to breathe through it.

Suddenly, Ash stood up. "I'll be right back. Don't go anywhere by yourself. You'll fall on your face again."

Rose watched him leave, wondering what he was up to. But before she could venture a guess, he returned with a tray in his hand. On it was a bottle of water, a sandwich, and a small bag of chips.

"Figured you're hungry." He set it on the bed table and rolled it over to her. He had never been this kind to her before, and she didn't know how to react. Probably better not to cry the tears suddenly blurring her vision.

"Thank you."

The smell of fresh bread and roasted turkey wafted from the sandwich. She took a small bite, savoring the flavors as they exploded in her mouth. It was then that she realized just how hungry she was. Despite her efforts to keep them back, the tears streamed out anyway, dripping down her cheeks as she ate. They were made of equal parts gratitude and shame. She had always prided herself on being strong and independent, but now she was reduced to a shell of her former self. She couldn't even think of a decent insult for Ash, and insulting him was one of her favorite pastimes.

Ash watched silently as she ate. His expression gave nothing away, stern as always, but there was something in his eyes she'd never seen before—a softness, maybe even a flicker of understanding.

When she finished, he asked, "Feeling better?"

The food had helped to distract her, and a small spark of hope warmed her chest. She *could* get through this. The crawling, itching, aching—it wouldn't last forever. She just had to hang on until her body detoxified. "Yes. Thank you."

"All right." He gathered the tray. She couldn't read his expression and his voice was cop flat again. "I'll be right outside the door if you need anything else."

She didn't want to be alone again with the cravings and caught his arm. "Why are you here?"

He looked down at her fingers wrapped around his wrist,

then carefully extracted himself and stepped back. "You're under twenty-four-hour guard until we can be sure the men who attacked you won't try again."

"But you're the sheriff. You have deputies for this kind of thing."

"I do," he said with an edge of annoyance in his tone. "But I wanted to make sure you were safe myself."

Rose studied him for a moment, searching for any hint of insincerity, but found none. There was a softness to his expression that she had never seen before, and it made her heart race in a way that had nothing to do with withdrawal.

"Why are you being so kind to me?"

"Maybe I'm a decent guy."

"You're a lot of things, Ash Rawlings, but decent isn't one of them."

"Then maybe I just don't like to see you suffer."

"That's funny because I suffer every time you walk into my pub and threaten to pull my liquor license."

Was that a twitch of a smile under his beard? "Yeah, well, I have a job to do."

"And I have a business to run."

They stared at each other, neither willing to back down first. The smug bastard. How dare he act like he cared about her now when he had caused her so much trouble in the past? She opened her mouth to tell him off, but he beat her to it.

"I know we've never seen eye to eye, but your doctor told me what that fucker did to you and the next few days are going to be hell for you. I want to help you get through it."

"Why?"

"Because I know what it's like." Without another word, he walked out and positioned himself outside her door, a grumpy mountain of a sentry.

She gaped at his broad back. Ash was always so put together and in control. How could he know what withdrawal was like? Was he an addict? But he was the sheriff. He was supposed to be a pillar of the community, a role model for others to follow. If he was an addict, it would be a scandal that could destroy his career. And he'd be a hypocrite of the worst kind, forcing others to abide by his strict laws in public while breaking them in the privacy of his home.

But... no. She couldn't picture that. Maybe he meant he knew what it was like because as a cop, he saw people suffering from addiction and withdrawal all the time? That made more sense.

Either way, Ash Rawlings was not a man to be trusted, no matter how sympathetic he seemed to her plight. He'd put on the compassionate act once before and then destroyed her life.

Fatigue settled over her like a heavy blanket, sapping her energy and leaving her drained and hollow. She settled against her pillow and thought about all the times Ash had come into her pub, threatening to shut her down and take away her livelihood. But now, he was here, watching over her, making sure she was safe. It was a strange turn of events, one she never thought she would see.

As if sensing the direction of her thoughts, Ash looked at her through the small rectangular window in the door. Their eyes met and held for a moment before he turned away, his expression unreadable.

There was more to that man's story than he was letting on.

She shouldn't care. She had her own demons to battle and couldn't afford to get sidetracked by his.

The silence in the room was heavy, broken only by the occasional rustling of the sheets as she shifted in bed. She closed her eyes, willing herself to fall asleep, but her mind wouldn't quiet down. Jagged memories of the men attacking her kept replaying in her head, like a never-ending nightmare. And it only got worse when she finally fell asleep because then her imagination took over, filling the black hole in her memory with the worst scenarios it could come up with. She knew they'd pumped her full of drugs, but what else had they done to her in those two days?

When she woke from a restless sleep, Ash was gone. She wondered if it had all been a weird dream until she saw the deputy stationed in front of her room. It hadn't been a dream. Ash Rawlings *had* come to the hospital and sat with her overnight.

Surely a sign of an impending apocalypse.

chapter
seven

AUNT RAINBOW and Marcel stopped by mid-morning, and Rainbow flew into the hospital room on a comforting cloud of patchouli and pot, her bangles clicking together like castanets as she wrapped Rose up in a hug.

"Oh, my baby." She pulled back to examine Rose's face. Tears and anger filled her dark eyes. "What did they do to you?"

"I'm okay."

"You are most certainly not! Look at these bruises. Dammit, I should've stayed and helped you close. I just had a feeling. I know better than to ignore my feelings." She squeezed Rose again, too tight, making her wince. "I swear, if I find out who did this to you—"

"Rainy, let the girl breathe." Marcel gently pulled Rainbow back and Rose gave him a grateful look while her aunt turned her outrage in his direction.

"She needs care!"

"And she's getting the best care here." Marcel winked at Rose, but he wasn't quick enough.

Rainbow scowled at them both, then gave his long, wiry gray beard a little punishing tug. "Behave."

He held up his hands. "I always behave."

Rose smiled at the pair of them. They'd been a couple for years and had the easy intimacy that came with a long relationship. They were perfect for each other, though they couldn't be more different—Rainbow with her beads and feathers and bangles and Marcel in black leather, looking like an enforcer for an outlaw motorcycle gang. He was a stocky man, equal parts fat and muscle, and had hair everywhere except on his head, where a skull tattoo decorated his scalp over his left ear.

The sight of it sent Rose careening back to the bar, and the man with the skull mask standing over her, raising the bat. She curled her hands into the blanket beside her legs and tried to breathe. It wasn't even the same kind of skull. The mask had been very realistic, while Marcel's tattoo was almost cartoonish.

It. Wasn't. The. Same.

Shit, if every skull tattoo she saw set her off, she'd need to find another line of work. Just about every other man who came into her pub had one.

"You okay, Rosie?" Marcel asked.

She nodded, but it was a lie. Her head was pounding, and her stomach churning. She couldn't draw full breath. The walls felt like they were closing in on her.

"I need... I need to get out of this room." She swung her legs over the side of the bed and stood up, swaying slightly. Rainbow tried to help, but she waved her away. "I'm sorry, but I need to be alone right now." She couldn't hold herself together much longer and didn't want her aunt to see her fall apart.

Rainbow blinked in surprise, but stepped back and folded her hands in front of her.

"We'll come back later." Marcel slid an arm around Rainbow and guided her toward the door. As they stepped out, he added in an off-handed tone, "There's a nice garden out behind the hospital, Rosie. Nice place to walk."

God, she could kiss the sweet man for that.

Rose took a deep breath and steadied herself on her feet. She could do this. She needed to do this. She waited until she was sure they were gone, then slipped out of her room. In the hallway, the deputy that was supposed to be guarding her was nowhere to be seen.

Good.

She didn't want company. No nurses fussing. No aunts worrying. No deputies with their guns and their flat, scanning eyes. She needed solitude. Just for a few minutes, so she could process everything and breakdown if she needed to.

She shuffled unsteadily down the hallway towards the stairs. She made it down the stairs without incident and started to feel steadier, more like herself. She headed for a door marked EXIT, but as she reached for the handle, the door swung open, and Ash stepped inside.

"Where's your guard?" he demanded.

She crossed her arms defensively over her chest. "I hit him over the head and snuck away."

"You did *what*?" A vein throbbed in his temple. He looked about ready to pop an artery and she scoffed.

"Wow, you really have a low opinion of me, don't you? He's fine—I assume. He wasn't there, so I took the opportunity to slip out. I need some fresh air."

"You need to rest."

"Don't tell me what I need. I can't stay cooped up in that room all day. I'll go nuts." She tried to squeeze by him, but he blocked the door with his muscular arm and scowled down at her.

"I *will* carry you back upstairs."

"Touch me, Sheriff, and I'll scream rape. I doubt you'll win reelection if everyone in town thinks you're a pervert."

His eyes narrowed. "Don't test me, Ambrosia."

The way he said her full name sent a shiver of awareness down her spine and she stepped back in shock.

No, that wasn't desire.

Not for Ash Rawlings.

It had to be another withdrawal symptom.

She reclaimed the step. "I'm going outside."

"You shouldn't be alone."

"Then come with me."

His scowl darkened. She glared right back, undaunted.

A muscle jumped under his beard. "Fine." The word sounded like he'd had to rip it from deep inside his chest.

Rose rolled her eyes, but didn't protest. She needed to get out, and he was probably right—she shouldn't be alone, even as much as she wanted it. She wasn't the steadiest on her feet and what if the men came back to finish the job they'd started? She wasn't about to make herself an easy target.

They stepped outside into the bright sunlight, and she took a deep breath of the cold, fresh air. It was invigorating after a day of canned, antiseptic-stained hospital air. She felt alive again.

Ash motioned her over to a bench in the small garden. "Sit."

She obeyed without protest since her legs were starting to wobble, and sank down onto the bench beside him. They sat in silence for a few moments, watching cars go by on the busy street beyond the garden.

Before long, Rose found her gaze wandering to him. She knew women found him attractive—he'd been voted Most Eligible Bachelor in the county after his election. And, despite their contentious history, she could see why. He had broad shoulders and a hard, well-worked body. His eyes were a fascinating blue that sometimes looked gray, and his reddish-brown beard only added to the appeal of his rugged features.

Okay, bad blood aside, maybe she was attracted, too.

"You know," she said, breaking the silence. "Maybe you're not so bad, Ash Rawlings."

He raised an eyebrow. "Is that a compliment from the sharp-tongued Ambrosia Galasso?"

"Take it however you want. But..." She looked down at her lap and picked at a stray thread on her hospital gown. "Thanks. For being there last night. Watching out for me."

He shrugged. "It's my job."

"No, it's not. You could have assigned one of your deputies to guard me, but you didn't. You stayed with me all night. And now you're back."

Ash looked away, his jaw tense. "I know what it's like."

She frowned. He'd said that before, and it didn't make any more sense to her now. "What happened to you, Sheriff?"

Ash hesitated, his gaze laser-focused on the road. "Let's just say I've had my fair share of demons to battle. Some things you can never forget, no matter how hard you try."

"Yeah, I get that." He must know that he was one of her demons. He'd destroyed her life, taken away everything that had made her feel safe—but now, in a strange twist of fate, *he* was the only thing that made her feel safe. And, dammit, she was curious about him, wanted to know what made the man tick. "Do you... have experience with addiction?"

He grumbled like an annoyed bear. "I'm not going to bare my soul to you, Rose. This isn't group therapy. I'm only here as a law enforcement officer, protecting the victim of a crime."

She smiled. Honestly, she'd expected nothing less than that answer. "Fair enough."

They sat in silence for a few more minutes, which was fine by Rose. She was content to just enjoy the cool breeze and the bright sunshine. It was a welcome respite from the dark, dreary hospital room.

Suddenly, Ash stood up, his hand going to the gun at his hip.

"What?" She followed his gaze and saw a man walking toward them. For a moment, she flashed back to the skinny man watching her with wild, bloodshot eyes.

"Do you know him?" Ash asked.

She sucked in a sharp breath. "No, I've never seen him before, but—"

"But what?"

"Something's wrong."

"Yeah."

The man was tall and muscular, with a shaved head and a chin full of dark stubble. His eyes were dark and intense, and there was a wild look in them. "Little Rose Galasso," he said. "I've been lookin' for you."

"What do you want?" She was proud of herself for how strong her voice sounded.

He took another step closer, and Ash positioned himself in front of her with his gun now drawn.

"Sheriff's Department," he said, his voice cop-flat. "Stop where you are and show me your hands."

The man sneered and took another step forward. "This is between me and the girl. We have unfinished business."

A chill scraped down her spine. She couldn't remember ever seeing this guy before, but the way he was looking at her made her feel like he knew her intimately. Had he been there when she was held captive? Had he pushed the heroin into her vein? She took a step back, bumping into the bench, and almost panicked when she realized she was trapped.

"I said stop," Ash repeated.

The man laughed and a blade flashed in his hand. "Make me."

Ash didn't hesitate. He fired a warning shot above the man's head, causing him to duck and cover. Ash took advantage of the distraction and lunged forward, tackling him to the ground.

Rose watched in horror as the two men wrestled for control of the weapon, grunting and cursing as they rolled around on the pavement. She reached down and grabbed a nearby rock. She raised it above her head, ready to strike the man if he got the upper hand.

But there was no need.

Ash pinned him to the ground and handcuffed him before hauling him back to his feet. "Get up, asshole. What's your name?"

The man spat on the ground. "None of your fuckin' business."

Ash shoved him towards the street. "Fine. We'll do this the hard way."

For the first time, Rose noticed Ash's Tahoe parked in a space on the street. She watched in numb shock, trembling with the adrenaline rush as he shoved the man into the backseat and slammed the door shut.

Ash walked back to her, his gaze searching hers. "Are you okay?"

She couldn't find her voice right away and nodded. "Yeah. I just...who was that guy?"

"I don't know," Ash admitted, his gaze finally leaving her to scan the parking lot. "But let's get you back inside so I can find out."

chapter
eight

BACK AT THE STATION, Ash sat down across from Dirk "The Crusher" Whitfield. The Crusher had a rap sheet as long as the state of California and an IQ as small as his dick. He was a member of the Golden State Nationalists, a white supremacy group who believed heartily in God, Guns, and Freedom, and thought the Nazis were the good guys.

Ash had dealt with guys like him before. Dirk's stunning lack of intelligence, combined with his inflated sense of self-importance, made him either extremely dangerous or highly malleable.

Ash was hoping for malleable.

"I know my rights," Dirk sneered. "You can't hold me. I was just talkin' to the girl. I didn't do nuthin' wrong."

"You were planning on it."

Dirk leaned back in his chair, arms crossed over his massive chest. "Can't arrest me for plannin' sumthin', Sheriff."

"So you admit you were at the hospital today to hurt Rose Galasso," Ash said and opened the file he'd brought in with him. It was empty, only for show, but Dirk didn't know that. He pretended to make a note. "Who put you up to it?"

"Wait. What are you writin'? I ain't admittin' nuthin'."

Dirk glanced around like he expected help to materialize out of the walls, but no help was coming because he'd neglected to say the magic word: lawyer.

"Don't play games with me," Ash said very softly. "I'm not in the mood. Who sent you to take out Rose Galasso?"

Dirk's thick neck muscles bulged as he leaned forward. So he'd opted to try intimidation. Dumbass.

"I ain't sayin' nuthin'," he spat, his breath reeking of stale cigarettes and greasy fast food. "You can't prove any-fuckin'-thing. I was just mindin' my own business."

"I was there, asshole. I watched you approach her, and you had a knife in your hand. You wanna try that statement again?"

Dirk remained silent. Sweat beaded on his forehead. He swiped at it with one meaty arm. "I ain't no snitch. You can't make me talk."

"Let me remind you, Dirk, California has a three strikes law, and you have way more than three strikes in here." Ash leaned back in his chair and tapped a finger on the file. "That's a minimum of 25-years-to-life with no time off for good behavior. If I tack on attempted murder, you're going away for the rest of your miserable life."

Dirk's gaze flitted around the room again as if searching for a way out, and Ash could all but smell the fear rolling off the man in noxious waves. For all of his tough talk, Dirk Whitfield was not a tough guy. Misdemeanors and non-violent felonies littered his record. He was a lackey, and Ash would bet his inheritance that Dirk knew the skinny guy who attacked Rose. In his experience, lackeys tended to run in packs like hyenas.

"So," he prompted. "You wanna try again?"

"I don't know nuthin'," Dirk said after another stubborn moment.

Ash stood up, his chair scraping against the linoleum.

"You do know something. And you're going to tell me. Because if I like what I hear, maybe I won't add on an attempted murder charge. Maybe I'll change it to simple assault, a misdemeanor. That's six months in county jail. Your choice, Crusher."

Dirk shifted in his seat, his eyes darting around the room one last time. He was cracking and it only took another second of tense silence before he broke. "It was some rich guy called Chester, okay? Chester Duran. He paid us to do it."

"Chester Duran," Ash repeated. "Who is he and why would he want to hurt Rose?"

"I don't know," Dirk said, his voice sulky. "I swear I don't know. Someone just said he'd pay to make her go away, so I thought I'd make some easy money."

"Where did you meet this Chester?"

"I didn't. I've never seen the guy."

"So how do you know he'd pay?"

"It's all over at The Palace. Everyone's sayin' how he's stupid rich and needs the chick who owns the Mad Dog dead and he'll pay whoever makes it happen. That's all I know. I swear on my mother."

"You'd sell your mother for the right price."

Dirk flashed a mouthful of yellowed teeth. "Hell, yeah, I would. She's a bitch."

Ash sat back in his seat and processed this new information. He had never heard of Chester Duran before, but it was obvious that whoever he was, he had some kind of grudge against Rose. Was Duran the one who had attacked her? He'd have to do some digging and talk to Rose, find out what she knew about him. But for now, he had what he needed to put Dirk behind bars.

"Okay," Ash said and stood. "You're under arrest for conspiracy to commit murder and attempted assault with a deadly weapon. You have the right to remain silent. Anything you say can and will be used—"

Dirk exploded up from his seat. "Hey, wait. You said it would just be assault!"

"I lied." Two deputies burst into the room, and he motioned to The Crusher who looked... well, crushed. "Get him out of here."

When Ash emerged from the interrogation room a few minutes later, he found Callum Holden leaning against the wall, waiting for him.

"You know I could pull that lie apart in court and make you look like the bad guy," Cal said conversationally and took a drink from the bottle of Diet Coke in his hand.

"You his lawyer?"

"Fuck no. I don't defend scumbags."

Ash raised a brow at him. "You're a defense attorney. Aren't they all scumbags?"

"No, not all of them. Donovan isn't. Zak ... sometimes isn't."

Ash snorted a soft laugh at that. Somehow, Zak had roped the infamous Cal Holden into working as Redwood Coast Rescue's lawyer.

"But," Cal continued, "I do have a list of no-gos so I can do my job but still sleep at night, and white nationalists are near the top of it right under child rapists."

Ash nodded in agreement. "Dirk Whitfield is a piece of shit, but he's just a low-level criminal hired to do someone else's dirty work. Have you heard the name Chester Duran?"

"No, can't say I have. You think he's the one who attacked Rose?"

"News travels fast."

"Small town, my man. It's all anyone's talked about since yesterday and people are pissed. Everyone likes Rose— well," he added with a smirk, "everyone except you. But I know you wouldn't hurt her, so is Duran the guy or what?"

"It's possible. Hell, probable. The chances of two different people trying to kill her in the same week are slim. It's looking like someone has a contract out on her head, but I need more information."

"I can do some digging on my end for you. See what pops out of the muck?"

"I'd appreciate that."

Cal took the final swig of his drink before tossing the empty bottle into a recycling bin. "No problem. But I have a fee, you know. Can't afford to work pro bono with a gazillion dollars of student loan debt hanging over my head."

"Give your receipts to payroll and I'll make sure the department approves it."

"Good man." Cal clapped him on the shoulder before heading for the door. "I'll be in touch."

"Hey," Ash called after him. "Why were you here if not to defend Dirk? We don't have any other potential clients for you here right now."

Cal just grinned over his shoulder and pushed through the door.

Ash grumbled under his breath as he headed back to his office. He needed to draft up some kind of zero tolerance fraternization policy before Cal fucked his way through all the women employed by the Sheriff's Department.

Not that it would help.

He'd seen the guy work and, along with being a hell of a defense attorney, Cal was as smooth as Casanova. All he had to do was grin with that mischievous twinkle in his eye and women flocked to him. And, somehow, shockingly, he was still friends with every single one of his ex-lovers, so at least when he moved on to his next flavor of the week, Ash wouldn't have to deal with any lovers' quarrels in the office.

The fraternization policy could wait.

He dropped behind his desk and pushed aside the pile of administrative tasks he had to do. The list of sex offenders his chief deputy had gathered for him days ago sat on top. Maria Socktish's file had also appeared while he was out, but he had to back-burner the serial killer theory for now, because as much as his gut told him the podcaster was right, he had no solid evidence to investigate yet. And Rose's attackers were still out there, apparently now hiring other people to do the job they'd botched.

Ash pulled up Chester Duran's name on his computer. Not much came up in the search results. There was a Chester Duran listed as a real estate agent in Eureka, but that didn't seem right. Why would a moderately successful, thirty-something real estate agent with a wife and two young kids want Rose out of the way?

Still, he should look into the man just to be safe.

Next, he found a Lester Duran with a long criminal record who had done time for assault and battery. And look at that. He also had ties with the Golden State Nationalists out in Sacramento. Dirk might have been confused or misheard, and *Lester Duran* was the one who had offered money for the hit. The shared connection with GSN even made it likely. Ash made a mental note to look into it further and then kept digging.

Another name popped up—Chester "Chet" Montgomery-Duran, fifty-two years old, heir to the Duran Fitness empire and the vast portfolio of Montgomery Industries, LLC.

Interesting.

Ash knew nothing about Montgomery Industries, which appeared to be a multi-billion dollar manufacturer of sealants and adhesives, but he probably still had some Duran Fitness DVDs packed away in the back of his TV stand. For a while there in the mid-teens, Duran's program was a huge fitness trend, with everyone from soccer moms to A-list celebrities and sports stars singing its praises. He'd bought the DVDs from a Facebook ad during a bout of insomnia late one night and then never used them.

Chet Montgomery-Duran stood to inherit two fortunes, one from each of his parents. So why would he want Rose, a nobody pub owner from a small town, dead?

Ash scrolled through Chet's social media, but it was full of mundane posts about golfing and dinner parties and fancy charity galas. He had no criminal record, and his home address was in Los Angeles. There was nothing to indicate he had any connections in Lost County or to Rose.

Dead end.

Frustrated, Ash leaned back in his chair and rubbed a hand over his face. He wasn't getting anywhere. At this rate, he'd have better luck knocking on every Duran's door in the county and demanding answers.

Just as he was about to give up, his phone buzzed with a text from Cal.

Found something interesting. Meet me at
the brewery in a half hour

What the hell? Just tell me now

Arrow Tree. Half hour.

"Jesus." Ash pulled on his jacket and grabbed his keys from his desk. Whatever Cal had found must be something big if he wanted to meet in person instead of just sending a message.

When he arrived at Arrow Tree Brewery, Cal was already there, nursing a stout at the bar while he scrolled on a laptop. He nodded as Ash approached and gestured for him to sit.

Ash waved off the bartender and sank into the chair. "Why meet here?"

"Because your office walls have ears," he said, sliding the computer across the bar. "And not all of them are friendly, if you catch my meaning. I'd rather word not get back to this guy that I've been fishing for information about him. He's got some seriously powerful connections."

Ash scanned the documents on the screen, but he already knew what he'd find. "Chester Montgomery-Duran."

Cal nodded. "Better known as Chet. Is that not the most pompous name you've ever heard?"

Not anymore pompous than Ashley Sutton Rawlings III, but he didn't like reminding people of his full name, so he kept his mouth shut and continued scrolling.

There were photos, surveillance footage, and even some transcripts of phone calls. Duran had some shady dealings with a number of known criminal organizations, including the Russian mafia.

"Son of a bitch," Ash said under his breath. "So he is behind this."

"It certainly seems that way," Cal agreed.

"Where did you get all of this information? Nothing popped on him in my searches."

"A magician never—"

"Don't finish that sentence." Ash sent him a glare, and he snapped his mouth shut, then shrugged.

"Okay, ruin my fun. One of my clients is going into witness protection after testifying in a federal case and I got to know the agent in charge quite well."

"Let me guess, the SAC is a woman?"

Cal grinned. "She owed me a favor. I asked her to look and *voila*."

"But what does any of this have to do with Rose?"

And why would Duran's first hitman threaten Ash, his family, and the rest of Redwood Coast Rescue?

It didn't make sense.

He shook his head. "Why would an heir to a billion dollar empire want a small town pub owner dead badly enough to send multiple hitmen after her?"

Cal raised his beer in a salute. "That, my friend, is the multi-billion dollar question."

chapter
nine

ASH OPENED his eyes and was blinded by the splash of morning light spilling through the windows. He blinked and rubbed a hand over his face, glancing blearily around a room that was all bland whites and blues with too-harsh overhead lights.

Where the hell...?

Then his brain kicked online.

Hospital.

Rose.

After his meeting with Cal, he'd returned to his office to tackle the administrative work piling up, then dug into all of the information Cal had given him on Duran. He'd left work late and stopped by the hospital on his way home to check in with the deputy guarding Rose's room.

All quiet. Nobody else suspicious made an attempt on her life, which was a relief.

Then, against his better judgement, he checked on Rose and found her deep in the throes of withdrawal. She'd begged him to stay, and so he had. He must have fallen asleep in the chair beside her bed.

Damn.

His back protested as he sat upright, and he massaged a crick from his neck muscles. He shouldn't have come here. Shouldn't still be here. And definitely should leave before Rose woke up...

But she looked small and fragile in the bed. Her complexion, usually a glowing bronze, was too pale against the bright white sheets. Her black hair stuck to her face in sweaty hanks. His heart squeezed uncomfortably as he watched her chest rise and fall with each breath.

At least she was finally sleeping.

At least, according to her doctor, the worst of the withdrawal was probably over.

Last night had been hell for the both of them. Watching her suffer had conjured up all the memories he'd shoved into a box in the back of his mind and locked away. Memories he had no intention of revisiting.

He took a deep breath and stood, the stiffness in his joints protesting. He walked over to the window, squinting against the bright sun. He stood there for a long time, hands linked around the back of his neck, just breathing, exhausted despite having just woken up. The view was nothing special—a parking lot and some trees with slivers of a pale blue morning sky visible through the branches—but it was a relief to focus on something other than Rose for a moment.

Seeing her like this wasn't right. Rose was loud and annoying and brazenly sexual. She should be arguing with him, needling her way under his skin in the way only she could, not curled into a tiny ball in a hospital bed, begging him to stay with her. The memory of her desperate sobs pissed him off, sparking a flame of rage inside his chest that he mercilessly squashed.

He turned around to look at her again. She was still sleeping peacefully. He walked back over to her bed and took her hand in his. It was cold, even though the rest of her was sweating.

"I'll find whoever pumped all that poison into you."

But to do that, he had to leave. Go home, shower, and head into work.

Why was it so hard to release her hand?

Ash forced himself to let go of her, walked out of the hospital room and took a deep breath, the smell of disinfectant and sickness thick in the air around him.

"How is she, Sheriff?"

He shifted to look at Mike Conti. The deputy sipped from a cup of coffee emblazoned with the logo of the hospital's cafe. The sight of it made Ash desperately crave a cup of his own. "She's sleeping now."

Conti sucked on his teeth. "Poor thing." Then he eyed Ash. "You should go home and get some sleep, too. If you don't mind me saying, you're looking rough, Sheriff."

"Yeah, I'll do that."

He had no intention of doing that.

He made his way down the sterile hallways and out to his Tahoe, moving on autopilot. As he drove, his thoughts turned to the past, to the memories he had buried deep inside. Memories of a time when he had been young and stupid, cocky and entitled, and desperately in love with a girl who was taken from him.

The rage inside him burned hotter with every passing mile, and by the time he arrived home, he was practically shaking with it.

He had to get control.

Bad things happened when he lost control.

Ash stumbled into his home, slamming the door shut behind him. He went straight to the shower, stripping off his clothes and letting the water wash over him. It was scalding hot, almost too hot, but he didn't care. He needed to feel something other than rage and despair, but the roiling emotions were relentless, pounding inside his skull like a hammer against steel.

As he stood under the water, his mind drifted back to her. Mandi. The girl he had loved with every fiber of his teenage heart. A young woman lost to the same drug that had nearly taken Rose.

He closed his eyes and let out a guttural scream, the sound echoing off the tiles. He wanted to smash, break, hurt just to release the anger that threatened to consume him.

Something knocked into the bathroom door.

He froze. Was someone here, coming for him now? Naked and unarmed, he was at a distinct disadvantage. He shut off the water and listened. For several long seconds, he heard nothing but the water dripping off him onto the tile under his feet.

There.

There it was again.

A scratching sound, like a dog was—

Fuck.

Dante.

He'd been so consumed with Rose's case, he'd forgotten about the damn dog.

He wrapped a towel around his waist, his muscles still taut with tension despite the heat of the shower. He opened the bathroom door and found the German Shepherd waiting for him, brown eyes narrowed in annoyance.

"Hey." He stared down at the dog and guilt heated the back of his neck. "Sorry I forgot about you."

Dante huffed with disapproval and walked away.

Ash took a deep breath and strove for calm. He couldn't afford to lose control again, not with Rose in the hospital and a killer on the loose. Or potentially killers if Duran decided to hire the job out again.

He had to get back to the office.

In his bedroom, he pulled on a pair of jeans and a long-sleeve Henley, then headed to the kitchen to make himself a thermos of coffee. He stopped dead in his tracks in the hallway.

"What. The. Fuck?"

His living room was trashed. Holes chewed in the drywall, end tables upturned. His leather couch had been shredded to ribbons, the stuffing scattered across the room. He'd been too up in his head to notice the chaos earlier, but now he wondered how he'd missed it. It looked like he'd been burglarized by a tornado. He scowled down at the dog. Dante hacked up a big pile of vomit at his feet.

Was drywall poisonous?

Shit, Anna was going to kill him.

He scooped Dante up, carried him out to the Tahoe, and drove straight to his sister's.

Redwood Coast Rescue was still recovering after the fire that had devastated town last fall, but Zak and Anna had made fast progress. They'd opted to buy a prefabricated house to replace the old Rawlings' family farmhouse and then threw all of their time, money, and effort into rebuilding the dog kennels, Dr. Sasha Scott's vet clinic, and a search and rescue training center. After only five months, they were almost up and running again.

And Anna called him a workaholic. He was pretty sure neither she nor Zak had taken a moment's break since the fire.

He remembered the day he and Anna had founded the rescue. It was originally just a non-profit organization dedicated to rescuing animals in need and had been a dream of hers since she was a kid. After their parents died, he'd helped her turn that dream into a reality by giving up his half of the land they'd inherited. They'd worked tirelessly together to convert the old barn from the defunct Rawlings Ranch into dog kennels and the old corrals into agility yards.

Now, Redwood Coast Rescue was one of the most successful animal rescue organizations in the country, with a team of dedicated volunteers and a soon-to-be state-of-the-art facility. Zak's team of tactical K9s were also gaining national recognition even though they'd only been training together since last summer.

With everything destroyed in the fire, Zak and Anna had been able to build exactly what they needed this time, instead of retrofitting a ranch. The new facility was a series of buildings laid out in a sun pattern, connected by walkways, with the welcome center in the middle. The doggie daycare and hotel—the money-makers that helped pay for everything else—were front and center when Ash pulled his Tahoe into the bigger, newly paved parking lot. Sasha's vet clinic was off to the left with its own designated parking spaces and the training facilities for Zak's tactical K9 team were tucked back behind the other two buildings. Beyond, the team had constructed different environments to train dogs in, including a large rubble pile they called "The Pit" and a simulated city nicknamed "Dogville." They'd planted trees and reseeded the grass and now Redwood Coast Rescue was a sprawling, shiny new beacon of hope on a landscape still blackened by wildfire.

He hadn't thought to bring Dante's leash, so he draped the dog over his shoulders in a fireman's carry and found Anna alone in the vet clinic, painting colorful paw prints on the wall. She had headphones in.

"AJ."

She didn't hear him and continued bopping to her music.

He raised his voice. "Anna!"

She spun around and almost slapped him with the paintbrush. "Ash! What the hell?" She pulled out her headphones. "Warn a girl next time."

"I need help. Is Sasha here?"

She narrowed her eyes at him and his cargo, then sighed and put down the paintbrush. "What did you do?"

"I didn't do anything." He set Dante at her feet. "This aptly-named demon dog destroyed my house."

His twin smirked. "C'mon. You're being dramatic."

"AJ, he ate my couch."

She looked down at the dog with a soft expression. "Did you snack on his couch?" she asked in the tone women only used for babies and cute things as she ruffled Dante's big ears.

"And the drywall. Then he threw up, so Sasha needs to make sure he's not going to die on me."

She scowled up at him. "Have you been feeding him?"

"No, Anna. I thought he could feed himself." He scoffed. "Yes, of course I've been feeding him."

"Walking him?"

He snapped his mouth shut.

"Training with him?"

Shit.

"Taking him to work with you? He's a working dog, Ash. A highly trained police K9. He gets bored when he has nothing to do. And when he gets bored, he gets destructive."

Ash grumbled, his frustration mounting. "I've had a lot going on. You know that."

"I do know that, which is exactly why I gave him to you. He forces you to slow down to not only take care of him, but yourself." She looked him up and down. "You look like shit, Ash."

He grunted in response, trying to keep his face impassive. His twin could read him like nobody else on Earth, and he didn't want her to know he felt like he was losing his mind.

Anna fisted her hands on her hips. "You need to slow down," she said, enunciating each word. "When you get like this—"

"I know, I know." He dragged a hand over his beard, smoothing down the flyaways. "But I don't have time for the dog right now."

Anna's gaze softened. "Okay, this isn't your normal overdrive mode. What's going on?"

He hesitated, considered lying for a half second, but then sighed with resignation. He never could lie to his sister. "They drugged Rose with the same shit that killed—" He stopped himself from saying her name, but Anna already knew.

She set a hand on his arm. "I'm so sorry, Ash. Are you okay?"

"I'm not the one in the hospital going through fucking withdrawal."

Anna flinched. It was a small movement, but it made him feel like an ass. He hated hurting his sister in any way, and reminding her of that turbulent era of their lives always hurt her because she'd had her own demons to slay at the time.

"Sorry, I—"

She waved him off. "Is Rose okay?"

"She's stable, and the doctors think she's through the worst of it now."

"Then why so glum?"

"Because I can't fucking find the bastard that did this to her."

"And you think losing your shit is going to solve that?"

His frustration boiled over. "Anna, I can't deal with a lecture right now. I just... I have to get to work."

She sighed and rubbed her temple. "Okay, fine. The clinic here isn't quite finished, so Sasha's still working in town for the next few weeks. I'll take Dante there for a check-up. But you need to sort your shit out, Ash. You can't keep going like this."

"You're one to talk. Have you stopped for even a second since the fire?"

"No, but the difference is, this was only a short term project, and the end is in sight. We had a goal to rebuild in six months and, once it's done, we plan on taking a few weeks off before reopening. But you? You don't stop. Ever. You're going to work yourself into the grave just like Dad did."

He pressed his palms to his tired eyes, then dragged his hands up over his head, scooping back his hair. "AJ, that's not fair. Mom and Dad died because a drunk driver—"

"No, they died because he was such a goddamn workaholic that he had to drive three hours in the middle of the night to get back to the ranch. They wouldn't have been on the road at all if he just would've taken one day off."

"Anna—"

"I do not want to watch you destroy yourself like that." She shoved through a door and disappeared deeper into the unfinished clinic with Dante trailing after her.

Ash stood there for a moment, staring at the empty space where his sister had just been, feeling like a piece of shit. Anna was right. He was spiraling out of control, and he knew it. He couldn't keep ignoring the fact that he was barely holding it together. He needed to take a step back and reassess his life. But he didn't know how to do that.

He didn't know how to stop.

chapter
ten

13 Years Ago

GRAVEL CRUNCHED under Ash's new boots as he approached the house a half-step behind Sheriff Jerry Tennison. He tried not to let his nerves show, but his hands were sweating. It was only his second day on the job and his khaki uniform shirt felt too stiff. The wide-brimmed hat was awkward on his head, and the green tie was strangling. He'd only found out this morning that most deputies wore their collars open and kept the tie only for more formal events. As soon as he got back to the office, he was taking the fucking thing off.

The shiny badge on his chest seemed to weigh fifty pounds.

"All right," Tennison said, pausing on the sidewalk in front of the Galasso house. "Missing person: Harmony Galasso, thirty-five, mixed race, Hispanic and Native American. She was last seen yesterday afternoon around 1400 by her husband, Peter, before he went to work at the Mad Dog in town. We get a lot of missing persons calls—usually it's bored housewives running off with their lovers or hikers who don't return on time. The Redwood parks have rangers to handle most of those kinds of calls, but everything else in the county falls to us. And we're still called in to assist the rangers occasionally."

Ash studied the house. It was small and old, desperately in need of a new coat of paint and new windows, but it was clean. Brightly painted flower boxes overflowed with blooms on the porch rails. Someone obviously loved the place and cared for it as best as they were able. "Is this a missing hiker?"

"No. Just giving you an overview of the kinds of missing persons calls we get. Keep up, son."

Ash clenched his jaw at the sheriff's condescending tone and reminded himself he was lucky Tennison had agreed to take him on as a deputy trainee, given his turbulent past as a juvenile delinquent constantly running afoul of the sheriff. He'd only gotten into the academy in the first place because Tennison had some friends in Sacramento and put in a good word.

"This," Tennison said on a heavy sigh and hiked up his pants by his belt loops, "is probably a case of a disgruntled housewife. Harmony Galasso has a... reputation. She's fucked around on her husband for years and I'd bet my badge she's shacked up somewhere with some guy. She'll turn up. I'd say in ninety percent of these cases, the quote, unquote missing person reappears as soon as they realize we're looking for them."

"And the other ten percent?"

"We either find their remains or don't find them at all."

Before joining the Sheriff's Department, Ash hadn't realized that sometimes people just vanished and are never found. And it happened with alarming—to him—frequency, though the sheriff didn't seem too perturbed by the fact. Even one of his high school classmates, Darcy Cantrell, had vanished almost two years ago. He thought she'd be found sooner or later, but now, given the time that had passed, he doubted it. He learned at the academy that the first forty-eight hours were the most critical when someone goes missing—if no solid leads were found in that time, their chance of recovery was cut by half.

Tennison stepped up onto the porch and knocked on the squeaky screen door. A girl with big blue eyes and long black hair answered. Barely a teenager, she was skinny with knobby skinned knees under ripped shorts. She all but disappeared inside a too-big *Twilight* T-shirt. She was as pale as one of those vampires, too, save for the delicate skin around her eyes, red and blotchy from crying.

"Hi," she said softly. "I'm Rose. Are you going to find my mom?"

Ash's chest tightened, old grief welling up like bile in his throat. He knew that raw, hollow look in her eyes. He saw it every time he looked in the mirror.

"Yes, we will." He ignored Tennison's glare. Yeah, maybe it was a lie, but the girl needed reassurance right now, not the harsh truth.

"Okay." Rose held the door open, letting them pass. "Dad's in the living room. He's pissed off."

A lanky man with long hair and bloodshot eyes paced the threadbare carpet, clutching a half-empty bottle of whiskey. Peter Galasso. Ash knew him from all the times he, Zak, and Donovan had tried to sneak into the Mad Dog as teenagers.

Rose perched on the arm of the sofa and watched her father pace. "Daddy, the cops are here."

"About fucking time," Galasso muttered and took another drink from his bottle. "Though I don't know what good it'll do."

Rose's gaze slid to Ash, and for a moment, he glimpsed a flicker of hope behind the sorrow. His resolve strengthened.

I will find your mother, he vowed silently.

No one deserved to live with the torment of uncertainty.

Tennison cleared his throat. "Mr. Galasso, this is Deputy Trainee Rawlings. We have a few questions about your wife's disappearance."

Pete whipped around, eyes blazing with fury. "I called hours ago. Where have you been?"

"We got here as fast as we could, Pete."

Ash scowled at the back of the sheriff's head. That was a lie. Before coming here, they'd been on an extended lunch break, with Tennison spending a good hour flirting with Rainbow Rodriguez at the coffee shop, and before that, they had been puttering around the office. If Peter Galasso really called hours ago, they could've been here right after his call.

Apparently, Peter sensed the lie, too, because he snorted with disbelief and took another drink. "Typical."

"Dad." Rose leapt up, grabbing his arm. "Please, just talk to them. For Mom. So we can find her."

Pete whirled on his daughter, face reddened. "Face it, Wildflower. Your mom ran off with one of her boyfriends. She abandoned us."

Rose flinched back like he'd slapped her. She dropped her hand from his arm and with fresh tears streaming from her eyes, ran deeper into the house.

Ash exchanged a glance with the sheriff. Tennison pulled him out of the living room, back into the foyer hallway.

"Go deal with the kid," Tennison said under his breath.

Ash glanced down the hall. "Uh... shouldn't a female deputy—"

"Do you see any female deputies here?" When Ash didn't respond, Tennison nodded. "Go talk to the kid. Kids always know more than the parents think. Find out if there was trouble in the marriage."

"You think he knows where his wife is?"

"If he does, it's because he put her there."

"Oh."

"Yeah. Rule of thumb, son. If the wife didn't leave of her own accord, it's always the husband's fault. So go talk to the kid and find out what Pete Galasso doesn't want to tell us."

Ash watched Sheriff Tennison return to the living room, then sucked in a breath and headed down the hall where he saw the girl disappear. He found her in a room so full of color it burned his retinas. The walls were bright purple, decorated with twinkle light strands of various colors and more *Twilight* posters—what was it with that movie and preteens?

Rose sat on her bed with her legs curled up to her chest and her face pressed into her knees.

He tapped on the door frame. "Hey there, Rose. Mind if I come in and talk to you about your mom?"

Rose sniffled and swiped at her huge, impossibly blue eyes. "Uh, yeah, sure. Come in, Deputy Rawlings."

How strange to hear himself called that. *Deputy Rawlings.* It was a joke. He still felt like a kid himself—he couldn't even have a legal drink for another two months—and now he was meant to keep the citizens of this county safe?

Jesus.

He cleared his throat, stepped into the bedroom, and took off his hat. "I know this is a tough time for you, but I'm here to help. Can you tell me what happened and when you last saw your mom?"

"I..." Her voice trembled. "I don't know exactly. Last night, she was here. But when I woke to go to school, she was gone and she wasn't here when I got home, either. Her car's still here, and she left her phone at home, too. I'm really scared, Deputy Rawlings. Something's wrong, I just know it."

"I get it. This is a scary situation, but we're doing everything we can to find your mom. Can you think of anything unusual that happened before she went missing? Anything that seemed off yesterday before you went to bed?"

Rose chewed on her lower lip. "Well, she was acting different lately. She seemed upset sometimes and was always on the phone, but it was like she didn't want me to see her. She always hung up real fast. I thought it was just... I don't know. Grown-up stress or something."

Ash nodded and pulled a brand new notebook out of his jacket pocket. It was a refillable one with a dark green leather cover that his mom had bought for him when he graduated from the academy. He flipped open the stiff cover to the first page. "Good, that's important information. Thank you for telling me. We can look into it and see who she was talking to. Did your mom have any close friends? Or maybe not even friends, but people she spent time with recently?"

"I guess... there's Auntie Rainbow. Her sister. They used to talk a lot, but I haven't seen her around lately. Maybe she knows something?"

Ash jotted down a note. "Okay, your aunt is Rainbow Rodriguez?"

"Yes."

"We'll reach out to her for sure. Anyone else your mom spent time with or mentioned often?"

"No."

"Okay." He hesitated. Now came the tricky part. He tried to gentle his voice. "How are your mom and dad together? Do they fight a lot?"

"Not really."

But her gaze slid away as she spoke and Ash thought, *shit*. Tennison was right. She knew more about her parents' marriage than she was letting on. He pulled the chair out from her desk and sat down, trying to make himself look smaller, as non-threatening as possible. It wasn't all that long ago that he'd been thirteen. He hadn't been much older than Rose the first time he, Zak, and Donovan had a run-in with the sheriff's office, and he clearly remembered how intimidating it was talking to the deputy while he waited for his parents to come get him. He didn't want her to be afraid of him.

"You know," he said conversationally. "It's okay if your parents fight. My parents love each other a lot, but even they still fight sometimes. One time, my mom kicked my dad out of the house all because he kept tracking mud into her kitchen from the barn. But he apologized and they made up. Fighting's just something married people do occasionally. It's normal, but I do need to know if your parents fought recently. It could be important to finding your mom, okay?"

Rose hesitated and rolled her lower lip between her teeth again, then nodded. "Okay."

"So do they fight sometimes?"

Another nod.

"Recently?"

"Last night, when they thought I was sleeping, I heard Dad yelling at Mom. He called her a—" She stopped. "A bad word. Something I'm not supposed to say."

"You can say it to me. You won't get in trouble. I'm sure I've heard it and worse."

She picked up a cat-shaped pillow and hugged it to her chest. She looked so very tiny in that bed surrounded by pillows and stuffed animals, with her black hair falling in a curtain over her face. His heart hurt for her. If Tennison was right, her life as she knew it was over. He wished he could shield her from the nightmare, but that wasn't his job. His job was to protect the community and if Peter Galasso was a killer, then he'd have to shatter this girl's life to keep everyone else safe.

She sucked in a sharp breath and let it out in a rush. "He called her a slut."

Ash tried to keep the surprise off his face. "Does he often call her names like that?"

"No. I think that was the first time."

"Do you know what they were arguing about?"

"No." She stared at him with those startling blue eyes. "My dad didn't hurt her, if that's what you're thinking. He would never."

Ash held up his hands in a calming gesture. "I'm just trying to figure out what happened to your mom, and we need to consider all possibilities, no matter how scary or unrealistic, okay?"

"Okay," Rose said, her voice barely above a whisper. "But I'm telling you Dad wouldn't do something like that. He's too nice and he loves my mom."

Her words held the ring of truth. Was the girl just in such deep denial she believed it? Or was she right, and Tennison was already focused on the wrong person? Ash wasn't experienced enough to know, but his gut said something about this situation wasn't right. "Can you think of anyone else who might know something about your mom's disappearance?"

"No, I don't think so."

"If anything comes to mind, call me or Sheriff Tennison. We're here to help you."

Rose nodded, but she still looked scared and uncertain.

Ash wished he could do more to reassure her, but there wasn't much he could do at the moment. He squeezed her shoulder gently before standing up. "I'll let you get back to resting. Try to take care of yourself, okay? If there's anything you need, don't hesitate to ask."

"Thank you, Deputy Rawlings," she said softly, her gaze fastened on her cat pillow.

Ash headed toward the door.

"Deputy?" she called.

He glanced back. Her eyes were red and puffy, her voice hoarse like she was trying to hold back tears. "I just want my mom back. I want everything to be like it was before."

"I know, Rose. I'll do everything in my power to make that happen. I promise."

She nodded. "Thank you."

Ash made his way back to the living room where Tennison was still talking to Pete Galasso. He caught the tail end of their conversation.

"...and you need to come down to the station for questioning," Tennison was saying.

Galasso paled. "What? Why? I've been here this whole time."

"We have reason to believe you may know something about your wife's disappearance that you haven't shared with us. We need to ask you some questions and get your statement on the record."

Galasso looked like he was about to bolt.

Ash stepped up, blocking the doorway. "Sheriff's right, Mr. Galasso. We need to talk to you about your wife. It'll be easier on your daughter if you come willingly."

"I haven't done anything!" he protested, but his voice wavered.

"We're not saying you have," Ash said, deciding to play the young, understanding deputy to Tennison's harsh, jaded old-timer. "But we need to investigate all possibilities. It's in your best interest—and your daughter's—if you cooperate with us. She's shaken up. She wants her mom back."

Galasso glared at him, but then his expression crumpled into grief. "You don't think she ran off. You think she's dead." He looked at Tennison. "Oh, Jesus. You both think she's dead and I killed her."

"Did you?" Tennison asked, point-blank.

Ash managed to keep his wince off his face. He was so new his uniform buttons still had a shine, but even he could see the sheriff was approaching this family all wrong.

Galasso's jaw tightened. "I want a lawyer."

"As is your right. Deputy Rawlings, take him to the station and make sure he's allowed to contact his lawyer."

"Yes, sir," Ash said, and motioned Galasso out the door. As he folded the man into the backseat of the squad car, he glanced up at the house.

Rose watched them from her bedroom window. Tears trailed down her cheeks, but she wasn't sad. She was pissed.

Fuck.

Ash shut her father into the car and felt her gaze burning into his back as he circled the trunk and climbed into the driver's seat. Guilt twisted his gut into knots.

As he drove away, he tried to shake off the feeling that he was doing more harm than good. Rose was just a little girl, caught in the crossfire of her parents' issues. He didn't want to cause her more sorrow, but it was his job to find out what happened to her mother...

No matter how uncomfortable or painful it might be for her.

chapter
eleven

Present Day

ROSE GRIPPED the cold metal doorknob of The Mad Dog, her knuckles turning white. Her heart pounded as she stared at the familiar red door and flashes of her abduction played on a loop in her mind.

The skinny man...
The struggle...
Liquor bottles shattering...
The skull mask...
The bat coming down...

No.

She *had* to go back to work. She loved this pub and wouldn't let them steal this from her.

"Are you sure you're ready for this?" Rainbow asked for the millionth time.

She didn't look back at Rainbow, too afraid her aunt would see the stark fear in her eyes. Summoning every ounce of courage she possessed, she twisted the knob and stepped inside. She'd expected to find a mess, but the floor was clean, the shelves behind the bar tidy.

"Marcel and I cleaned up for you," Rainbow whispered.

Rose blinked back tears and breathed in the familiar scents of old wood and stale beer and, for the first time since this nightmare started, she relaxed.

She was home.

She finally faced Rainbow and smiled. It didn't feel forced, but she also knew it didn't quite reach the normal wattage of her smiles. That would change, though. With time, she'd be herself again. "It's okay. I'm okay. You don't have to follow me around. I know you have work to do."

Rainbow looked around the pub and twisted her hands together. She rocked anxiously from side-to-side, her long skirt swishing around her legs. The woman was never still or silent. She was always swooshing and clinking and chiming and jingling.

Rose crossed to her and grasped her hands, stilling her anxious movements. "Auntie, I *am* okay. I promise. I'm stronger than this. They can't break me."

"Oh, I know you are, baby." Rainbow's eyes filled with tears, and she gently touched the bruise Rose had tried to hide under layers of concealer. "You're the strongest person I know, but it's my job to worry."

Rose kissed their clasped hands before releasing her. "Well, worry from your shop. I'm opening soon and I can't have you infecting the patrons with your nervous energy."

Rainbow exhaled and stepped back, waving a hand at her face to dry her tears. "You're right. You're right. I'm giving bad vibes." She glanced back at the door where the newest sheriff's deputy stood guard, silent as a statue. "You're well protected and Marcel will be in later, so I need to chill. I'll go to my shop, have an edible." She held up a finger. "But you call me if you need *anything*, understand?"

"I will."

Rainbow fussed for a minute more, then thankfully left.

Rose breathed a sigh of relief, turned toward the bar—and spotted the empty place on the shelf behind where the bottle of Johnnie Walker King George V once sat. The memories came crashing back, blinding her with the intensity.

The bottle slamming into her head.

The metallic taste of fear in her mouth.

The sour smell of his breath...

Rose blinked, forcing the flashback away. It was just an echo, a ghost that couldn't hurt her anymore. She was safe now. In her own pub, the one her father had loved and left her when he went to prison. She needed this place, needed the routine and purpose it gave her life again. If it meant facing shadows around every corner, she'd face it with a smile.

They. Weren't. Going. To. Win.

Shoulders back, she walked behind the bar and lost herself in the mundane tasks of opening. She took inventory and put in an order with her supplier to replace all the broken liquor bottles. She dusted and ran a damp rag over the scarred oak surface of the bar, finding a new divot where the skinny man's knife had hit during the fight. She traced it, fingers trembling slightly as panic flared in her chest. She dropped the rag over the fresh wound and stepped back, wrapping her arms around herself.

Breathe.

She sucked in a breath and held it until she got light-headed. Her heart pounded as she gripped the edge of the bar, her knuckles turning white. The panic was right there, lurking beneath the surface of her fragile composure, waiting to pull her under again.

You're okay.

Breathe.

She exhaled in a rush.

Just then, the pub door swung open, and Ash walked in.

Rose jumped, then cursed herself.

Dammit, she *was* okay.

She plastered on a scowl even as her heart banged around in her chest. "What are you doing here?"

Ash paused on the threshold, scanning the dim interior, his brow furrowed. "You're not supposed to be back at work yet."

"What, did my babysitter tattle on me?" She thought of the string of deputies who had been her constant companions over the last week since she left the hospital. She hadn't even known the current one could talk. He'd trailed her silently from her apartment above the bar to the front door of the Mad Dog, where he planted himself like a bouncer at an exclusive club.

Ash's face remained stoic. "Deputy Conti reported when you left home, as is his job."

She bristled and snapped up the rag. "I'm fine. The doctors cleared me."

"Like hell they did." Ash strode toward the bar, boots thudding ominously on the worn floorboards. "You can't even go into town without having a panic attack."

"So he told you that, too, huh?" Her attempt at grocery shopping last night had been a nightmare. She'd jumped at every unexpected sound and all of the concerned well-wishers had worn on her last fragile nerve. She ended up abandoning her basket and running out of the market near tears.

Ash's scowl only darkened. "What makes you think you're ready to run the pub again? Not to mention, someone out there still wants you dead. You're not opening tonight. You need to lock up and go home."

Anger ignited in her chest, thankfully burning away the fear. Anger, she could handle. "I don't need you telling me what I can and can't do, Sheriff." She flung the rag onto the bar with a defiant snap. "This is my pub, and I'll open it whenever I damn well please."

Ash stopped in front of her, close enough that she could see the concern etched into the lines around his eyes. It softened her, and then pissed her off because she softened. His concern for her well-being stemmed only from his obsessive need to protect everyone in the county. It had nothing to do with her personally, and it shouldn't make her feel all soft and melty inside.

She *hated* this man.

He'd ripped her family apart.

She had to remember that.

He bladed his hands on his hips and stared at her for a long time. "Ambrosia." His voice was soft, but still held the snap of command. "You've been through hell, and you need time to heal."

"Look at you, pulling out my full name. You're not my father, *Ashley*." Because she knew he hated it, she leaned on his name. "You took my father from me when I was barely thirteen, and I don't need your pity now. What I need is for you to leave me the hell alone and let me get to work."

Ash sighed and ran a hand through his hair. "I'm not going anywhere until I'm sure you're okay."

The rage bubbled over. "You want to know why I'm really not okay?" She leaned across the bar, heart pounding, but whether from the lingering effects of panic or anger she didn't know. "You. Took. My father. From me!"

He shook his head. "I was just doing my job."

"By railroading an innocent man?"

Annoyance snapped in his eyes. "By arresting the man all the evidence pointed to."

"Whose?"

"What?"

"Whose evidence pointed to him? Yours? Did you personally collect it?"

"No, of course not. I was a deputy for all of two days

when it happened. I only did as I was told."

Rose trembled, unable to contain the fury and anguish. The panic had retreated for now, eclipsed by the storm of emotions churning in her. "Well, did you ever think maybe what you were told was wrong? Maybe my mother's killer is still out there and *he's* the one who attacked me."

She'd surprised him. She could see it, though his face had gone blank. He honestly hadn't made that connection.

"Your dad was convicted for Harmony's murder," he said finally. "*I* didn't do that. A jury of his peers did."

"He was convicted because you and your incompetent Sheriff's Department decided thirteen years ago that he did it and made sure all the evidence backed you up."

"I would never manufacture evidence."

"What about the former sheriff?" She crossed her arms over her chest. "We all know how honest he was."

"And I'm doing everything in my power to right his wrongs. I understand you're hurting, but that doesn't change the fact—"

"Do you?" she interrupted. "Do you really understand what it's like to have your life torn apart?"

A muscle ticked in his jaw. He was striving for patience, but she didn't want his equanimity. She wanted his annoyance, his temper—one he so rarely unleashed, but that she knew burned as hot as her own.

Anger was easier than fear. Easier than the messy mix of emotions this man evoked every time he scowled at her.

"I've seen my fair share of tragedies, Ambrosia," he said, his voice low and even. "And as for your mother's case, we followed the evidence we had at the time. If new evidence comes to light, I'll reopen the investigation."

Rose scoffed. "Like you're going to take the time to investigate anything more complicated than a traffic violation."

Something that resembled anger flashed through his carefully neutral expression and vicious satisfaction surged in her. At least she had finally gotten a rise out of him.

"You know I take my job more seriously than that." The words were coated in ice.

"Then prove it. Test my DNA against the Jane Doe you found last fall. The one from the fire." She stared at him, daring him to refuse her request. "If you find a match to my mom, then explain how Dad killed her and buried her up on the mountain when he only had a half hour gap in his alibi for that day."

He was silent for a moment, then exhaled hard and dragged a hand over his beard. "Fuck." He paced a few steps away. Stopped. Swung back. "It never even crossed my mind Jane Doe could be Harmony. Come with me to the station and give the sample. I'll put a rush on it and if it's a match, I'll reopen the case."

She should feel triumphant. Finally, after all these years, she might get some answers. But she was just exhausted by it all, and then the fear crept back in.

What if the DNA didn't match?

What if it did, but it also proved her father really was the killer?

If that was the case, who else would want her dead?

During the long hours of suffering in her hospital bed, she'd convinced herself that the men who attacked her had to be tied to her mom's case somehow. It was the only thing that made sense. But if Dad was guilty...

No. She pushed the thought away. She knew her father. Yes, he used to drink too much, and party too hard—but he was gentle at heart. He wasn't a killer. She couldn't think anything else. Not if she wanted to keep her sanity.

"Fine," she said, pushing herself away from the bar. "But I'm coming back as soon as we're done. The pub is opening tonight, with or without your approval."

chapter
twelve

ASH HAD every intention of returning with Rose to the Mad Dog and convincing her to keep the pub closed, but as soon as they arrived at the station, work inundated him. His secretary reminded him he had to be in court that afternoon to testify about a drug bust, then he had back-to-back meetings until dinnertime, and he was overdue on half a dozen administrative tasks.

He couldn't leave and Mike Conti's shift was just about over, so he sent Ralph Jenkins with her—not his first choice for a bodyguard, but everyone else was already out in the field. Jenkins was nearly at retirement and had given up on any kind of fitness regimen years ago, but hopefully just having a deputy stationed at her door would act as a deterrent.

By the time Ash finally left work at almost one a.m., his mood had gone from salty to sour. His head ached. All he wanted was to go home, take a hot shower, and scrounge up some food. Maybe drink a beer and plant himself in front of the TV for some mindless entertainment until he fell asleep.

But someone needed to stay with Rose, and he didn't trust Jenkins.

Rightfully so, as it turned out.

The pub was closed, so he took the steps up the side of the building to Rose's apartment and found Deputy Jenkins slumped in a chair by her door, head lolling to the side and mouth gaping open as he snored like a goddamn foghorn.

Ash gritted his teeth, fury simmering in his gut. The lazy bastard was part of the old guard, and had escaped the purge after the last sheriff's corruption had been exposed precisely because he was too lazy to have been involved in any of the shoddy police work—but this was the last straw. Ash had decided to give him the benefit of a doubt, but he didn't deserve to reach retirement.

Ash strode over and roughly shook the deputy awake.

Jenkins startled, blinking blearily. "Wha—what is it?"

"Badge," Ash growled and held out a hand.

"Sheriff." He scrambled to his feet and his belly jiggled under his sloppily buttoned uniform shirt. He swiped a sleeve over his sweaty face. "I-I-I was just—"

"And gun. You're fired."

"Wait, what? I—"

"Now."

Jenkins looked stunned, and a hint of anger blazed in his eyes. But he was too lazy to act on it. He'd probably be at the Arrow Tree talking shit tomorrow, but Ash didn't care. He was done tolerating incompetence and laziness on his watch.

Jenkins hesitated for a moment, then fumbled with his holster, unclipping the weapon and handing it over to Ash. His eyes darted around nervously, as if searching for some way to talk his way out of this, but Ash wasn't in the mood to listen. He took the gun and tossed it onto the chair where Jenkins had been sleeping.

"Go home, Jenkins. You're done here."

Jenkins shuffled away, his head hanging low. Ash didn't feel any satisfaction from the man's shame. He was too preoccupied with the anger and frustration that had been building up inside him all day.

The door creaked open behind him.

"What's going on?" Rose emerged from the apartment in an oversized T-shirt, tousled hair tumbling over her shoulders. Her gaze landed on the badge and gun, and she arched a brow. "Did you fire him?"

"It was long overdue."

"I can see why. He was... unpleasant. He smells like onion and snores like a chainsaw symphony."

"Well, he's gone. You can get some rest now. I'll keep watch."

"My hero."

He ignored the snide remark and stepped forward, forcing her to back into her apartment. "Get inside. It's not safe for you to be answering the door."

She visibly bristled. "I don't want a babysitter."

"Too bad. You're stuck with me until we figure out who attacked you."

"I can take care of myself."

"I know you can. But I'm still responsible for your safety."

"Even if I don't want your help?"

"Especially then."

She rolled her eyes and turned away. "Fine. If you're staying, you're not sitting out on the landing snarling at everyone like a gargoyle. You can have the couch."

Ash followed her to the living room, taking note of the way the T-shirt clung to her large breasts as she walked. She wasn't wearing a bra and her nipples poked against the thin cotton, inviting his mouth to—

No.

Shit, what was he thinking?

He forced himself to look away and studied her apartment. A chaotic clash of colors and quirky flea market furniture, it reminded him of her childhood bedroom, only without all the teenage fandom memorabilia. Though he recognized the cat-shaped pillow in the papasan chair. It was the same one she'd hugged during his interview with her all those years ago, now faded and frayed.

The sight of it made his brain short-circuit for a minute. Of course he knew this Rose with her fuck-me body and sassy mouth was the same Rose as the skinny girl with the skinned knees and *Twilight* obsession, but seeing the childhood pillow in her adult living room really hammered that fact home.

He had *no right* to look at her as anything other than a victim who needed protection.

He did a quick patrol around the small space, peeking into her bedroom and bathroom—ignoring the dark floral spice of her scent clinging to the air in both places—and checking to make sure all of her windows were shut and locked.

"So, what now?" she asked when he returned to the living room. "Do we just wait for someone to come after me again?"

"We're not waiting. I'm going to find out who attacked you and make sure they can't hurt you again."

Rose raised an eyebrow. "And how do you plan to do that?"

"I've got a few leads I need to follow up on, but I need your help." He pulled out his notebook. "Let's go over everything again."

She pressed her palm to her forehead like he was giving her a headache. "I don't remember anything. I told you that."

"Maybe something will come back to you. Or maybe there's something you didn't think was important at the time, but could be the key to solving this."

She looked skeptical, but he saw the gears turning.

"Let's start with enemies. Do you have any?" he asked, pen posed above a fresh page.

"Besides you?"

"You know what I mean. Anyone that would want to cause you harm? Patrons of the pub you pissed off? Old boyfriends?"

She flapped her arms in exasperation. "Oh, c'mon. We went over all this in the hospital."

"You were also recovering from a vicious attack and dealing with withdrawal at the time." He decided to ignore the way she rubbed self-consciously at the track marks on her arm. "Going over it again might shake something loose."

She sighed heavily, went into the kitchen and grabbed a bottle of rosé from the small beverage fridge tucked into the island. "Wine?"

"I'm on duty."

"When aren't you?" She poured herself a full glass and took a deep drink.

He glanced away because the long line of her throat led his gaze down to her nipples. It wasn't the first time he'd noticed how attractive Rose was, but he'd always pushed those thoughts aside. It wasn't appropriate, especially not with their age gap and history. But with her scent still lingering in his nose and the way that T-shirt clung to all the right places... he was having a harder time ignoring the attraction.

"You wear that badge like a shield, Sheriff," she said and topped off the glass before returning to the living room. "Anyone ever tell you that?"

His sister.

All the time.

But he wasn't about to get that personal with her. "Can you think of anyone who might want to hurt you?"

"I told you before, no." She sank into the papasan chair and picked up the cat pillow, hugging it to her chest just as she'd done at age thirteen. "I don't have problems with anyone. I like everybody."

"Except me?"

She smirked and curled her legs up under her nightshirt before picking up her wine glass again. "Except you. But unless you hired a hitman…" She let the thought trail off.

"It wasn't me."

She shrugged. "Well, I guess we're out of luck. I honestly don't know who would want to hurt me."

"What about ex-boyfriends?"

"I haven't dated in… God, three years? And my last ex and I weren't serious enough to lead to this. I think he's married now." She shook her head. "No, this must have something to do with Mom's murder. The night I was attacked, my aunt and I were talking about the Jane Doe and about me giving my DNA for comparison."

"In the bar?"

"Yes. Maybe that sparked something. Made someone nervous."

"Was there anyone around to overhear?"

"I mean… maybe? It was right before closing and we weren't busy. There were five or six people in there, including my aunt and the skinny guy who first attacked me."

Ash scribbled the information, flipped to a new page, and realized he was running out. He'd need to buy another paper refill soon. "Who else was there?"

"Uh. Let's see." She looked up at the ceiling as if trying to bring memories of that night back into focus. "We closed at midnight that night. Sophie Foley and May-Lynn Tapia were there from eight until about eleven-thirty-ish. They were drinking those light seltzers that taste like someone is whispering the flavor from the next room over. Sophie just had a break-up. It was a guy-bashing girl's night, but May-Lynn didn't want to corral kindergarteners while hungover the next morning, so they left before last call."

Ash looked up from his notes. "You remember all that, but can't recall anything after the initial attack?"

She shrugged, drank more of her wine. "I'm a bartender. I'm trained to remember patrons. Their favorite drinks, their food orders. Their spouses' and kids' names if they have them. Their hopes and dreams and worries. People drink when they're sad and when they're happy, so I'm there during all their ups and downs. And," she added with a smile, "they tip better when they feel valued." Her smile faded. "As for the attack... part of it is the drugs they gave me inducing amnesia, or so says my doctor. But I think another part of it is I just don't want to remember."

He stared at her for a beat. She looked fragile, curled up like that in the chair, hugging the cat pillow. God knew she wasn't—farthest thing from it—but seeing her like that put a need inside him to wrap her up in a bubble so nothing could hurt her again.

He didn't like it.

He cleared his throat, looked back down at his notes. "Who else?"

She exhaled a sharp breath. "Um... Larry Lamb and Gordon McDaniel. They're two of my regular seat warmers and left right before last call."

Ash looked at her again. "Did you say Larry Lamb?"

"Yeah." She set her wine on the end table and uncurled from the chair. "Why?"

"He was the main eyewitness against your Dad."

"What? Larry?" A frown creased her forehead. "I never saw his name in any of the reports."

"Yeah, that was Tennison pulling his usual shit, keeping his buddy's name out of it. He was Witness A for the prosecution."

"Wait, that was Larry? But Witness A said he saw Dad putting something that looked like a body into his trunk. He lied. Dad wasn't even home when he said he saw him."

Dread unfurled in Ash's chest. "How do you know he lied?"

"Because I was there. I was home alone at that time. I even talked to Larry. He was out gardening."

"And you told Tennison?" Because, dammit, it was the first time he was hearing any of this.

She nodded. "And Dad's public defender, but it never came up again after that. They wouldn't let me in the courtroom for the trial, so I didn't know. God. Larry? And now that bastard comes into my bar every night. He looks me in the face and jokes with me and—and he's one of my best tippers. How could he...? You don't think he...?" She trailed off and abruptly shoved to her feet. "I'm tired. Can we finish this some other time?"

Ash closed his notebook. "Sure."

She didn't look at him as she walked by. "There are blankets inside that ottoman. If a fat furball tries to smother you in your sleep, it's just Fanta, my cat."

"I don't plan to sleep."

"Fine. Do whatever."

Because he wanted to reach out and catch her hand, he stuffed both of his into his jacket pockets along with his notebook. But he couldn't help calling out, "Rose."

She stopped in the doorway of her bedroom, but didn't look back.

He suddenly couldn't think of what he'd meant to say. Something comforting, or reassuring, but he'd never been great at that. So he settled on, "Good night."

She murmured something that might have been a "good night" then disappeared into her room, firmly shutting the door behind her.

Ash exhaled and leaned back on the couch. As he did, the cat she'd mentioned poked its head from behind the chair she'd just left. It was fat and as orange as a blazing fire, with a thin white stripe under its nose that looked like a cartoon villain mustache. It eyed him like it was waiting for him to sleep so it could attempt murder.

He eyed it back. "Don't get any ideas. I'm not falling asleep, cat."

Fanta padded over and jumped up on his lap. It circled a few times then curled up, purring happily. He rubbed a hand down its back and thought of Dante. He hadn't asked Anna how the dog was doing, and guilt ate at him for it.

"I think I'm more of a cat person," he told Fanta.

The soft warmth of the cat's body combined with the hypnotic motor of its purr eased the tension from his neck and shoulders.

Yeah, he decided, leaning his head back against the couch. He was definitely more of a cat person.

chapter
thirteen

SOMETIME IN THE middle of the night, the sound of the front door opening startled Ash out of a doze. He wasn't asleep, but he wasn't fully awake when the man stepped over the threshold.

Ash jumped to his feet and raised his gun, feeling fuzzy and sloppy. He was moving too slow. If this was the guy he'd faced in the woods, he might have just gotten both himself and Rose killed.

Fuck.

"Hands up! Get down! On the floor now!"

The shadow froze, then slowly raised his hands. "Ash?"

Wait. He knew that voice.

He turned on the light. "Zak?" He lowered his gun and stared at his brother-in-law in disbelief. "What the fuck are you doing here?"

Zak looked like hell, his eyes red-rimmed and puffy, his hair standing up like he'd assaulted it with both hands. His shoulders drooped in defeat. "I just... needed somewhere to crash."

"So you came *here*? Why aren't you home?" A knot of dread twisted up his stomach as he glanced between Zak and

Rose, who had appeared in her bedroom doorway still wearing that thin oversized T-shirt. Her nipples pebbled in the cool air. He had an irrational urge to throw a blanket over her and that pissed him off.

He turned that anger on Zak. "You better not be fucking around on my sister, Hendricks."

"What? No! That's not— I just—" He lifted his hands in defense, but didn't seem to know what to do with them and dropped them back to his sides.

"Wow, Sheriff. You think so highly of me." Rose disappeared into her room for a second, then came back dressed in a robe. She went to Zak's side, taking his hand and leading him over to the couch. "I told Zak—*and* everyone else in his therapy group—that my couch is always open to them. Judgement free, so put that scowl away."

As she passed, Ash caught her scent—that heady, feminine spice that had his cock swelling inappropriately. Thankfully, she'd put on the thick robe that covered her down to her knees, so at least those nipples couldn't distract him anymore.

He holstered his gun and, while her back was turned, surreptitiously adjusted himself. She didn't notice but Zak did, and a small smile ticked up the corner of his mouth.

Dammit.

"Did you and Anna have a fight?" he asked before Zak could open his mouth and say something stupid about his unruly dick.

Zak groaned and buried his face in his hands. "It's my fault."

"Why?"

Zak just groaned again and leaned back against the couch cushions, eyes closed.

Rose headed toward her kitchen. "How about a drink?"

"Not everything can be solved with alcohol," Ash said. Zak hadn't had a drop of alcohol in nearly two years and, if nothing else, Ash planned to keep the man dry for his sister's sake. "He's sober."

Rose made a face at him over her shoulder and pulled a six pack of cola from her fridge—the good stuff in glass bottles. "I'm well aware he's sober, Sheriff. I was there when he bought his last drink." The soda bottles clinked gently as she extracted three from the cardboard carrier and returned the rest to the fridge. She picked a magnetic bottle opener shaped like the Mad Dog's bulldog logo from the fridge's door and expertly flicked off each of the caps. "I watched him make the choice that it was his last and was so damn proud of him for it. Then I watched you finish the beer for him so he wouldn't feel obligated, and I was damn proud of you for that, too."

She pushed one of the sodas into his hand, careful not to let any part of their skin brush, then continued on to the couch. "But Zak's not falling off the wagon tonight. I've been a bartender long enough to know when someone's at that edge, and he isn't. He's just pissed at himself and afraid he fucked up the best thing in his life and needs someone impartial to talk to. Since I was his bartender during some of the worst years of his life, I felt like the safest choice." She knelt in front of Zak and offered the bottle. "Isn't that right?"

Zak smiled faintly as he accepted the soda and clinked the neck of the bottle to hers. "Nailed it."

"So." She sat down on the carpet in front of him and pulled her legs up under her robe, looping her arms loosely around her knees. Her drink dangled from one hand. "What's up?"

Zak glanced in Ash's direction and, if he wasn't mistaken, that was shame on the guy's face.

"Nah, ignore the broody Neanderthal in the corner. Just pretend we're sitting at the bar late one night after closing and I'm feeding you glass after glass of water to sober you up. It's just us again. Talk to me like that."

Zak took a long drink of his soda. "It was easier to talk when I was wasted."

"I know," she said sympathetically. "But I also know you prefer your life now that you're sober."

Zak nodded, his eyes fixated on the bottle in his hand. "Anna... she just... wants me to be healed."

"Of course she does. She loves you."

"No, not like—I'm not saying this right." He set aside his drink and rubbed his hands on the thighs of his cargo pants. "Okay, let me start over. Last fall, I overheard her telling Sasha that I was in a good headspace, like my baggage didn't exist anymore. Which, some days, it's true. I feel great and I can forget what those bastards did to me over in Afghanistan. But that's not every day. And ever since I heard her say that, I've been... I guess, hiding."

"Have you mentioned this in group?"

He shook his head. "I'm supposed to be the poster child of success. I pointed to all the training I did with Ranger and told them all this K9 shit works. That having this purpose with the dogs helps. That it heals."

"It does," Ash said and returned to his seat on the couch. "I was the most skeptical of everyone and you proved me wrong. I watched it heal you. And Donovan. I've watched Pierce come out of his shell because you gave him Raszta and freaking Sawyer attempting things a blind man probably shouldn't be doing. The training you guys are doing with those dogs does heal."

Zak looked at him again but this time, there was no shame in his eyes. It was all misery. "But it's not the miracle pill I made it out to be. I still have nightmares. I still wake up soaked in a cold sweat, desperate to not fall back asleep. I still flash back to my captivity—all those moments I thought I was dead, all the moments I *wished* I was dead. It's all up here still." He tapped his temple. "But Anna thinks I'm healed. I'm all better now because I have her and the girls and Ranger and the group. So I've been hiding all that darkness. It's eating me alive and I'm taking it out on her and the girls. They don't deserve that."

Rose nodded. "And, tonight, you said something you regret."

"Yeah." He looked away and swallowed hard. "I told her that I didn't want to be with them anymore."

"Ah, shit." Ash scrubbed his hands over his face, then let them fall to the back of his neck. "That's why she was crying when I called earlier. I knew something was wrong, but she wouldn't tell me."

"They deserve someone who isn't living a lie," Rose said firmly. "Your wife and daughters deserve to know every part of you, Zak. They deserve the good, the bad, and the ugly. They deserve you—all of you."

"I'm not sure I know how to be all of me."

"Jesus, you're an idiot," Ash said. "AJ doesn't care if you're a little fucked up. If we're honest, she likes fucked up. My sister knew exactly what she signed up for when she married you."

"The Queen of Lost Causes," Zak murmured with a faint smile. "But what if..." He trailed off, then exhaled and tried again: "I'm not sure I can do this. I'm not sure I can be the husband she wants or the father the girls need. What if she gets sick of the night terrors and mood swings and the constant war I'm fighting with myself? What if I backslide so far that I take a drink? We have Bella and Poppy now. She has to put their needs first—and I'm not saying she shouldn't because I love those girls and want nothing more than for them to be safe and happy. But if I fuck up, she'll have to make a choice between me and them."

Rose reached out and took his hand, squeezing his fingers gently. "It's bad, isn't it? The nightmares?"

His eyes were full of anguish. "I can feel myself spiraling and I'm afraid to reach out for help. I'm afraid I'll drag them down with me. I won't expose them to this. I won't poison them with my darkness."

"You're not alone, you know. You've got me. And Ash." She nodded in his direction. "And you've got the guys from group, too."

"What if they can't help me this time?"

"They won't be able to fix you," Rose said. "That's not their job. They won't fix your nightmares or take away the panic attacks. They won't give you a magic pill that takes away the memories. Those things don't exist. But they will be there for you and if one person can't help, then we'll get you someone that can. But, Zak, if you don't reach out and try, then you're going to lose everything."

"You're right," he said, his voice hoarse. "I can't keep hiding like this. I need to face my demons and talk to Anna. I need to tell her everything and hope that she understands."

"She will," Ash said with absolute certainty. He knew his sister better than anyone. Zak might not be able to see it, but his worries were unfounded.

"She loves you," Rose added. "She'll understand."

chapter
fourteen

POOR GUY.

Rose walked Zak out and waited until she heard his truck's engine roar to life before shutting and locking the door. She turned and found Ash right behind her, his arms crossed over his chest. His face was a carefully blank mask, which she was learning meant he was pissed.

A muscle flexed under his beard. "Exactly *how many* other people have keys to this place?"

She shrugged and tried to shoulder by him. "Just friends."

He caught her arm. "So you don't know."

"I never needed to know. My door's usually open. Now let go of me."

As if just realizing he held her arm, he released it and stepped back. "Jesus. Why do I have to keep reminding you that someone tried to kill you?"

"You don't. I'm well aware."

"Twice," he stressed, holding up two fingers.

"Yes, I know."

"I don't think you do, Ambrosia. Once is usually all it takes. You got lucky twice. Odds say you won't get lucky a third time, which is why I'm trying to prevent the bastard from having another shot at you." He dropped his head forward and sighed in exasperation, rubbing a hand around the back of his neck. "All right. Pack a bag." He eyed her cat, who was sitting on the back of the couch, watching Ash like he was a god. "And the orange beast."

"Why?"

"You're staying at my place until we can get someone in here to change your locks."

Rose frowned. "I don't need to stay at your place. And I don't need you to stay here. I can protect myself."

He raised an eyebrow and motioned toward the door. "Clearly not if everyone and their fucking brother-in-law has a key."

Rose bit her lip. She knew he was right, but she hated the idea of being dependent on anyone, especially Ash.

"Fine." Without another word, she headed to her bedroom, grabbed a duffel bag from her closet and tossed in a few essentials. She wouldn't be gone long. She'd call a locksmith first thing and schedule an appointment to update her locks.

She hesitated, then grabbed a small handgun from the drawer of her nightstand and slipped it into her bag. She had never used it before, but she felt better knowing she had some form of protection besides the grumpy sheriff. She didn't want him to know, but she *was* scared.

Before leaving her room, she took a moment to pull on jeans and a hoodie over her nightshirt.

Ash was waiting for her by the door, his own duffel bag slung over his shoulder. Fanta was clinging to his chest, looking up at him with adoration. He stroked a hand over the cat's head and his expression was as gentle as she'd ever seen it. He was so handsome when he smiled like that, all his hard edges softened.

A weird warmth spread through her chest. She wished he'd smile at her like that.

Wait.

Oh, hell, no.

She just had to zip her libido back up because she wasn't going to fall for the fucking sheriff.

"Huh." She opened the hall closet and pulled out Fanta's carrier. "Always knew that cat had horrible taste in men."

It really wasn't Fanta's taste she had to worry about.

She pulled Fanta out of his arms and tucked the yowling feline into the carrier, then went to the kitchen to grab several cans of cat food from the pantry to add to her duffle.

His expression shifted back to grim cop. She couldn't see him as Ash when he looked like this. Ash was the guy who'd been snuggling her cat moments ago. The man in front of her now was The Sheriff, capitalized. Gruff and flat-eyed. All business.

"You ready?" he asked.

Rose nodded, slinging the bag over her shoulder and picking up Fanta's carrier.

The night air was cold and crisp, but Rose barely felt it as she hurried to keep up with Ash's long strides. His Tahoe was parked in the alley behind the bar, and he opened the passenger side door for her before circling the hood to the driver's seat.

The drive was mostly silent, except for the occasional protesting meow from her cat. Rose couldn't shake the feeling of unease blossoming in her stomach. She knew she was safe with Ash, but the fact he thought she needed to leave her home was unsettling.

Ash's house was a sprawling ranch tucked on a gated property deep in the redwoods. It sat at the end of a long dirt driveway, with a wide, welcoming porch and a large yard. The wood siding was such a deep, rich color, it looked black in the moonlight. In the valley below the house, the town's lights sparkled. She bet if she walked out onto his back porch, she'd clearly see the Mad Dog at the edge of town.

Ash led her inside, flicking on the lights as they entered. The house was tastefully decorated, with neutral colors and modern furnishings, but it lacked any personal touches. It felt empty and sterile compared to her cozy, cluttered space and she felt a pang of sympathy for him. No doubt he was too busy working to bother with furnishing his home.

"This is nice," Rose said, trying to make conversation. She paused and looked at the living room. A brick fireplace dominated the wall between two floor-to-ceiling triangular windows, and a large-screen TV hung over the mantel. There were two leather chairs in a neutral beige and a coffee table, but—

"Where's your couch?"

"Dog ate it."

"A dog ate your couch?"

Ash grunted in response, setting his bag down in the entryway. "I'll go get you some towels and show you where you'll be sleeping."

Rose nodded, setting Fanta's carrier down on the floor. She unzipped it far enough to reach a hand inside and rub the cat's head. "It's okay, buddy," she whispered. "We're safe."

She didn't know if she was trying to convince Fanta or herself.

When Ash returned with the towels, he led her across the living room and down a short hallway to a spare bedroom. "You can sleep here," he said, opening the door. "You'll want to keep the cat in here when Dante gets home. I don't know how he'll react."

"Dante?"

"One of my sister's pet projects she railroaded me into

taking. He's kenneled at the rescue because he ate the couch. And the drywall. For all I know, he might eat the cat, too."

"Okay."

"The bathroom is back through the living room, just off the foyer. My room is here on the left if you need anything."

Rose nodded, taking the towels from him. "Thanks."

Ash hesitated for a moment, as if he wanted to say something, but then he just nodded and left, closing the door behind him.

Rose took a deep breath and exhaled slowly. She was relieved to be in a safe environment, but it was awkward being in Ash's house, especially with the weird sexual tension that had been crackling between them all night. She set the towels on the bed and crossed to the window. From here, she could see nothing but the dark, dense trees that surrounded the house. She should feel safer out here, in the middle of nowhere.

She didn't.

She shook her head, trying to dislodge the creeping fear.

She *was* safe here with Ash.

Untangling the cat from his carrier, she set him on the bed and began to unpack her bag. She pulled out her laptop, charger, and a few books, but hesitated when she reached the handgun.

Should she tell Ash she had it?

If she did, would he take it from her?

But she needed to feel safe, and the gun was the only thing that made her feel even remotely secure. She tucked it under her pillow and tried to convince herself that she wouldn't need it.

chapter
fifteen

ROSE BOLTED AWAKE, scaring Fanta off the end of her bed. No, wait. This wasn't her bed. Wasn't her room.

Where was she?

Panic grabbed her in a chokehold.

Oh, God. She hadn't gotten away. Her captors still had her, and they were going to do horrible things—

But... no, that wasn't right either.

She stared at the outlines in the unfamiliar room and her suitcase by the dresser slowly came into focus. Fanta peeked out from behind it, his eyes reflecting back the soft moonlight filtering in from the window, wide and wary.

She was at Ash Rawlings' house.

She was safe.

Shivering from a cold sweat, she pulled her knees to her chest and buried her face in them. The nightmares were getting worse as the weeks dragged on, not better. She'd told Zak to reach out for help, while here she was, drowning.

Now who was a hypocrite?

But the difference was, Zak had the Paws for Vets therapy group to lean on. She wasn't a veteran, so that option was out. She couldn't talk to her family. She didn't want Rainbow to worry, and no way was she telling her dad she'd been attacked and was now suffering a traumatic stress reaction.

No. She had to handle this on her own. Which was usually how she preferred it, but right now, she ached to confide in someone.

As if sensing her thoughts, Fanta padded across the floor and leapt onto the bed, pushing his head under her arms, seeking a scratch.

"Yes," she told him and rubbed a hand over his head. "I know I have you, but sometimes I need someone other than a cat."

Someone who could hold her through the worst of the after-nightmare fear and tell her it would be okay.

Someone like Ash.

No.

God, where had that thought come from?

She didn't even like the man.

Disgusted with herself, she flung off the covers and pulled on her robe. She crossed to the door and when she opened it a crack, realized that the house wasn't silent. A low buzz of conversation floated from the living room. She backtracked for her phone and checked the screen. It was almost 3 a.m.

"He's not still working, is he?"

Fanta mewed and patted down her pillow before curling into a fluffy orange ball in the divot where her head had been. She smiled at the cat then slipped out into the hall and followed the sounds. As she got closer, she realized he wasn't having a witching hour meeting with one of his deputies, after all. The TV was on, casting a blue glow over the otherwise dark room, the volume low. He sat in one of the leather chairs with his back to her, dozing if the angle of his head was any indication. He was going to have a hell of a neck ache when he woke up.

She moved closer.

On the coffee table in front of him sat more paperwork. Seemed like any time she saw him lately, he was surrounded by stacks of it. She turned one file toward her and read the name on in. Maria Socktish. Under that was one labeled Harmony Galasso.

Mom.

She itched to open it up and read what was in the official police reports, but she knew better. It'd just piss her off and she was too exhausted.

Ash jolted awake with a snort. Which was adorable, but she wasn't about to tell him that.

I don't like him, she reminded herself firmly.

"Rose?" He came half out of the chair, but sank back when she curled up in the other chair across from him. He fumbled through the files for the remote and paused the TV. "Did I wake you?"

She had no intention of telling him about her nightmares, so she just shrugged and looked at the frozen image on screen. A pretty, blood-spattered blonde ran from a hoard of zombies, screaming silently. It was very low budget, but, she realized, it wasn't just something that had come on while he was sleeping. It was a movie, a DVD he'd deliberately chosen. The case sat open on top of the player, and she walked over to pick it up.

She smirked at him. "*Zombocalypse Wow!* Isn't this awfully lowbrow for you, Sheriff Rawlings?"

"You're one to talk." His voice was rough with sleep. "I seem to remember a bright purple bedroom plastered in *Twilight* merch."

She rolled her eyes. "I was a kid. You're allowed to like dumb things as a kid. But this?" She held up the DVD case. "I expected better from you."

He groaned and rubbed both hands over his face, mussing his beard. "Can we not do this? I'm too tired."

She frowned down at the bad artwork on the DVD's case, then set it aside. "I wasn't making fun."

"Yeah, you were."

"Okay, fine. But I didn't mean—"

"Yeah, you did." He reached for the remote again, presumably to turn the movie off, but she got to it first and held it out of his reach.

"Why horror?" she asked, suddenly intrigued.

He leaned back in the chair, and glared at her with bleary eyes. "What do you mean?"

"Why do you watch horror movies? You're a cop. You see the real thing all the time. You don't need fake scares."

Ash shrugged. "It's a way to escape. To feel something other than the constant stress of this job. And it's not like I can't handle the sight of fake blood and gore."

"I'm not saying you can't."

"You're saying it's lowbrow."

"I didn't mean it like that. I just... it surprised me."

"Why?"

"I don't know." She turned the remote over in her hands a couple times. "You seem like the type that would watch documentaries on the evolution of the justice system or something."

He laughed softly. "Jesus. I'm not that boring."

"I didn't say boring."

"But that's what you meant."

"Stop telling me what I mean." She rolled her eyes. "But, yes, I thought you were as boring as white bread."

"White bread is good."

He said it so deadpan, she couldn't help but laugh. "Was that a joke?"

"I don't joke." But his cheek twitched under his beard. "I'm boring, remember?"

"You're not boring... exactly. You're just so serious all the time, I never expected to find you enjoying campy, low budget horror movies."

"It's mindless," he said abruptly and motioned to the stacks of files on the table. "This fucking job. There's always something else to do, something else to worry about. Sometimes I feel like I'm drowning in it, like there's no end to the darkness, but these dumb movies help me forget about the real horrors out there. I don't have to think about murder or corruption while watching zombies get their brains bashed in. It's... perversely soothing."

She held out the remote, allowing him to take it from her. "I get that."

"Do you?" He sounded skeptical.

"I mean, not exactly the same thing, obviously. But I do know what it's like to have your mind running in circles. To feel like you're drowning in... stuff."

"Stuff," he repeated, a hint of a smile tugging at the corner of his mouth.

"Yeah. Stuff." She turned to go back to her room. "I'm sorry. I shouldn't be barging in here in the middle of the night."

He waved away the apology. "I wasn't sleeping anyway."

She raised an eyebrow. "You looked pretty out of it to me."

"I was just resting my eyes."

"Uh huh. Then I'll go so you can continue resting your eyes."

He stared at her a beat. "Stay. Please."

She ignored the flutter in her belly at his soft words and sank into the empty chair again, pulling her legs up under her robe to keep them warm. She looked at the stacks of paperwork. "Are you sure you're not overworking yourself?"

He sighed, a deep, heavy sound. "You sound like my sister. I'm fine."

"You don't look fine."

"I'm a mess, okay?" he snapped, his frustration palpable. "Is that what you want to hear? That I don't have my shit together? Because I don't. The more I look into your mother's case, the more I think we fucked it up and sent an innocent man to prison. And I can't seem to get any leads on who attacked you. And I have to review every single case my mentor ever breathed on because I can't have his stink on my department. Then there's that podcaster running around town, chasing serial killer urban legends and the kicker is, I'm afraid she's actually on to something. And tonight I find out my brother-in-law is thinking of leaving my sister. It will destroy her. I had to watch that destruction the first time he walked away when we were teenagers. I won't watch it again. I'll have to kill him and then I'll end up cellmates with the former sheriff. Hell, maybe that would be for the better." He exhaled a hard breath that sounded like a bitter attempt at a laugh. "The tighter I try to hold this town and my family together, the more they both fracture."

The pang of empathy for him caught her by surprise. It must be hard, carrying the weight of the town's problems on your shoulders day in and day out. She didn't envy him that burden. "Maybe you're hanging on too tight."

"What do you mean?" Exhaustion weighed down his voice.

"You're trying to control everything and everyone around you, and it's driving you insane. You can't carry the burden of everyone's mistakes and problems on your shoulders. It's not fair to you, or to them. Sometimes, things just happen, and you have to roll with it."

"Do I look like the kind of guy that can just roll with it?" he asked. "If I let go, everything falls apart. I'm the only thing standing between this county and lawless chaos."

At first, she thought he was joking again—it was so hard

to tell with him and his deadpan humor—but then she realized he truly believed that. She shook her head in awe.

God, the ego on this man!

"You're such a hypocrite. You broke the law. Many times, if local gossip is to be believed. And you weren't punished."

"No, I wasn't, but I should've been. Someone should've held me to the same standards as everyone else and not put me up on a fucking pedestal because of the family I was born into. Someone should've told me no, and they never did, and someone I cared about died because of it. So, yes. I'm a hypocrite, but I'll be damned if I let some stupid kid make the same mistakes because I didn't tell him no."

"What mistakes?"

He shut down. "Forget it."

She studied him for a long moment. She was usually good at getting a read on people—came with the job—but he was still a complete mystery to her. "You don't actually believe you're the only thing standing between us and chaos?"

He didn't respond.

She rolled her eyes. "You have a whole team of deputies who are more than capable of handling things when you can't. And you have to trust that the county, the town, and your family, are strong enough to handle their own problems sometimes."

When he opened his mouth to argue, she cut him off. "I'm not saying to let chaos reign. I'm saying that you can't control everything, and you'll exhaust yourself trying. You can only do your best and trust that others will do theirs."

He rubbed a hand over his face, then eyed her with suspicion. "You're being nice. Why are you being nice to me?"

Her stomach twisted. "I don't know," she said honestly. "Maybe because you stayed with me when I was hurting. And because I know what it's like to feel like you're drowning, and no one seems to notice. Or maybe because you're a good man, even if you drive me fucking crazy most of the time."

He chuckled softly. "*I* drive *you* crazy?"

"You know you do."

"Ditto, Ambrosia."

The soft, growly way he said her full name sent a bolt of lust through her belly. She uncurled from the chair. "I'm going back to bed."

She had to get away from him before she did something entirely inappropriate.

"THE SHERIFF WON'T BE HAPPY."

Rose sent Deputy Mike Conti a big smile over her shoulder as she unlocked the front door of the Mad Dog. "Is he ever?"

Conti tilted his head in consideration. "Point to you. But I'd still prefer not to piss him off. I'd like to keep my badge."

"Jenkins only lost his because he was sleeping on the job."

"That doesn't surprise me at all. His lazy ass should've been fired years ago. Here, let me go in first." Gun in hand, he nudged her aside and pushed open the door. He came back a moment later. "It's clear."

She rolled her eyes and stepped through, flicking on the light. "I could've told you that."

"Better safe than dead."

"Point to Deputy Conti." She sketched it in the air and started back to her office.

He took up his position on the stool by the door. "Just Mike, please."

"Okay, Just Mike." If she had to be stuck with a babysitter, she could do worse than the affable Mike Conti. Like Jenkins. Or Ash. She definitely couldn't deal with him right now. She was too raw, too wired, too... everything. "Do you want a water or soda? Coffee?"

"Nah, not yet. Thanks, though." He watched her start her opening procedure: checking stock, giving the bar another wipe down, counting the cash drawer. "Need help with anything?"

"Nope." She needed the busy work. She hadn't slept a wink after leaving Ash last night, too twisted up about the weird bolts of lust she'd experienced around him and too afraid the nightmares would drag her under again.

Mike looked at the sign on the front door. "I thought you opened at one. Do you always get in three hours before opening?"

"Not always. On Wednesdays, I have a group that comes in to use the multipurpose room." She didn't tell him it was a therapy group. The Paws for Vets group was the main reason she was so determined to open today. After Zak's visit last night, he needed the session today.

And so did she, if they'd have her, because she couldn't keep living with panic constantly humming under her skin, ready to rear its ugly head at the slightest provocation.

The first to arrive was Sawyer Murphy with his seeing eye dog, Zelda. He was always early, and they'd fallen into playing a "guess that drink" game—she'd mix a new mocktail for him and he'd have to guess what it was by smell. Today's concoction was pineapple-ginger punch: pineapple juice and ginger beer, blended with a little bit of lime juice and garnished with mint.

All of the group were recovering addicts, so she'd made sure to beef up her non-alcoholic drink menu when they'd started using her pub as their meeting place after the fire last fall destroyed Redwood Coast Rescue. With RWCR's new facilities about finished, she imagined they'd go back there for meetings before long. She'd miss them all when they did.

Sawyer paused at the end of the bar and grinned in her direction. "I smell pineapple and ginger and a hint of lime."

She set the finished drink in front of him. "From all the way across the room?"

He tapped his nose. "I have a super sniffer. Like my dog."

Zelda's tail whipped the air and Rose bent down to give the chocolate lab some love while Sawyer tested the drink.

"Shit, Rose. That's good."

"It's pineapple-ginger punch. I'm thinking of adding it to the menu. Both an alcoholic and the non-alcoholic version."

"You should. What are you thinking for the alcohol?"

"Maybe tequila? Make it margarita-ish."

He took another drink. "It'll sell. In both forms."

"Can I try it?" Mike asked and Sawyer jolted, spilling his drink on the bar.

"Jesus." He looked toward Mike's voice. "I didn't realize anyone else was here."

"My babysitter," Rose said and grabbed a towel to wipe up the spill. "Ash's orders. That's Deputy Conti."

"Mike," Sawyer said in greeting and raised his glass in his direction. "Make some noise or move next time I come in, unless you wanna give me a heart attack."

"Sorry, Sawyer."

He turned back to the bar and slapped down a twenty. "Get the man a drink. On me."

Rose sighed and tried to push the money back at him, but he wouldn't take it. "You know you don't have to pay during group."

"Consider it a tip then. For your beauty." He blew her a kiss, then followed his dog back to the multipurpose room.

"You can't even see me, you shameless flirt. For all you know, I'm cross-eyed and snaggle-toothed."

"Beauty goes beyond looks," he called back. "And you *are* beautiful."

And she melted. If she were a different person, she'd snap the sweet man up before another woman got to him. But given the star of her recent fantasies—Ash freaking Rawlings—her libido apparently wasn't interested in sweet.

As she made the ginger-pineapple mocktail for Mike, Dr. Amelia Firestone arrived at the same time as Pierce St. James. Both liked coffee—black for Pierce and cream and sugar for the doctor.

"Hi, Rose," Dr. Firestone said. "How are you?"

Oh, that was a loaded question. There was so much she could say to answer that, but she wanted to wait until everyone arrived before she asked to join them. "I'm okay."

The doubt in Dr. Firestone's kind eyes said she didn't believe that for a second, but she didn't press. She accepted her coffee with a smile and headed back.

Pierce lifted his mug and nodded his thanks as he followed the doctor. He couldn't speak and Rose didn't know the sign language he used to communicate, so their interactions were always brief.

Next to arrive was Donovan Scott. He was a simple drink kind of guy—club soda and lemon. He eyed Mike as he came in, then hitched a thumb over his shoulder at the guy. "Ash's idea?"

"How'd you guess?"

"I know Ash."

She studied him as she prepared his drink. He'd been seriously injured during the fire, but he looked good now. Maybe a little less muscular than he used to be, but healthy and happy. She nodded toward his wedding band as she set his drink in front of him. "Marriage looks good on you, Van."

He grinned. "It does, doesn't it?"

She laughed. "How's Sasha?" His new wife was the town's best veterinarian.

"Good. Busy getting ready to move back to the Rescue.

She can't wait to get into her new clinic. Dr. Richards is wearing on her last nerve at the hospital in town."

"Well, it's hard working for someone else when you're used to being the boss." She'd been her own boss since she took over the Mad Dog and couldn't imagine answering to anyone else. It was difficult enough following Ash's rules, and those were meant to keep her safe.

"Don't I know it," he said as the door opened, and Zak stepped in. "Especially when that someone else is a tyrant."

"If my employees weren't such assholes, I wouldn't have to be a tyrant," Zak said. He looked haggard and drawn, more like the man he'd been two years ago when he'd been at rock bottom. He nodded at the deputy. "Hi, Mike."

"Zak." Mike nodded a hello, then went back to reading something on his phone.

"Asshole is my default setting," Donovan said good-naturedly and took a swig from his glass. "You knew that when you hired me for your doggie A-team." He started back to join the others, but stopped and spun around. "Oh, Rose. Before I forget, Sasha wanted me to remind you your cat is due for some vaccines."

Tears rushed into her eyes and clogged up her throat. She was so grateful they were all treating her like normal. She hadn't known what to expect, but this simple, every day interaction was such a relief. She didn't want to be handled like fine china, because the more delicate people were with her, the more she felt like she'd break.

"I'll make an appointment," she finally managed.

"No need. Just pop in to see the new clinic when you get the chance and Sash will squeeze you in." He walked away, leaving just her and Zak in the bar. And of course Mike, but he was ignoring them.

She turned to Zak. "How—"

The door opened again, and the final member of their

group walked in. Veronica Martens never asked for a drink. She rarely ever spoke. She kept her head down, her shoulders hunched, and hurried into the back room.

That woman had shields for her shields.

Zak tapped his knuckles on the bar. "I should get back."

He made it to the door of the multipurpose room before she worked up the courage to speak again. "Wait."

His shoulders stiffened. "I don't want to talk about last night."

"It's not that." She stepped out from behind the bar and walked over to him, her heart pounding so hard he must have heard it. "I..." She looked at the closed door in front of them and felt ridiculous. "Never mind."

Zak studied her for a long moment, then pulled open the door. "You want to come in?"

"I..." She bit her lip and glanced inside. She'd recently purchased a long reclaimed wood table for the room, but the group members had pushed it against the wall and were busy placing the chairs in a circle. "Will they have me?"

"Ask them."

chapter
seventeen

"HEY, GUYS," Zak said, taking his usual seat between Sawyer and Dr. Firestone. "Rose wants to ask us something."

Everyone turned to look at her. She took a deep, steadying breath. "Uh, I know I'm not a veteran, but I was hoping I could sit in on these sessions? Because—" Her voice broke, and she cleared her throat. "Because I need help and I don't know where else to go."

"Of course," Dr. Firestone said. "You're more than welcome, as long as nobody has any objections."

"It's okay if you do," Rose added quickly. "I get it. I won't hold it against you."

"You've helped all of us plenty in the past," Zak said. *Including me last night*, his eyes said, though he didn't add that out loud. "None of us would ever object to helping you just because you didn't serve."

A murmur of agreements went through the group. Pierce jumped up and grabbed another chair, inserting it into the circle between his seat and Sawyer's. He waved her toward it, his hazel eyes solemn but earnest. She resisted the urge to hug him.

"Thank you."

"Do you want to start by telling us a bit about yourself?" Dr. Firestone asked. "What brought you to us? You can go into as much or as little detail as you want."

She took a fortifying breath and sat in the offered chair. "I'm sure you all know I... I was abducted." She motioned toward the door. "Right out front there while I was closing one night. They had me for a couple days and we're pretty sure they meant for me to die. They even sent someone after me at the hospital, but Ash was there and stopped him before he got close enough to try anything."

A low growl rumbled through the room. She glanced up, startled, but couldn't pinpoint which of the men it came from. But for the first time, she saw their rage on her behalf. The four men all but steamed with it. They'd done such a good job hiding it outside this room, she hadn't realized how much her abduction had pissed them off. Even Veronica and Dr. Firestone looked upset, though Dr. Firestone did a much better job of keeping her expression pleasantly neutral.

"Ash better catch the bastards who did it before we do," Donovan said. "They'll fare better with him."

She blinked at them, then glanced over at Zak. "You have RWCR looking into it?"

"Of course I do, Rose. You're one of us." His lips quirked. "But maybe let's not tell Ash? It'll piss him off."

Sawyer held out his arms as if embracing the whole room. "This is the chamber of secrets. Nothing said here leaves these four walls."

Donovan snorted. "Of course you're a Harry Potter fan."

"Hey, you caught the reference."

"Anyone born in the nineties would catch that reference."

Sawyer's pale eyes narrowed. He wasn't quite looking at Donovan, but in his direction. "I bet you're a Slytherin."

"I have no idea what that even means."

Sawyer leaned toward Rose as if to divulge a secret. "Definitely a Slytherin."

"Boys. Focus." Dr. Firestone shifted toward Rose and smoothly guided the conversation back on track. "That was a very traumatic event for you. How are you coping?"

She tried for a smile. It felt weak and tired. "Okay I think? I don't remember much, but I'm having nightmares about what I do remember. And maybe about stuff I don't. It's all twisted up in my head and I don't know if what I'm dreaming is real or if I'm just imagining the worst case."

"It could be a bit of both. That's very normal," the doctor said gently. "You're processing the trauma."

"Yeah, I figured, but..." She brushed a strand of hair away from her face as the memories clawed at the edges of her mind. "During those days they had me, they kept me subdued by injecting me with heroin against my will." She pushed up her sleeve and held out her arm so they could see the fading bruises.

"Fuck," Donovan said and popped to his feet, pacing away from the group.

Rose watched him go. He'd lost a close friend—a former member of this therapy group—to a heroin overdose. And like Rose, Chrissy had been injected against her will.

"I'm sorry," she whispered.

He swung back, his jaw set, his expression a storm cloud. "Don't you dare fucking apologize. Not to me, not to your-self. You didn't ask for any of this. It's not your fault."

Rose lowered her gaze to her lap as a strange mix of grati-tude and guilt washed over her. "I know it's not," she said, her voice small. "But... but sometimes I can't help feeling like it is. Like I could've done something to prevent it. Or like I brought it on myself somehow."

Donovan shook his head. "You couldn't have prevented it and worrying about whether or not you could've is a waste of time and energy and sanity. Believe me, Rose. I know what it's like to blame yourself for things beyond your control. But the truth is, sometimes you just have to take the punches as they come and then find a way to get back up on your feet when it's over."

Hadn't she said something very similar to Ash just last night? It had been so easy to dole out that sage bit of advice, but not so simple to follow it herself.

She touched a spot on her face where one of the bruises had turned a sickly yellow. She'd done her best to hide it with make-up that morning, but she knew it was still visible. "How do I get back up?"

Donovan shook his head. "Unfortunately, I can't tell you that."

"It's for you to figure out," Dr. Firestone said. "But we can help. How are you feeling?"

"I guess I'm getting better," she hedged. "Everything is healing like it's supposed to."

"Physically, yes. But what I meant was how do you feel inside? Bodies heal faster than minds, so other than the night-mares, how has the experience affected you? How do you feel about it?"

Rose searched for words to express the cauldron of emotions bubbling over inside her. "Helpless, violated, angry, scared— there's no easy way to sum up how bad it feels. With-drawal is hard enough on its own, and then every craving I have feels like another violation all over again. I've never even smoked pot before, and now suddenly my body is telling me I need this drug that terrifies the hell out of me."

Dr. Firestone leaned in, her voice still like a gentle, moth-erly caress. "Rose, what happened to you is... unimaginable. And your feelings of helplessness and confusion are completely valid. But remember, you don't have to go through this alone."

Rose's heart swelled with gratitude for the empathetic

response of the group. She hadn't expected this kind of acceptance. Not that she thought they'd turn her away, but she figured there would be an invisible, impenetrable wall between them because she wasn't a veteran and had never seen war like they all had. But they had opened their arms and, amazingly, she felt safe here when she hadn't felt safe anywhere since waking up in the hospital.

Except, maybe, in Ash's presence.

"Thank you," she said, her voice barely above a whisper. "I just... don't know what to do. I can't stop thinking about it. I'm afraid to go to sleep."

Sawyer reached out, seeking the arm of her chair. When he found it, he trailed his fingers down her arm until he landed on her hand. He gave her fingers a reassuring squeeze. "I know how you feel. I was afraid to sleep for a long time, but Zelda, here, helps me with my nightmares."

At her name, Zelda's tail thunked on the floor.

Sawyer smiled at the sound, his love for the animal plain in his sightless eyes, then asked, "Have you considered getting a therapy dog?"

Rose shook her head. "My cat would never forgive me."

"Huh. I never pegged you as a crazy cat lady."

"Well, I may be crazy, but I only have one cat."

Everyone chuckled and the tension in the room eased slightly.

Donovan sat back down, his expression softening as he studied her. "Have you talked to anyone about it? About what happened to you?"

She swallowed hard. "Not really. I mean, the police, obviously. And Ash." She realized her voice had gone weirdly soft and dreamy on his name and cleared her throat.

Dammit, she didn't like the man.

"My aunt knows I was attacked," she continued. "But I haven't told her all the gory details. She's already worried enough. And my dad... if you don't know, he's in prison, so it feels cruel to tell him when he's stuck there and can't do anything to help."

"That's understandable," Dr. Firestone said and adjusted her tidy wireframe glasses. "It's very common for victims to want to shield their families from the trauma, but it's important to reach out to those around you who care about you. And if you don't feel like you can tell your friends or family everything, then I urge you to find someone you can talk to."

"You talk to us," Zak said, then leaned forward, his eyes bright with intensity. "And never forget you're a fighter, Rose. You survived this, and if you ask me, what you went through was more horrific than any war because you didn't sign up knowing you could pay the ultimate price. We all knew we could come out of the military broken or not at all. We accepted the possibility of trauma when we enlisted. But it was forced on you, so that makes you more of a warrior than any of us."

Pierce waved to get her attention, then pulled his phone out of his jacket pocket. His thumbs worked furiously over the screen, his eyes darting between the letters and her face.

After a few moments of silence, he held the phone out to her. In bold letters on the bright screen, it read:

> Zak's right. I served in Iraq. Shrapnel from an explosion injured my neck and I lost my ability to speak, but I knew it was dangerous going in.

A mix of frustration and acceptance flickered across his expression before he continued typing.

> During my recovery, I became addicted to pain pills. For years, I needed them to function. When I finally decided to get clean, withdrawal almost killed me.

Rose's heart went out to him as she studied the scars that cut across his neck. With an injury like that, it was no wonder he became hooked on pills. She couldn't imagine what getting clean must have been like for him. Her own experience had been hell, but the doctor told her she was lucky she had only been exposed to the drug for a few days—long-term opiate addicts had a much harder time with withdrawal and eighty-five percent of them relapsed within a year.

Pierce returned his attention to the phone.

> It was my own stupid choices that put me in that situation. You were violated. You didn't choose any of this, but you're handling it better than I did.

Tears brimmed in her eyes. She felt raw and exposed, but also comforted. There was solace in knowing that she wasn't alone in her turmoil. "I'm so sorry for what you've been through. To have your voice taken away, and then to struggle with addiction... it must have been incredibly difficult."

Pierce nodded and typed a response.

> It was brutal. I had to re-learn to communicate.

He set down the phone and signed something, then looked at Donovan.

"He said that it was a long and hard road," Donovan translated as Pierce continued to sign. "He had to first figure out he wanted to live, then he had to learn to communicate again before he could kick the addiction. But he made it through with the help of therapy and support groups like this one."

Pierce picked up his phone again and looked up at her directly while he typed.

> You can heal, too.

"Thank you for sharing your story," Rose said, touched by his honesty. "It gives me hope. And thank you all for your understanding and offers of support. It means... so much to me."

Pierce's hazel eyes were warm as he looked up from the keyboard and smiled, then he went back to typing.

We're all in this together. Each of us carrying our own burdens, but we find strength in the bond we've formed as a therapy group and a team. When one of us is feeling weak, the rest of us step in and share our strength. So whenever you need someone to lean on, know that you have us. We'll support you while you try to find your footing again.

Rose lifted her gaze from the phone's screen and without saying a word, extended her hand towards Pierce. He took her hand and gave her fingers a gentle squeeze.

She looked at each person in the room, taking in their battle scars—Sawyer's sightless eyes, Zak's missing leg, the rope of scar tissue running down the side of Donovan's head, and Pierce's destroyed neck. Veronica, who hadn't spoken once since she entered the room, whose scars were all internal and so deep, she hid under oversized sweaters and tried to make herself as small as possible. And, still, she was here. She was trying.

They were all survivors, in their own ways.

Maybe Rose could be, too. She'd already lived through the hardest part—the attack. She could defeat the nightmares. She could conquer the constant, low-level pull of her body toward a drug she didn't want. And whoever was trying to kill her— well, she was prepared now. They wouldn't catch her off guard again. If they tried, she'd beat them, too.

"I got back on my feet with exercise," Donovan said after a

moment. "It's not a cure-all, but I find it helps. I like to run with my dog. It's a chance to work out the frustration and anxiety and clear my head."

"It's hiking with Zelda for me," Sawyer said.

Pierce mimed strumming a guitar.

Donovan's brows shot up. "I didn't know you played guitar. Are you any good?"

Pierce shrugged.

"It's Ranger for me," Zak said, his voice just a bit strained. "Training him, watching him learn new skills." A smile ticked up the corner of his mouth. "And also helping the rest of these assholes train their dogs at the Rescue. I like having a purpose."

Except, she knew, even having found his purpose, he was struggling. She opened her mouth to urge him to lean on the group, but she didn't get the chance.

"Reading," Veronica murmured, surprising them all. "I like light, fluffy rom-coms. It's escapist and I always know it's going to have a happy ending, so there's no anxiety."

"I read, too," Dr. Firestone said. "Cozy mysteries—for the same reasons Veronica likes romantic comedies. I also love mindless reality TV. It's a guilty pleasure. We all have our coping mechanisms. You just have to find what works for you."

Just like Ash and his campy horror movies.

Rose considered it. She'd never been much of a runner, and she liked to read occasionally, but definitely not rom-coms. She didn't have a dog and doubted Fanta would be good at search and rescue. Reality TV was a big no, as was learning an instrument. While her Dad could play anything he picked up, the musical gene had skipped a generation with her.

"I'll try hiking," she decided. It was something she already knew she enjoyed, so maybe it could be her escape, her coping mechanism.

"I'll go with you." Ash's low voice rumbled through the room, flushing her with an uncomfortable warmth. She looked up to see him staring at her intently from the doorway.

"If you want," he added.

Her heart leapt into her throat. The idea of being alone in the mountains with Ash, doing something not related to her abduction or his investigation—something that was dangerously close to a date—was both thrilling and terrifying. But maybe it was exactly the distraction she needed. Someone to help chase away the demons.

Except this man was one of her demons.

She couldn't let herself forget that.

"No thanks." She was thrilled when her voice came out steady and just a bit icy. She stood and addressed the group. "Thank you all for listening to me."

"Come back next week," Dr. Firestone said.

"I'll think about it, but I have to get the bar ready to open now. Thanks again." She started toward the door, but Ash still blocked it. She stared him down. He stared right back, his face set in stone, until Dr. Firestone delicately cleared her throat.

"Sheriff. Rose has work to do."

He finally broke the staring contest to glance over at the doctor, then stepped aside.

Rose hurried out of the room, bypassed the bar and ignored Mike's questioning look. She shoved into the kitchen and leaned on the prep table, sucking in multiple steadying breaths. Marcel wouldn't be in for another hour, so she was blissfully alone amid all the cold stainless steel appliances. It was a fitting place for her, because now that she was away from the cozy embrace of the therapy group, she felt all cold and echoey inside just like the empty kitchen.

chapter
eighteen

OF COURSE she went to work.

Ash didn't know why he was surprised. The woman was too damn stubborn and determined to make herself a target.

Or give him a heart attack.

Which was nearly what he had when he walked into the Mad Dog to find the door unlocked and the pub empty.

No Rose. No Deputy Mike Conti, who was supposed to be guarding her with his life.

Ash's blood pressure shot through the roof, and he thumbed his radio with the intent of calling an 11-99 and getting every LEO within radio distance here—but then he heard the toilet flush in the men's bathroom. He whirled toward it as Mike stepped out, wiping his hands on a paper towel.

"Where is she?"

Mike frowned. "What—?"

"Rose! Where is she?"

"Sheriff, she's—"

"If something happened to her while you were taking a shit, Conti, I will not only have your badge, I'll make fucking sure you never work in law enforcement again."

"Rawlings!" Mike made his name into a whip. "Relax. She's safe. She's in the back room with Zak, Donovan, and the rest of them. I figured nobody would get to her through them, so I took a bathroom break."

Oh, Jesus. Why couldn't he breathe? "She's...?"

"Safe. I wouldn't leave her unguarded." Mike nodded toward the back room. "Go see for yourself."

Heart still pounding in his ears, he walked over to the door. He would've shoved it open, if not for recognizing Zak's voice, followed by Rose's and then Donovan's. He took a second to calm himself, leaning his head against the wood and letting the sound of her muffled voice slow his heart rate.

"Man," Mike muttered. "You got it bad, Sheriff."

"Shut up, Conti." He drew another deep breath, released it, then cracked the door and slipped inside. Pierce was typing on his phone, then showing it to Rose. She wore her cropped, too-tight Mad Dog t-shirt, but had thrown one of his flannels over it. The sight of her in his shirt unlocked that fierce protectiveness again. She looked small and sad and vulnerable. She was none of those things—not the Ambrosia Galasso who poked and needled and teased him until he didn't know if he wanted to kiss her or bend her over his knee.

Or both.

He hated the fear he saw in her. He hated that the sick bastard who put it in her was still out there, and he was no closer to catching him.

Then Donovan said something about exercising, and his mind dove straight back into the gutter as he pictured Rose sweat-slicked and panting. The only man exercising with her in any capacity would be him.

"I'll go with you."

Rose looked up at him with wide, startled eyes. He chose to ignore Donovan's knowing smirk and Zak's soft snort.

"If you want," he added, realizing he'd sounded too possessive.

"No thanks." The ice in her tone should've frozen the flames inside him. Unfortunately, all it did was make him burn hotter.

He was tired of her not listening. Tired of her testing him at every turn. She would listen. She would submit.

As she said her pleasant goodbyes and made her escape, he stalked after her... and found her in the kitchen looking like one strong wind would blow her apart.

He muttered a curse under his breath and went to her. "Rose."

She sucked in a breath and looked up. Her eyes were hollow, the bruises on her cheeks bleeding through her makeup.

Ash's heart clenched at the sight of her battered face. He reached out to touch her cheek, but she stepped back.

"Don't," she said, her voice barely above a whisper.

He dropped his hand. "I'm not your enemy, Ambrosia."

She shook her head and turned away. "What are you doing here, Sheriff? I'm plenty protected without your sparkling presence."

He hesitated. Maybe now, with her so vulnerable, wasn't the best time to do this. But then, was there ever really a good time to find out if a long-buried body belonged to your mother? No, probably not.

He reached into his jacket pocket and pulled out a folded sheet of paper. "I have the DNA results."

She whirled back to face him, her eyes wide. "Already?"

"I told you I put a rush on it."

She reached for the paper, but stopped. "Have you looked?"

"No. I printed off the email and brought it to you. Figured you'd want to know as soon as I do."

She stared at the paper, her hand still half-outstretched to take it. Then she sucked in a breath and snatched it. Seconds ticked by in silence as she read.

The longest seconds of Ash's life.

"It's her," she whispered, and tears flooded her eyes, spilled over. "Oh my God. It's Mom."

Ash shut his eyes and saw the blackened, grinning skull of Jane Doe on the backs of his lids.

No. Not Jane Doe anymore. Harmony Galasso.

He opened his eyes and took the paper from Rose's trembling hand, read it through. The results were about as conclusive as DNA got. The Jane Doe was maternally related to the provided DNA sample.

He nodded. "All right. I'm reopening your mom's case."

She laughed, but it was all bitterness. "So, wait. You tore apart my family, and you expect me to just forgive you for that because you've decided to actually investigate?"

"No, I don't expect forgiveness, but I also won't feel guilty for doing my job."

"See, that's your problem, Sheriff. You think your job is black and white. Someone breaks the law, and they go to prison, end of story. But you forget that's never actually the end of the story." With that, she turned and walked away.

Ash watched as her long strides carried her across the kitchen toward her office. He had always believed that his duty as a sheriff was to uphold the law, no matter the costs. But maybe, sometimes, the costs were more than justice was worth.

"Rose, wait."

She turned back to face him, her expression guarded as he caught up to her.

"I know I can't make up for what happened to your family," he said, his voice low as the noise level at the front of the bar grew. The therapy group was leaving. "But I want to try.

I'm reopening your mom's case because I want to find out what really happened to her. I need to know how she ended up on the mountain and if your father didn't put her there, I need to find who did."

Her eyes narrowed. "Why is it so important to you?"

He wasn't about to tell her that the betrayal on her face when he showed up to arrest her dad had haunted him for thirteen years or that every time he closed his eyes, he saw her mother's blackened skull grinning at him.

He skimmed his knuckles across her cheek. "Because it's important to you."

Her too-red lips parted in a soft gasp. "I don't like you, Sheriff." But even as she said the words, she leaned into his touch.

"I know. I don't like you very much, either." He circled a hand around the back of her neck and dragged his thumb over her bottom lip, smearing away the lipstick that somehow both irrationally infuriated him and tantalized him.

Jesus. He shouldn't be touching her like this, but he needed to. Because while the girl she'd once been haunted his nightmares, the woman she was now had starred in all of his recent fantasies.

"I hate that I'm so damn attracted to you," she whispered.

"I know."

Her exhale ghosted over his thumb. "I don't understand why we're doing this."

"Neither do I." He bent his head and pressed his lips to hers, tasting the bitterness of her anger and the sweetness of her mouth.

She didn't respond at first, but then her fingers curled into the fabric of his uniform shirt, pulling him closer as she angled her head to deepen the kiss.

It was wrong, so wrong.

Dammit, he was a lawman, and he shouldn't be getting

involved with a victim like Rose, especially not while he was investigating her mother's case. But he couldn't help himself. The pull between them was too strong, too intense.

When they finally broke apart, they were both panting for air. Ash looked into her eyes and saw a mixture of surprise, desire, and something else he couldn't quite place.

"I shouldn't have done that," he said, his voice rough.

"No," Rose agreed, but she didn't move away from him. "But you did."

He didn't know how to respond, so he just stood there, their bodies pressed together so tightly he could feel the excited beat of her heart against his chest.

It was a mistake.

A huge mistake.

But as Rose looked up at him, her blue eyes shining, he realized it was a mistake he desperately wanted to make again.

Ash forced himself to release her and step back. "I need to go. I have work to do."

Rose nodded, not looking at him. "Yeah. I have to open the bar."

"Don't go anywhere without Conti," he said. "He's glued to your side, got it?"

"Yes, sir."

The way she said that had his cock stirring behind his fly. He had to get out of here before he bent her over that prep table and did indecent things to her right here in her pub's kitchen.

He spun on his heel and marched resolutely toward the door.

"What about my mother's case?" she asked suddenly. "Does this mean my dad will get an appeal?"

"I don't know yet." His tone was gruffer than he'd intended, and she deserved a better answer. He stopped and turned back. "It won't make up for what happened to your family, but I'm going to do everything in my power to find out what really happened to her."

She nodded again, her expression unreadable. "Okay. I'll see you at home."

The words sent a weird thrill through him. Home. Of course, it wasn't really her home. It was only a temporary arrangement while he tracked down the bastards who hurt her.

Jesus, he had so much work to do.

"Yeah. See you at home." He didn't look back, but he could feel Rose's eyes on him as he walked away.

Outside the bar, he climbed into his Tahoe, his head filled with thoughts of the woman he shouldn't be attracted to. Kissing her had been a mistake, but his self-control was non-existent when it came to her. She was smart, tough, and fiercely independent. Annoying and infuriatingly sexy. A woman who knew exactly what she wanted and weaponized her beauty to get it. He admired her for it, even as he struggled to reconcile the woman with the girl she'd once been. The girl whose life he'd ruined.

She was eight years younger than him—twenty-six to his thirty-four. Did that make him a cradle robber? Was she too young for him? But age didn't seem to matter when they kissed. Their chemistry was undeniable, and he found himself drawn to her like a bug to a zapper.

Likely with the same disastrous results.

Jesus.

He shook his head, trying to dislodge her from his thoughts. It didn't matter if he was too old for her. Yes, he was attracted—with that body and those lips, every straight man in town was—but so what? He didn't like her as a person. He felt bad for what happened to her when she was a kid, for losing both her parents in such a traumatic way, but he. Didn't. Like.

Her. And he wasn't going to let his self-control slip around her again. He refused to be controlled by his dick.

He parked in his space in front of the Sheriff's Department and headed inside. There were a few deputies milling about, but Ash ignored them and made a beeline for his office. He closed the door behind him and sank into the chair behind his desk.

Time to focus.

Now that he had a name for Jane Doe, he planned to go over Harmony Galasso's case with a fine-tooth comb.

Someone in that file had to know what really happened to her.

chapter
nineteen

13 Years Ago

ROSE'S HEART raced as she opened the door to find Deputy Ash Rawlings and Sheriff Tennison standing on her doorstep.

Her dad came to the door behind her, and she'd never seen the look on his face before as he stared at the two cops. "Rose, please go back inside."

"What's going on?" Confusion and fear mingled in her belly, making her nauseous, and she wrapped her arms tightly around herself. "Is there any news about my mom?"

Deputy Rawlings met her gaze and his sad expression had tears rushing into her eyes. "Hi, Rose. We need to talk. Can we come in?"

"No." Letting them through the door felt like she was inviting in something bad, something potentially evil like the vampires in her favorite TV show.

"Let them in, Wildflower." Dad set a hand on her shoulder and gently pulled her back, allowing the two cops to enter the living room. The air grew heavy with tension, the familiar space suddenly suffocating.

This was wrong. They shouldn't be here. They should be out looking for Mom.

Sheriff Tennison's gaze hardened as he addressed her dad. "Pete, you know why we're here."

"No," Dad replied but something in that one soft word said otherwise.

"You're under arrest for the murder of your wife."

Dad didn't look surprised. Tears glimmered in his eyes and his voice quivered. "I didn't... I would never hurt Harmony. If you think she's dead, then her killer is still out there. Please, don't do this, Jerry."

"You have the right to remain silent..." The sheriff repeated the words she'd heard on so many cop shows and snapped a pair of handcuffs around Dad's wrists.

No. This couldn't be happening.

"It's okay, Wildflower," her dad said in the same soothing voice he used when she had a nightmare.

Yes. It was just a nightmare and she'd wake up at any moment.

Just a nightmare.

"Call Auntie Rainbow," Dad called over his shoulder as the sheriff pushed him toward the door. "Tell her to come get you. It'll be okay. I promise."

It wasn't a nightmare.

Tears welled up in Rose's eyes as her world crumbled before her.

"You can't take him!" She turned to Deputy Rawlings. "Please, tell them. Tell them my dad couldn't have done anything!"

He stepped forward, his eyes filled with compassion. "I know this is hard to accept, but—"

"You promised to help us. You promised to find my mom!"

"We're doing our best to—"

"Arresting my dad is your best? He didn't do anything! Please—" Her voice cracked, and her knees wobbled.

Deputy Rawlings caught her arm before she collapsed and gently guided her to sit down on the couch. He got her a glass of water and knelt in front of her. "Rose, we're not giving up on finding your mom."

"But you think she's dead. If Mom's gone, Dad's all I have."

"I'm so sorry."

He was so nice. Soft-spoken and gentle, with kind blue eyes.

And how she hated him.

She threw the water in his face and jumped to her feet, bursting through the front door in time to see the sheriff drive away with her dad in the back of his car.

"Rose, stop!" Hard arms banded around her and dragged her back inside. She kicked and clawed and felt blood well under her nails. Good. He deserved to hurt just as much as she was.

He dumped her back on the couch and stepped away before she could kick him. His cheek was bleeding, but his eyes were still soft and filled with sorrow. It made her despise him even more.

"You stupid fucking cop! I *never* should've trusted you! I hate you!"

He dodged the pillow she threw at his head. "I understand your anger and confusion, but we have to follow the evidence and unfortunately the evidence right now points at your dad. We owe it to your mom to find the truth."

She glared at him, her chest heaving with sobs. "You owe it to my mom to find her killer, not arrest my dad for something he didn't do!"

Deputy Rawlings sighed and ran a hand through his hair.

"I know this is hard for you, but we have to be thorough in our investigation."

"All you care about is your stupid investigation. You don't care about my mom or my family."

"That's not true," he said firmly, his eyes locked on hers. "I care about finding justice for your mom and for your family. For *you*. But sometimes justice is hard and painful. Sometimes it means facing the truth, even when it hurts."

She hated the tears streaming down her face and swiped at them. "I just want my dad back."

"I know," Deputy Rawlings said gently. "And we'll do our best to find out what really happened. If your dad is innocent, we *will* prove it. But we can't ignore the evidence we have now."

"What evidence? You haven't even told me what it is!"

He hesitated, his eyes flickering with guilt. "I'm sorry. I can't share that right now, but please know we are following all leads."

Rose scoffed, pushing past him and pacing the room. "You don't even know for sure that she's dead. Maybe she ran off like Dad said. Maybe she just got tired of living here and fighting with Dad and taking care of me and—"

"I'm sorry, Rose."

She wanted to scream at him, to lash out again and hurt him, to give him some of the pain eating away at her heart. But she was suddenly too tired. Broken. Lost. She sank back to the couch.

"Can I at least go with him?" she asked in a whisper.

"I'm afraid that's not possible," Deputy Rawlings said, his voice tinged with regret. "But I promise to keep you updated on the investigation, okay?"

Why did he have to be so nice? She wished the crusty old sheriff were here instead. She wouldn't feel guilty for scratching Sheriff Tennison.

The screen door squeaked, and Aunt Rainbow burst into the room in a cloud of pot smoke and patchouli oil, her face twisted with worry. She rushed to Rose's side and pulled her into a tight hug, the bangles on her wrists jangling.

"Oh, baby, what's going on?"

Rose buried her face in her aunt's chest and cried.

chapter
twenty

Present Day

THE ITCH WAS BACK.

It woke Rose out of the first sound sleep she'd had in over a week, clawing at the back of her mind, whispering ugly, seductive things to her. She could take a pain pill. That wasn't as bad as sticking a needle in her arm. People took pain pills all the time. It would ease the itch. Settle her mind.

What could it hurt?

Then she remembered Pierce's story. His addiction.

Everything. It would hurt everything. If she caved, they won. Whoever they were. Her attackers may not have killed her, but if she gave in to the itch, then they would accomplish something even worse. They would destroy her.

And she refused to let them have that.

She lay in bed and breathed through the withdrawal pangs, focusing on Fanta purring on her chest. Her dreams came back to her in bits and pieces. She'd dreamt about Dad's arrest. She hadn't done that in years.

God, she'd hated Ash that day.

And every day after.

Until recently.

It wasn't hate anymore. Was it even still dislike? She wasn't sure, and couldn't pinpoint exactly when her feelings had changed. Or maybe they had been changing, softening for all these years.

She got out of bed and walked to the window, her bare feet cold on the hardwood floor. Ash's property lay several miles north of town, nestled deep in the redwoods. His house had been one of the lucky ones last year, escaping the fire that scorched acres of land to the south and east of town, and the forest around the cabin was still lush with life. Silver mist curled through the trees as gray clouds, heavy with rain, hung low in the sky.

She loved this kind of weather. Cool and foggy with misty rain. It was one of her favorite parts of living in Northern California. The perfect day to stay inside and indulge in a little self-care.

But if she stayed inside today, she'd lose her mind.

She rubbed her arms, trying to shake off the tingling sensation crawling beneath her skin. She couldn't do this on her own anymore. She needed a distraction.

She slipped into her robe and cracked open her bedroom door. Ash's door was shut, and she heard no sounds inside. It was almost nine a.m. Would he sleep in this late?

No way. Not Sheriff Ash Rawlings. He was probably already at work, and she'd find the affable Mike Conti posted up in the living room.

To her shock, it wasn't Mike she found asleep in one of the two chairs that Ash owned—he really needed to buy another couch—but rather the sheriff himself. Like her first night here, Ash was slumped over a stack of paperwork, his neck bent at an uncomfortable angle. No horror movie on the TV this time, though.

She stood in front of him, watching his chest rise and fall

with each deep breath. Did the man ever stop working? Did he ever sleep in his own bed, or did he always fall asleep in front of mounds of paperwork?

She studied his face. A square, too-serious face. He didn't always have all those frown lines, she remembered. When they first met thirteen years ago, he'd still been boy-like in many ways. Unjaded and clean-shaven—hadn't started growing the beard yet—with a deputy uniform so new it had sharp creases from the package it had come in. Asleep, he looked more like that younger version she remembered, less weighed down by the responsibilities of his job and his role in the community.

She'd been too young at the time to appreciate his rugged handsomeness, but as an adult she thought about him more often than she cared to admit. His lips, especially. He had lips made for kissing, the bottom slightly fuller than the top.

A thin, barely noticeable scar sliced down his cheek, disappearing under his beard. She traced it with her finger and his eyes opened. Dark blue, like the ocean sky as a storm rolled in. He stared at her for a groggy second before his gaze sharpened.

He sat up and winced, rubbing at his neck. "What's wrong?"

"Nothing." She again traced the scar. "Is that from me? When I scratched you the day you arrested Dad?"

Lust flickered in his eyes. She saw it clearly before he shuttered his expression. She also noticed the growing tent at the front of his sweatpants.

"Something to remember you by," he murmured.

"Like you could forget me."

"Christ knows I've tried." As soon as he spoke, his eyes widened like he hadn't meant to say that.

Huh. She liked sleepy Ash. His guard was lower than fully awake Ash. "Really? Because I never got the impression you've thought about me at all."

"I don't," he said brusquely. "I didn't. You were a kid."

"I'm not anymore."

"You're still nearly a decade younger than me."

"Eight years."

"Exactly. So I don't think about you in any way other than as a member of this community I need to protect."

Her gaze dropped pointedly to his lap. "Uh-huh."

Ash sighed and adjusted his position in the chair to make his erection less noticeable. He scrubbed his hands over his face. "Stop it. I can't spar with you right now. I've been up all night dealing with paperwork. So much fucking paperwork."

"Right," she said, feeling awkward all of a sudden. "Sorry. I didn't mean to wake you."

He looked at his watch. He was the only thirty-something man she knew that still wore a watch. Not a fitness tracker, but an actual silver watch with a black leather band. "I should've been at work hours ago."

She rolled her eyes. "Not if you didn't sleep."

"I slept."

"No, you catnapped over a pile of paperwork."

He frowned at the papers strewn about, then gathered them up and set them aside. He stretched and yawned, and his T-shirt hitched up, showing off corrugated abs and a line of hair that disappeared into his sweatpants. Her pulse quickened at the sight, and heat pooled in her belly.

"Did you need something, Rose?" he asked. If he noticed the sudden flush in her cheeks, he didn't acknowledge it.

She quickly looked away. Why was the sight of his abs more of a turn on than his morning erection? She'd been amused by the tent in his pants. But that hard stomach and line of hair did all kinds of things for her.

"I just..." Her voice came out strangely husky and she swallowed. "The itch."

She knew he'd understand without more explanation.

His expression softened. "Is it bad?"

"It's not bad. More... annoying," she decided.

He said nothing for a long moment. "I've been where you are."

Rose turned to look at him, surprised. "What do you mean?"

"Withdrawal." His eyes fixed on some distant point over her shoulder, like he was staring into the past. "It started as a social thing when I was a teen—someone would show up to a party with a handful of pills from their parents' medicine cabinet, and we'd all take them. I thought it was harmless fun. Then my sister lost her baby when we were eighteen, and she was so sad. Just a... shell of herself." He rubbed a hand over his heart. "It hurt me, seeing her like that, so I gave her all of my strength during the day, then fell hard into the drugs and partying at night to cope."

Rose couldn't believe what she was hearing. He'd hinted at it back when she was in the hospital, but she hadn't believed it then. She still couldn't wrap her mind around it. The Ash Rawlings she knew was always in control, never showing any vulnerability. And now he was confessing to her that he had been an addict? It didn't make sense.

"Why are you telling me this?"

He shrugged. "I don't know. Guess I want you to know that it gets better. That itch might not ever go away completely but it becomes easier to ignore."

"Do you still have it?"

"Sometimes."

Rose stared at him, taking in the lines etched into his rugged face. She saw a hint of the pain he had endured, the battles he had fought, and the strength it took for him to open up to her.

"I had no idea," she whispered, in awe of him.

He shrugged again, his expression guarded once more. "It's not something I talk about."

And that, she realized, was the end of the conversation. She wanted to ask more questions, but knew he wouldn't answer them. He'd pulled those shields of his back up.

She looked down at the stack of case files on the coffee table and picked up the top folder. It was the same one she'd seen her first night at his house.

She held it up. "Who's Maria Socktish?"

Ash let out a breath that sounded a lot like a sigh of relief. He leaned back in the chair and rubbed at his eyes. "That podcaster, Alexis Summers, thinks there's a serial killer in Lost County, and that Maria was the first victim."

"Wow. And you believe her?"

"Not entirely, but her research is compelling," he admitted, his tone full of grudging respect. "I haven't had a chance to look too far into it. That's what I was doing when I found you out on Route 10—walking through Maria's last steps. That gas station was her last known location."

"She was never found?"

"No."

"Huh. That does seem to happen a lot around here." She dropped the file back on the stack. "My line of work can get hectic, but even at my busiest, my to-do list has never included hunt down a possible serial killer."

He yawned again. "It'd be weird if it did. You're a bartender."

"Pub owner," she said with mock outrage. "And it'd be like one of those cozy mysteries. The scrappy pub owner getting reluctantly sucked into a murder investigation." Which, she realized, wasn't too far off from her real life and the reminder sent a sizzle of panic down her spine.

Coping mechanism, she reminded herself. Like Pierce's guitar or Dr. Firestone's reality TV. She just had to find her own. "I'm going on a hike."

Ash's drooping eyes popped open. "It's supposed to rain."

She grabbed her phone from the pocket of her robe and checked the weather. "Not until this afternoon."

"That's not a good idea. It's not safe."

"If you don't think so, you could come with me. Protect me from any big, bad trees that might want to hurt me." When he looked about to protest, she added, "You said you would."

He groaned and pinched the bridge of his nose like he had a headache. "Jesus, Ambrosia. Why do you insist on making yourself a target?"

She thought she'd pinned down his moods when he called her by her full name— annoyed, frustrated, angry. But she heard something else in his tone this time: fear.

"That's not my intention." She swallowed hard to dislodge the sudden lump in her throat. "I don't plan to give them another shot at me, but I can't sit around this house any longer when my skin is prickling, and my mind keeps telling me it wouldn't hurt if I took something just once to make it all stop. I need a distraction. So." Her laugh came out more bitter than she'd planned. "We can either fuck or go on a hike."

Ash's gaze was electric as he rose from his chair, and her heart suddenly hammered against her ribcage. She yearned for him to cross the space between them and pull her against his hard chest. Her mind replayed the kiss yesterday and a tingling sensation swept through her as her nipples hardened in anticipation.

"Hiking it is," he said, voice rough, and turned away.

She told herself not to be disappointed. But... why shouldn't she be? She saw his desire in his eyes. The heat had nearly scorched her robe right off her body.

"Or..." She caught his hand. "We could do both."

He sucked in a sharp breath. "Rose, we can't... I can't get involved with you."

"Involved?" She scoffed. "That's such a complicated word.

Neither of us wants involved, but I think we're both adult enough to admit we want each other. We're consenting adults and we want each other. So give me one good reason why we shouldn't."

When he met her gaze, his eyes were flinty again, cop hard, no hint of the heat left. "I don't fuck women who are vulnerable."

She dropped his hand and crossed her arms over her chest. "I'm not."

"Yes, you are."

The flush that washed through her had nothing to do with desire. It was all anger now. "No, I'm the queen of the vulnerable. I'm the person everyone else comes to when they need comfort or advice. But who do I go to when I need help? Who helps me when I'm the one who's hurting? No one. I'm not vulnerable because I can't afford to be, so don't you dare use that as an excuse."

"It's not an excuse. It's a boundary. I won't take advantage of you."

"I'm not a child," she snapped. "I know what I want. And right now, what I want is you."

"I can't give you what you want." The words rumbled out of him as he prowled toward her. She'd never seen this side of him before. He looked dangerous, like a predator zeroed in on easy prey.

Heart racing, she backed up until she hit the wall by the fireplace. "Why not?"

"Because you have no idea what you're asking for." He trapped her against the wall with a hand on either side of her head and leaned down until his lips almost brushed hers. "I'm not gentle."

"What if I like it rough?"

"You've been hurt enough."

"I dare you to hurt me, Sheriff."

He caught her chin between his fingers and tilted her head up. "No." His voice was all edges, little more than a growl. "If we ever fuck, it'll only happen because you finally shut that smart little mouth and submitted to me."

The heat emanating from his body was scorching as he pressed up against her, pinning her to the wall. The anger she had seen in his eyes earlier had been replaced by a white-hot desire that sent a thrill racing through her, burning away the lingering craving for that damn drug, and the ever-present cold tendrils of fear.

She knew she should still be scared. Someone wanted her dead, and her only protection was this gruff mountain of a man who had ripped her family apart. She'd never met anyone who could simultaneously piss her off and turn her on like Sheriff Ash Rawlings. It was maddening and thrilling and exhausting all at once.

She pushed up onto her toes and sank her teeth into his lower lip. "I don't submit."

His too-serious eyes raked over her, and she was half-surprised her robe didn't disintegrate. He caught her around the neck and pinned her to the wall to keep her from biting him again. His lip was bleeding, and he ran his tongue slowly over the cut.

"We'll see about that."

The words sounded like a promise, even as he released her and stalked toward his bedroom. The door shut behind him with a resounding thud.

She sagged against the wall and sucked in a breath, pressing a hand to her thundering heart.

We'll see about that.

Oh, she was going to take great pleasure in proving him wrong. Control freak that he was, he thought he was at the wheel of this thing between them, but he wasn't. Not with the way he'd looked at her, held her...

He thought he was dangerous, but she knew the difference between a man who intended to truly hurt her and one who simply wanted to blur the line between pleasure and pain. She held his reins, and he was going to submit to her first.

He just didn't know it yet.

chapter
twenty-one

ASH EMERGED from his room a half hour later, showered and dressed in his uniform, to find Rose in the kitchen waiting on the coffee pot to finish brewing. She'd set out two mugs—a ceramic one for her and his stainless steel travel tumbler. She'd also changed into her "uniform"—if you could call it that. Her breasts strained the limits of the Mad Dog Pub top. The shirt's cropped hem showed off her tight stomach and the tendrils of a tattoo on her ribs. Her jeans hugged her hips and ass like a second skin. The "uniform" left little to the imagination. She'd put on make-up, somehow making her eyes look bigger and bluer, and the bold red of her signature lipstick drew his gaze as she closed her mouth around a banana.

Fuck.

He glanced away as he crossed to the fridge and grabbed a yogurt. He couldn't look at her or the erection he'd dealt with in the shower would pop right back up.

His lip still stung from where she'd bit him. He ran his tongue over the spot and despite his efforts in the shower, his cock stirred. It had a mind of its own lately.

This wasn't going to work.

Hell, he couldn't even breathe the same air as her without

getting hard. He'd been an idiot to think he could keep her here and still do his job with a level head. He had to get her out of his house.

"I'll call the locksmith today about replacing the locks at your place." Then he'd assign more deputies—capable, married ones like Mike Conti—to protect her until this was over.

"I already called a couple days ago," she said. "They're booked up for the next two weeks. I took their first available appointment for the eighteenth."

He could not wait that long. "I'll call in a favor."

"Ready to be rid of me, Sheriff?"

"Yes." He didn't turn around to see her reaction, but felt the air change like an electrical storm was gathering. The hair on his arms stood at attention in warning. She was going to try something, push all his buttons again until she found the one that made him snap like he had in the living room.

The way he'd backed her into the wall and told her she'd submit...

Jesus.

It went beyond unprofessionalism and into exploitation. Whether she wanted to admit it or not, she was vulnerable. And the things he'd wanted to do to her whenever she challenged him had to be borderline illegal.

He'd wanted to order her to her knees and make her suck his cock. He'd wanted to bend her over the chair and spank her ass until it was as red as her mouth. He'd wanted to order her to spread her legs so he could bury his face between them and eat her pussy until she came all over his face.

He wanted to make her beg for him.

By God, he wanted to hear her beg.

He'd imagined it all in vivid detail as he'd stroked himself to an unsatisfactory climax in the shower.

At the memory, a hot pang of longing shot through him.

It would have been so easy to give in to that desire. She was willing, he was willing... they were alone.

He closed his eyes and told himself—again—he could not go there with her.

Not with Ambrosia Galasso.

Never with her.

Too bad it wasn't tourist season. He could take a night off, walk into the Arrow Tree Brewery, and find a willing woman to help sate this need Rose had awakened in him. Except when he tried to insert a nameless, faceless tourist into his fantasies instead of Rose, he didn't get the same visceral, gut-punch surge of need.

Then his brain inserted Rose right back in—*where she belongs*, it insisted—and his cock stirred again.

She touched his back and a bolt of heat sizzled from her fingers, through his blood, and down into his cock. He almost groaned. Just barely bit it back before the sound escaped his throat.

"Why the uniform today?" she asked, her voice like a seductive caress.

Yes.

Work.

He had to focus on work.

It took every ounce of strength he possessed to step back out of her reach. He grabbed the carafe and filled his travel mug to the brim with coffee. "I'm going to the prison."

"What?" She retreated and he could draw a full breath again without her scent invading his head. He finally faced her.

She crossed her arms over her impressive breasts and glared at him. Fury snapped in her bright blue eyes. "You're not talking to my dad."

"He's already agreed to meet me."

She scoffed. "He's in prison. You think he has the choice to say no when the sheriff wants to talk to him?"

This was better. He could handle angry Rose. It was sassy, seductive Rose he couldn't deal with. "I gave him the choice. He agreed."

She held up a finger in warning. "You are *not* telling my dad about the attacks."

"I'll tell him whatever I need to get answers."

"No." She threw the banana peel in the trash, then grabbed another of his travel tumblers and poured her coffee from her mug into it. "I'm going with you."

He eyed her. "Not dressed like that."

"No shit." She shoved her cup at him as she passed. "Give me five minutes."

chapter
twenty-two

PETE GALASSO LOOKED nothing like Ash remembered.

Thirteen years ago, he was the typical coastal hills hippie. His hair had been a sandy brown, long but well cared for. Likewise for his beard. He'd worn tie-dye Grateful Dead T-shirts, "drug rug" sweaters, a floppy wide-brimmed hat, and sandals year round. He'd always had a wide, toothy smile for anyone who walked into the Mad Dog, even for three underage boys looking to sneak a drink with fake IDs—not that Ash, Zak, and Donovan would know anything about that. Pete's laugh had been the kind that made everyone around him join in.

But now, he looked...

Old.

Beaten down.

Exhausted.

His hair was still long, but now a greasy yellowish-gray. His smile was half the wattage as it used to be. Deep lines grooved his mouth and eyes.

Blue eyes, the same color as Rose's.

"Wildflower," Pete said with obvious surprise when the

guards led him in and sat him down across the table from Ash and Rose. "What are you doing here?"

Rose waited for the guards to lock his cuffs to the table, then reached for his hands. "Hi, Daddy. I was overdue for a visit."

Pete's gaze slid to Ash. "Yes, but why...?" He let the question trail off and squeezed her hands back. "It doesn't matter. I'm glad you came. I've missed you."

"I know. I'm sorry it's been so long. I've been... busy."

Pete's expression clouded at the short pause in her words. "Oh, my little wildflower. You're lying. I can always tell when you're lying." He looked at Ash again. "What's going on?"

"Daddy—"

"Sweetheart, let the sheriff answer please."

Ash cleared his throat and pulled out the case file he'd brought with him. He set it on the table and opened the cover.

Pete turned a sickly yellow color. "That's Harmony's file."

Rose squeezed his hand to get his attention. "We found Mom."

"You—" Pete blinked, and tears flooded his eyes, spilled over in a rush. "You finally found my Harmony, Sheriff? You brought her home?"

"We did," Ash said, making sure to keep his voice even. The man's genuine show of emotion touched him more than he'd expected. "We discovered her remains near Bear Gulch Road after the wildfire last fall. She was a Jane Doe until Rose offered a sample of her DNA earlier this week for familial testing and her identity was confirmed."

"Dear God." He laid his head down on the table and sobbed. "You found her," he repeated over and over, his voice muffled by his arms. "You found her."

Rose was crying now, too. She obviously wanted to hug her father, but the armed guard by the door stopped her when she stood. All she could do was hold on to Pete's hands over the table and cry with him.

"Mr. Galasso," Ash said when the tears slowed. "I have some questions if you're willing to talk to me."

"I've been willing to talk for thirteen years." Pete swiped at his eyes, making the chains around his wrists rattle. "The problem was always nobody was ever willing to listen."

"I'm listening now."

Pete lifted his soaked, bloodshot gaze to Ash's face and studied him for several long minutes. "I believe that. Okay. Ask your questions."

Ash took a deep breath before starting. He knew this would be a difficult conversation for Rose to hear, but it needed to be done. "Can you tell me about the last time you saw Harmony?"

Pete sighed heavily, his whole body seeming to deflate with the weight of the memory. "The night before I reported her missing. Harmony and I had been fighting because—" He glanced at his daughter, who gave an encouraging nod.

"Whatever happened between you, I can take it. I'm not a kid anymore."

"Oh, my girl. All grown up." Pete nodded and wiped away a stray tear. "Harmony wanted a divorce. She had a lot of affairs throughout our marriage, and she was seeing someone in LA. She wanted to leave me for him and take Rose with her. We were both pretty drunk. I know I said some awful things to her, but she was there when I went back to the pub. I didn't get home until almost 4 a.m."

"Was she in bed when you got home?" Ash asked.

"I honestly don't know. I slept on the couch."

"What about the next morning?"

"No. I never saw her again."

"What did you do that morning?"

"I woke him up," Rose said. "I was getting ready for school and needed lunch money and Mom wasn't there."

Pete nodded in agreement. "I had a massive hangover. No, that's not true. I was still drunk. I spent more time drunk than not in those days. One of the hazards of running a bar." He gave Rose a smile full of shame. "I'm so sorry for that."

She returned his smile. "It's okay. You were never a cruel drunk and all I have are fond memories of those days before —" She stopped and glanced at the case file. "Before Mom died. Besides, I think I turned out okay."

Pete grunted. "No thanks to me. That was all Rainbow."

"It was both of you."

"So Rose woke you," Ash said, steering their attention back to the question. "Then what?"

"I was awake long enough to see Rose off to school, then went back to bed since I didn't need to open the bar until the afternoon. But I only slept for a half hour longer. Or maybe an hour, tops. My neighbor started working in his yard and it woke me up, so I went to the pub and started drinking again with some friends."

So far, his story lined up with the one he'd told thirteen years ago. It had always bothered Ash that there was only that one hour of time unaccounted for. Both the previous night and the rest of that day, Pete's whereabouts had been corroborated by many other people. "And you didn't see or hear from Harmony at all that day?"

"No."

Something in his voice dinged on Ash's cop radar. "Are you sure?"

He rubbed a hand over his face. "I don't know. I've replayed those two days over and over in my head for years and... okay, listen. It might be nothing. Like I said, I was still drunk, but I think she came back while I was in bed. I think I heard her voice and someone else's."

Ash studied Pete's face, searching for any sign of deception. All he saw was pain and regret and crushing sadness. He picked up the initial report and scanned it. "You didn't report that."

"It all happened so fast, I didn't remember until I was already behind bars for life."

"Memory can be faulty. People often recall things that didn't happen with startling clarity."

"I'm aware, Sheriff. I've read the studies— I have nothing to do in here but read. And, like I said, I was drunk. It's why I didn't mention it before."

Ash set the report aside. "Was it a man's voice? A woman's?"

"I don't know. I just heard voices talking. One was definitely Harmony because she laughed. She had a very distinctive laugh. I was still pissed off, so I rolled over and went back to sleep."

"Then what made you think she was missing if you heard her voice?"

Pete closed his eyes and pinched the bridge of his nose as if remembering that day gave him a headache. "When Rose got home from school around four, she called me at the bar and said her mom wasn't home. Harmony was supposed to be there in the evenings for Rose, and she wasn't. I tried calling her cell phone, but it went right to voicemail. It worried me. Despite the problems in our marriage, she was a good mother. She loved our girl and never would've abandoned her like that."

"What did you do when you realized she wasn't home like she was supposed to be?"

"I panicked. I called all her friends, all our family. Nobody knew where she was. Then I called the sheriff, and you know the rest."

Ash did know. Even without reviewing the file, he remembered it all. Maybe because it was his first case as a deputy. Or, more likely, because it had never sat right with him. "Do you know the name of the man Harmony wanted to leave you for?"

Pete laughed. It was soft and laced with old bitterness. "You wouldn't believe me if I told you."

"Try me."

"Chet Duran."

Rose sat back and blinked in shock. "Of Duran Fitness? The billionaire?"

"The one and only."

Ash had suspected as much. "One more question. Did you load anything into your car before leaving for the pub that morning?"

"No, I—" Pete frowned in thought. "Wait. It wasn't that morning, but later that afternoon. Before Rose got home from school, I stopped back in for a minute to pick up a delivery I mistakenly sent there rather than to the pub."

"What was the delivery of?"

"Napkins, straws, toilet paper, cleaning supplies—that kind of stuff. I loaded it up and left again. Was there all of ten minutes. Didn't even go into the house."

"Thank you." Ash stood and sent a meaningful look at Rose, silently urging her to tell her dad about the attacks. "I'll let you two talk."

As he stepped out into the hallway, he heard Pete ask, "What's going on, Wildflower?"

Ash walked into the observation room next door, where Cal Holden stood in front of the one-way glass with his arms crossed and a deep frown on his face.

"Well?" He tossed the file down and then propped his ass on the edge of the table and watched Rose through the window. Even without the intercom turned on, he could tell she'd decided to fill Pete in on the events of the last few weeks.

Frown still in place, Cal turned toward him. "He's innocent."

"I'm starting to think so, yes." Ash scrubbed his hands over his face. "Jesus. I put him in prison for life."

"Not you. Tennison." Cal spat the former sheriff's name like it tasted bad. "I reviewed the case and that bastard's stink is all over it. The convenient witnesses—one of whom stayed completely anonymous?"

"It was Larry Lamb," Ash said. "The neighbor doing yard work."

"What, did the judge conveniently forget the Sixth Amendment?" Cal looked even more disgusted. "And all the so-called evidence that suddenly showed up right before the trial? Circumstantial bullshit. I mean, so what if Pete purchased cleaning supplies and heavy duty garbage bags? The guy owned a bar. Sure, he did some shady deals at that bar, but it was all white-collar shit, and he had a gambling problem that, apparently, nobody thought to investigate. He definitely made enemies there that could've targeted Harmony to make a point. And of course he'd have a life insurance policy on his wife. Most married couples do. And don't get me started on that shit-for-brains public defender he was assigned. Pete never stood a chance at a fair trial."

"What are his chances of an appeal?"

"Hell, I'll get the conviction overturned on the Sixth Amendment violation alone. And then I'll help him sue everyone involved in this farce."

Ash winced, but he'd known that was coming. "So you'll take his case? I'll pay for it."

Cal held up a hand. "No, this one's pro bono."

"Thought you don't do pro bono work."

"I'm making an exception." He looked at the window again. "Are you going to LA to talk to Montgomery-Duran?"

"If I can get a face-to-face with him. I doubt he'll just agree to a meeting with a rural county sheriff, especially if he was involved in Harmony's murder. You worked in LA for a while, didn't you? You wouldn't happen to have any connections…?"

"If I had connections to a billionaire, do you think I'd be living here, defending drug addicts and petty criminals for what amounts to minimum wage?" Cal snorted. "If I could get a sit down with one of the world's richest men, I wouldn't have to worry about those student loan payments."

"Yeah, didn't think so."

"So, what are you going to do?"

Ash stuffed his hands in his jacket pockets. "I'll think of something." In fact, an idea was already brewing, thanks to something Cal had said.

One of the world's richest men…

Didn't Zak have a connection like that from his military days?

In the other room, the guard led Pete away. Rose sat at the table for a moment longer, obviously pulling herself back together. Then she swiped at her face with her sleeves and got up.

Ash met her in the hall. Her face was splotchy, her eyes red, and she looked unsteady on her feet. He wanted to pull her into his arms and hold her until she felt steady again.

Instead, he motioned to Cal. "Do you know Callum Holden?"

"He's come into the pub a few times, but I don't think we've ever been officially introduced." Rose sniffed and offered a polite, albeit watery smile. "I know you helped Zak and Anna with the girls' adoptions when they were hitting snags with the courts over the custody of Bella."

"I sure did. Hi, Rose. I'm Cal." He gave that charming, panty-dropping smile of his and instead of holding out his hand for a shake, he passed her a handkerchief.

Where the hell had that come from?

"Thank you." She wiped her face. "Are you here visiting a client?"

Ash curled his fists at his sides to keep from punching the man who was going to give Rose the thing she wanted most in the world—her dad's freedom. "He's taking Pete's case."

Her eyes widened. "What?" She turned to Cal. "Oh, no. I'm so sorry if Ash gave you the wrong impression, but I can't afford—"

"Ash offered to pay," Cal said.

"You did?" Those eyes swung back to him and filled with tears again.

He both loved and hated the reverence he saw there. "He turned me down. He's doing it pro bono."

She faced Cal again. "You are?"

"I can't take money from someone who has been wrongly convicted," Cal said softly. "It wouldn't be right. Your family has suffered enough."

"I-I don't know what to say."

And, in fact, Rose said nothing more as Ash led her out of the prison. She stared silently out the car window at the ocean as they twisted along the coastal road back to Steam Valley.

Ash let her have the silence and instead played over Pete's interview in his mind.

He knew Harmony had still been alive the morning of her disappearance because a couple who lived down the street were out for a run at dawn and had stopped to speak to her when they saw her watering the flowers on her porch. So at some point between then and when Rose woke for school, she left the house and was never seen again. That left only one hour of Pete's time unaccounted for that day—the hour he was supposedly asleep after Rose left for school. And he thought he'd heard Harmony at their home during that time speaking to someone.

Had she returned with the person who killed her?

The neighbor, Larry Lamb, out doing yard work later that morning, claimed he saw Pete load something that looked like a body into his car. But Pete wouldn't have had time to kill Harmony, load her body into his trunk in full view of the neighbor, drive her up the mountain and bury her, then return to open the Mad Dog early. But, Ash supposed, Pete could have stashed her body somewhere then buried her later. With nothing more than charred bones left of her, it was impossible to establish an exact time of death or whether she was moved after death.

But that scenario didn't ring true to Ash. Pete didn't kill her. His instincts had told him as much thirteen years ago, but he'd been too green to trust his gut back then. Now he knew better.

The whole conviction hinged on Larry Lamb's testimony.

Ash made a split-second decision and detoured off the main highway onto a road that would take them to the Galasso family's old neighborhood.

Rose finally looked at him. "Where are we going?"

"To talk to Larry Lamb."

She stiffened. "About?"

"What he really saw that day."

"It's a waste of time." She shook her head. "He won't change his story."

He changed his story.

Rose couldn't believe it.

Larry came out onto his porch when they pulled up, almost as if he'd expected them. He always looked a little sad with a hang-dog expression of droopy eyes and sagging jowls, but now he was downright grim as he watched them get out of the Tahoe.

He nodded to Ash. "Sheriff." Then he looked at Rose, but she noticed he couldn't hold her gaze. "Rose. I'm mighty sorry for what happened to you."

"Thank you. I'm okay now."

"Good." He still looked at everything but her. "That's good."

"You know why we're here," Ash said, making it a statement rather than a question.

Larry scrubbed a hand over those jowls, then gave a sigh that moved his shoulders. "Suspect so. You want to know what I saw the morning her mama"—he nodded toward Rose—"vanished."

"Why didn't you ever tell me you testified against my dad?" Rose asked.

He lifted his shoulders in a helpless shrug. "I felt bad. I felt stupid. Jerry Tennison—we went way back. We were in kindergarten together, for chrissakes. I've known him all my life, so when he took my words and twisted them to fit what he saw was the truth—well, I had no reason to doubt him. Maybe what I saw was what he thought I saw. Figured he knew better'n I did, so I said what I said. But, honest to God, I don't know what I saw. Pete was there and he was putting stuff in his trunk, but I didn't see what it was and couldn't tell you what time it was when I saw him. I was working in the yard. Always lose track of time out there, you know?"

Ash took a card out of his wallet and passed it to Larry. "You need to call this man, Cal Holden, and tell him exactly what you just told us."

Larry frowned at the card. "Am I in trouble?"

Rose glanced over at Ash. He was pissed. She could see it in the jumping muscle of his jaw, but he somehow managed to keep his voice gentle when he said, "You do the right thing, call

Cal, tell him what you told me, and as far as I'm concerned, we're good. Okay?"

Larry nodded. "I really am mighty sorry about all this."

Back in the car, Rose watched Larry through the windshield as Ash backed out of the driveway. He was pacing his porch, the card in one hand while he held a cell phone to his ear with the other. He looked worried, almost child-like, as if he still expected to be scolded.

"I never noticed it before because he's always drunk when I see him, but he's..." She searched for a way to put it that didn't sound cruel. "He has an intellectual disability, doesn't he?"

And there, finally, was the anger, thrumming in Ash's voice. "Making him the perfect witness for Tennison to mold." He banged a fist on the steering wheel. "Fucking Tennison."

She looked out the side window as they passed her childhood home. It looked nothing like she remembered it. The new owners had built on an entire second story and painted it a soft blue. The porch no longer sagged and had also been painted bright white—but, she noted, her mom's beloved planters were still there along the railing. She hoped they still bloomed with color in the spring and summer. Mom would want that.

At the thought, she smiled and looked at Ash. "Thank you."

He glanced her way, then did a double take and his expression softened, the anger draining out of him. "Just doing my job."

"No," she murmured. "You're doing so much more."

He said nothing for a long moment. "Thirteen years ago, I made you a promise to find out what happened to your mom. One I never intended to break. It was past time I did my job and fulfilled it."

She couldn't explain why her heart sank at his words. Of

course she was just another case for him, another victim he had to protect. She'd known that from the beginning, so she had no right to feel disappointed.

No.

That was bullshit.

After everything that had happened between them in the last few weeks, she had all the right in the world to be annoyed at the distance he was trying to put between them.

She crossed her arms over her chest and stared out the window. "I'm more than just your job, Sheriff, and we both know it."

part two
love

"Love makes your soul crawl out from its hiding place."
– Zora Neale Hurston

twenty-three

A WEEK after visiting her dad, life almost felt normal again. Of course, she still had Mike Conti shadowing her when Ash wasn't around, but there had been no new threats and, as far as Ash would tell her, no new leads.

Rose was thrilled. Maybe it was over. Maybe she could finally put it all behind her and focus on her dad's appeal. Cal Holden was pulling together an air-tight case of police corruption and wrongful conviction. He was confident they'd win. It was a hopeful spark of light at the end of a very long, very dark tunnel.

But Ash didn't think it was over yet, and he was frustrated. His mood darkened with each passing day, like a thunderhead building during the summertime, sizzling with electricity. She was holding her breath, waiting for the lightning strike. When it finally came, she had a feeling it was going to scorch them both.

Ash had taken to working at the pub when Mike's body-guard shift ended. He set up a mini office at the end of the bar with his laptop, radio, and stacks of files and paperwork. More than one patron had raised a brow at him when they walked in. Having the sheriff as a permanent resident in her bar probably hurt sales, but she had to admit—if only to herself—that she enjoyed having him there. Even when he was a grump. Which was most of the time.

Business was slow today, so as she washed glasses and wiped down the bar top, she kept one eye on him, watching him work. The way his eyes narrowed in concentration, the way his fingers moved over the keyboard with a practiced ease, and the way he muttered under his breath when things didn't go his way, all fascinated her. Tension radiated off him like a heat wave. His jaw was set, and his eyes were like flint, hard and unyielding. His deputies came and went throughout the day, bringing crisis after crisis, and he handled it all with cool, calm deliberation.

Around three p.m., a man she'd never seen before came in. He was tall—almost as tall as Ash—with short dark hair, dark eyes, and a fair amount of scruff on his chiseled jaw. He carried a leather laptop case on one shoulder, and wore ripped jeans and a dark green thermal shirt under a chunky cable knit cardigan. On any other man, that cream-colored sweater would look grandfatherly, but this guy more than pulled it off. On his muscular frame, it even looked sexy.

Her gaze slid to Ash again as she tried to picture him in a similar sweater. Nope. Didn't work for him. He was a flannel kind of guy when he wasn't wearing his uniform.

Sexy Sweater Guy glanced around, and she got the sense he was looking for something, but then he settled into the booth nearest the fireplace, where joyful flames danced and crackled, warming away the damp March chill.

Since he chose a booth instead of the bar, she grabbed a menu and a place setting, then poked her head into the kitchen. "Looks like you have a food order incoming."

Marcel slid off the stool he was perched on. "About time. I'm bored stiff."

"Slow day."

"Because your grumpy boyfriend out there is killing business."

She sighed in exasperation. "He's not my boyfriend. I don't even like him." *Much*, she added silently.

"Yeah, right," Marcel muttered and rolled his eyes as he stuffed his long graying beard into a hairnet. He waved her away. "Go get me a food order, Rosie. Before I start growing cobwebs back here."

Ash looked up from his work as she walked by, and she felt his gaze on her all the way to the corner booth.

"Hi," she said to the newcomer. "Can I get you something to drink? Anything to eat?"

Sweater Guy smiled as she set the menu down in front of him. He had a movie star smile of bright, even teeth that had to be the product of childhood braces. "I've heard the parmesan fries here are to die for."

"It's Marcel's specialty."

"I'll take a plate. And..." He studied the menu. "Do you have a beer suggestion?"

"What do you like?"

His polite smile spread into a grin. "Anything as dark as my soul."

She laughed. "Okay, then. You want the Bulldog Stout. It's *my* specialty."

He arched a brow. "You brew it here?"

"No, we don't have the space for it. Maybe someday, but for now I have a contract with the brewery outside of town."

"Okay, I'll try it." He handed the menu back to her. "You can wait and bring it with the fries. Thanks."

Once again, Ash's gaze tracked her across the room.

"Who's that?" he asked, his voice all growly possessive, as she walked past him to give Marcel the order.

She scoffed. "A customer. One you better not scare away."

A muscle ticked under his beard.

She ignored him, gave a crestfallen Marcel the order—
"Really? Only fries?" —then waited in the kitchen until it was
complete. When she returned to Sweater Guy's table with his
food and beer, he was typing intently on a laptop. He gave her
a distracted smile and another, "Thanks," but he seemed off in
his own world, so she left him to it and went back to cleaning.

An hour later, Marcel closed up the kitchen and left with
the promise to come back if business picked up that evening.
She doubted it. Nobody had come in since Sweater Guy, and
he was still typing away, oblivious to his surroundings.

Rose noticed his glass was empty and walked over to offer
him a refill. At first, he didn't seem to hear her, then he
blinked, and his gaze focused.

"Sorry." He winced, shook his head as if to clear it, and
closed the computer's lid. "I get caught up. Just the bill,
please."

She handed him the slip from her pad. "So, you must be
the writer my aunt was telling me about."

He smiled as he checked the total, then dug a twenty out
of his wallet. "Keep the change. How can you tell?"

"Thanks." She tucked the bill into her jeans pocket and
nodded toward the table. "The laptop. The notebooks. The
faraway look for the last hour, like you were in another world."

"Guilty as charged. And you must be Rose." His smile
turned into a charming grin. "Yeah, Rainbow has told me all
about you, too, but I doubt anything your aunt has said is the
truth."

"So you didn't ask her permission to date me?"

Another wince. "No, can't say I did, but she makes sure to
tell me you're single every time I go into her shop." His gaze
shifted over to Ash. "Except that doesn't appear to be true,
either, judging by the sheriff's scowl."

She glanced over at the bar. Yep. Ash was scowling.

Was he jealous?

Good.

She turned back to the writer and gave her most flirtatious smile. "No, that's just his normal expression. He only wishes we were together."

"Ah. You might want to tell *him* that."

"Oh, believe me, he knows. What about you, writer? Are you single?"

"Very." There was no mistaking the spark of interest in his dark eyes, but then his gaze strayed over her shoulder to Ash again. "But, while you're a beautiful woman, I, unfortunately, don't have time to date right now." He tapped his fingers on the lid of his computer. "Deadline."

"What do you write?"

"Horror, mostly, but my current work in progress is a police procedural." He held out a hand. "Connelly Davis."

"No shit?" Rose was never a horror fan, but her father was, so she tried to read whatever he was reading to feel closer to him. He called it the "Reading Between the Bars" Book Club, which she didn't find amusing in the slightest. "I read *Dreadwood Manor* with my dad a few years ago. Seriously creepy. It gave me nightmares for weeks."

"I always love to hear that, but...." Connelly winced. "Please tell me you've read some of my newer stuff. *Dreadwood* was my first, published when I was barely out of high school, and it's... immature."

"Honestly, I didn't know you were publishing anymore."

"I took a break for a while—bounced around a bit, did the college thing, did a stint in the military." He lifted a shoulder. "But I couldn't stay away from my first love, so here I am."

"Dad will be thrilled when I tell him I met you. He's a huge fan."

"Well, I'll be here most afternoons plugging away at this manuscript. Tell him to stop by, and I'll buy him a beer. Which was excellent, by the way."

Her heart twisted. Most people around Steam Valley knew her father was in prison, but every once in a while, she'd run into a situation like this with someone who didn't. She always found it was easier to bluff her way through the conversation than try to explain the truth. "He doesn't live here, but I'll tell him you said hi."

"In that case..." He dug in his bag and pulled out a hardcover, opening it to the title page. "What's his name?"

"Pete."

Connelly signed it, then held it out to her. "Give him that. It's my next release, out this fall."

She glanced down at the cover. It showed a shadowy figure rising out of a blue-gray mist. She read the title out loud: "*The Shadows Within*. Looks phenomenally creepy."

"It's about The Shadow Stalker. Have you heard the legend?"

"Of course. *In shadows so deep, the Stalker hides. Fear his presence, where moonlight dies,*" she recited the first verse of the nursery rhyme in an ominous tone, then laughed. "You can't live around here and not know it by heart."

He nodded. "That rhyme captured my imagination when I first heard it as a kid and never left my head, so..." He motioned to the book. "I wrote about it."

"My dad's going to love this. He used to scare me around the campfire with those stories."

A throat cleared. They both turned to see Ash standing there, his arms crossed over his chest. His scowl had deepened, and Rose had to stifle a giggle. She loved getting under his skin.

"Everything okay, Sheriff?" Connelly asked, his gaze flicking between the two of them.

"Just fine," Ash said, his tone clipped. "Rose, can I talk to you for a minute?"

"I'm busy with a customer," she said, all sweetness.

She didn't think it was possible, but Ash's scowl deepened further as he glowered at the writer. "I'll wait."

Connelly raised his hands in surrender. "I met my word count, so I'll get out of your hair. Nice meeting you, Rose."

"Thanks for the book for my dad." Rose smiled politely as Connelly gathered his things and headed to the door.

Ash stalked after him, and as soon as Connelly was gone, he locked the door, closing them into the empty bar together.

"What are you doing?" she demanded. "It's the middle of the day. We're not closed."

He turned his scowl on her. "What the hell was that?"

"What was what?" Rose asked innocently, though she knew exactly what he was talking about.

"You were flirting with him."

She shrugged. "He's cute, and he writes horror. What's not to like?"

"You're mine," Ash said, his voice low and possessive.

Rose rolled her eyes. "I'm not anyone's property."

"You're my responsibility."

Heat flashed through her in a weird mix of anger and want. This man really thought he could claim her in one breath and then walk it back to an obligation the next. He thought he could kiss her like he wanted to devour her, promise all kinds of dark, thrilling things, then pretend nothing had changed between them. He was an arrogant, uptight jackass, and if he thought he could control her, he had another thing coming.

"I'm not a damn job," she snapped. "You're in charge of the county, Sheriff, not me. And you made it quite clear last week you have no interest in fucking me, so I can flirt with whoever I want."

"Ambrosia," he began in a tone laced with warning. "Listen to me—"

"No. You listen. You don't get to have it both ways. You

can't have me on a leash when it's convenient for you, and then act like you don't care the rest of the time. It doesn't work like that."

Ash stepped closer to her, his eyes darkening. With anger or desire? It was anyone's guess. His gaze dropped to the signed book, and he plucked it out of her hand, set it aside. "Then tell me how it works."

She could feel the heat emanating from his body, and she couldn't help but move closer. "You either want me, or you don't. You can't have half of me."

"You know I want you," he said, his voice rough, his fingers clenching and unclenching at his sides like he wanted to grab her. "But I can't touch you for so many complicated reasons, and I'm doing my best to be responsible, even when your scent is all over my house, my clothes, filling my head and driving me crazy."

"Fine, be responsible." Rose took another step closer, her chest practically brushing against his. "Be cold and professional, but at least stop walking away every time I enter a room. Stop making me feel like I'm just some obligation you have to fulfill. Stop pretending like you don't feel anything for me."

His gaze dropped to her lips and then lifted back to her eyes. She saw the hunger there, the need, and it filled her with a sense of power.

She had him exactly where she wanted him.

"You want me to stop pretending?" Ash growled, his hand clamping onto her chin. "Fine. I'm done pretending."

ASH CAUGHT her chin in his hand and made her look up at him. The anger was still there, burning bright, but something else was behind it now. Something hotter and more dangerous than hate.

She smiled like a cat that had just caught the mouse in her claws. "You want to take out all of your frustrations on me, don't you?"

Desire and anger swirled inside him as he leaned in closer. "You have no idea," he growled, his hand tightening around her chin. "But it's not just frustrations I want to take out on you, Ambrosia. Trust me, you won't enjoy it."

Rose's smile only widened as she leaned in closer to him, her breath hot against his ear. "How do you know?"

"Because I want to punish you for flirting with that asshole in front of me. I want to show you just how much power I have over you." His grip tightened even more, and she let out a gasp of pain, but it only seemed to fuel her desire.

"You have no power over me, Sheriff." With a sudden movement, she broke free from his grasp and pushed him up against the wall, her hands roaming down to the buckle of his belt.

Ash let out a low groan as her hands worked expertly, undoing his pants and pulling them down to reveal his hard length. Without hesitation, she sank down onto her knees in front of him, taking him into her mouth and swirling her tongue around him.

Oh, Jesus.

He should pull her away. Put a stop to this before they crossed a line they couldn't return from. He should—

Her tongue swirled over his tip and his brain short-circuited.

Fuck it.

He tangled his fingers in her hair and pulled her up to her feet, slamming her back against the wall. She let out a gasp of surprise and pain, but it only seemed to excite her even more.

"You think you can just play with me like that?" he snarled. "You think you can just take what you want without consequence?"

Rose's eyes blazed with desire as she looked up at him. "Yes." She reached down between them and wrapped her hand around his throbbing shaft. "Because you like when I do."

"Fuck," he breathed, and his lips crashed down on hers in a fierce, hungry kiss.

It was a dangerous game they were playing, one that could explode out of control at any moment. But he didn't care. He wasn't a man right then—he was an animal that only knew one thing.

Her.

His mate.

He pulled her away from the wall and bent her over the bar, his hands cupping her breasts through the tight fabric of her cropped t-shirt. He skimmed his lips over her neck and bit down harder than he intended to, leaving a mark on her skin.

Rose cried out and shoved her ass against him, her fingers digging into the scarred wood of the bar top. "Yes."

"You like that, Ambrosia?" Ash slipped his hand down to the waistband of her jeans and popped the button open. He traced the line of her panties along her hip and leaned in to bite her shoulder as he slid his fingers under the damp fabric.

She moaned and pushed up onto her tiptoes as he parted her. She was hot and swollen and already so wet. His cock throbbed. He wanted to kick her legs open and bury himself to the hilt, but settled for rocking his hips against her ass as he slipped his fingers inside her.

"Yes," she said again, the word barely more than a whisper.

He pressed her clit with his thumb and a quiet, desperate sound slipped from her lips. She pushed her pants further down her legs and bent forward to pull them off, giving him a clear view of his fingers in her wet, dripping pussy.

Goddammit. He wanted to punish her, not pleasure her. He pulled his free hand back and smacked the round globe of her ass hard.

Rose gasped and whimpered and pushed her ass higher as if begging for more.

Ash paused, his hand raised. He needed to make sure she knew who was in control. "Do you want more?" he asked, his voice like ice cold steel.

"Yes," she moaned.

"Okay." He bent over and traced his tongue over the red mark he'd left on her skin. "But you're going to beg for it."

"Please, Ash," she said, her voice breathy and soft. "Slap my ass again. I want you to mark me like a fucking animal."

He rewarded her with a soft slap, this time on the other cheek, and she let out a guttural moan. "Yes. Again. Make me feel it."

With his teeth bared, he smacked her again, harder this time.

Rose cried out and her walls clenched hard around his

fingers. She was loving this, and he almost lost control. He was shaking the effort of holding himself still.

"Tell me," he growled. "What do you want me to do to you?"

"I... I want you to— to—" She looked over her shoulder at him, her eyes glazed with lust and something more. Submission, he realized, and his cock kicked in anticipation.

"You want it? You want me to fuck you hard, right here on the bar? Tell me you want me to fuck you like the bad girl you are."

"Yes."

"Yes, what?"

"Yes, Sheriff. Mark me. Make me your slut."

Ash groaned. It had been too long since he'd had a woman, much less one as responsive as Rose. She really was Ambrosia—a fucking taste of heaven and he couldn't deny himself any longer.

He smacked her again and as she moaned, he removed his fingers from her and positioned his cock at her entrance.

Rose cried out as he plunged in, her voice hoarse. "Oh, God. Finally."

"Shut up." He fucked her hard and deep, his hips smacking against her rear as his fingers dug into her waist. She wasn't gentle either. She pushed back against him, urging him deeper with each thrust. He pulled at her hair, her throat, her breast—whatever he could reach.

"I want to hear you," he growled in her ear, his teeth gritted. "Tell me you submit."

"Yes," she moaned. "Please, Ash. Anything. Just... harder. Fuck me harder."

"Good girl." He slammed into her until the bar was covered in a thin layer of sweat under her and he could feel it dripping down his back. "Now come for me."

Rose climaxed with her hands clutching at the bar top and her head thrown back as she coated his cock with her juices.

"Yes. That's it. I'm going to come on your back, and I want you to feel every drop." Unable to hold on any longer, he pulled out and his seed spilled across her back in long, thick spurts. She cried out and collapsed forward, leaning against the bar until her breathing slowed.

He stared at the red hand prints he'd left on her ass, and the cum pooling at her lower back, and thought, *fuck, what did I just do?*

"Wow," she murmured. "That was..."

"Yeah," he said, his voice thick as he grabbed a towel and wiped her off. "It was."

She pulled up her pants, then turned and took the towel from him, dropping it to the floor. "Do you want a drink? I need a drink."

Ash pulled up his zipper, wincing as it dug into his still-sensitive cock. "Yeah."

She grabbed a bottle from the shelf behind the bar. "Bourbon? Or would you prefer a beer?"

"Bourbon's good." He found himself staring at her ass as she poured them each a healthy dose of the golden alcohol. The way her jeans hugged that perfect inverted heart was almost as erotic as seeing her without them on. As was the knowledge that under that denim, her cheeks were pink with his handprint.

"So..." She turned to him and held out his glass. "Who knew the uptight sheriff was a closet Dom?"

"Fuck," he hissed and took the offered bourbon. He downed it in one gulp and then stepped around her to pour another. "That shouldn't have happened."

"But it did. And I liked it. A lot more than I expected, if I'm honest." She motioned with her glass, indicating the towel on the floor between them smeared with his cum. "And I'm pretty sure you did, too."

Jesus. Not only had he fucked the one woman in town he couldn't stand, but he'd done it in her bar. They must have broken all kinds of health codes. Maybe even a law or two.

"You don't know me well enough to know what I like," he said, keeping his tone cool and even.

"But I know men." Her gaze dropped pointedly to the towel again. "And most men don't spill like that if they're not having a good time."

Pain shot through his jaw as he snapped up the towel and stuffed it in the trash. He was grinding his teeth hard enough to crack a molar. He forced himself to relax and drew a calm, measured breath. "I don't like to lose control like that."

"Hm." She leaned against the bar that still sported her handprints and sipped her drink with a thoughtful expression on her face. "So what you're saying is it won't happen again?"

"It shouldn't have happened in the first place. I don't fuck women like—" He broke off, realizing a half-second too late that what he'd been about to say was cruel. Why did his mouth always spout off before his brain around Ambrosia Galasso?

"Women like me?" Rose smirked and set her glass down. "It's okay. I get it. I'm not your usual type. So, what kind of woman do you fuck, Sheriff?"

He downed the rest of his drink. "Women who don't demand more. Or ask questions."

"I see." She switched her glass to her other hand and held out her fist. "Fist bump?"

Ash stared at her. "What the fuck kind of thing is that to say?"

"Well, I know you're not a high five kind of guy." Her eyes glinted with laughter. "C'mon. Fist bump."

He continued to stare at her, at a loss for words. This woman was something else. "Why?"

"To break the tension and see how you respond to the unexpected. I'm trying to get a feel for who you are under all that gruff growliness." Her gaze was direct and unflinching. "You know everything about me—all of my deepest, darkest secrets. And you're right, I know next to nothing about you except you fuck like you're trying to exorcise your demons through your cock."

Heat rushed into his face. Jesus, was he actually blushing? She wouldn't notice it in the bar's dim light with his beard as thick and wild as it was, but he turned away on the pretense of dumping his empty glass in the nearby sink. He wanted another drink, but he knew better than to indulge. His parents had died when a drunk driver slammed into their car, and he'd seen too many friends in this town succumb to alcoholism. So, like everything else in his life, he kept a firm grip on his drinking habits, never allowing himself more than two.

"And, after what we just did, I think it's only fair I get to know you a little bit more, don't you?" She held out her fist again, waiting for him to bump it.

With a sigh, Ash faced her and hit her fist with his. To his surprise, she caught his wrist and stepped into his personal space.

"And maybe," she whispered, her breath hot against his lips, "you need a reminder that you can't control everything. Especially not me."

She stood on her toes and pressed her lips softly against his. He wasn't prepared for the bolt of heat that ran through him. It was hot and sweet, a forbidden pleasure that was like a drug. He closed his eyes and breathed in her scent, a warm, spicy smell that was going to be the end of him.

He tried to pull away, but her lips clung to him.

He gave up trying to escape and settled into the kiss. She

tasted like the smoky caramel of the bourbon, and it was only after he was able to tear his mouth from hers that he realized he was already drunk—not from the alcohol, but from her.

"You should go," she whispered, her fingers still wrapped around his wrist. "Before you do something you regret."

"I already regret it." His voice came out gruffer than he'd intended. He cleared his throat, extracted his wrist from her grasp, and stepped back out of her reach. "And I'm not leaving you alone when someone tried to kill you a few weeks ago."

She shrugged and took her glass to the sink to wash it. "I'm not worried."

"You should be. Someone tried to kill you," he repeated, enunciating each word. "Why aren't you more upset about what happened? You had a bottle smashed across your head. That bastard tied you up and dragged you out into the woods and pumped you full of heroin, for fuck's sake." He watched her as he spoke, looking for any sign of distress. But she appeared calm, her shoulders relaxed as she washed and dried their glasses. "Doesn't that bother you?"

"I mean, yeah, it hurt, and it was terrifying, but my sheriff in the shining Tahoe saved me before the sick fuck could do whatever else he had in mind." She replaced the clean glasses on the shelf, her cropped shirt riding up to show the thorny rose tattooed to her ribs.

He wanted to trace that design with his tongue and—

No.

He walked around the bar, putting another physical barrier between them before he did something stupid.

Again.

He rubbed a hand over his beard. Fuck, he was tired.

Rose grabbed a clean towel from the stack under the bar and started wiping away the last evidence of their mistake, buffing her handprints out of the oak bar top. "Besides, Sheriff, I'm a survivor. I survived losing both of my parents in one go. I survived multiple mystery illnesses in my teens that should've killed me. I'll survive this, too. It's what I do."

Wait.

What?

He didn't like the tone of her voice. It was... resigned. Like she expected to spend her entire life simply surviving.

"What illnesses?"

"Doesn't matter." She finished cleaning the bar and draped the towel over her shoulder. "It's nothing for you to worry about."

"If it has to do with your safety, then it is something for me to worry ab—" When she merely smirked at him with those ungodly sexy lips, he broke off and shook his head in exasperation. "Jesus, I don't know why I'm wasting my breath arguing with you. You're never going to listen. You're a stubborn ass, and you're going to do whatever the fuck you want."

Her expression didn't change, and her answer was simple. "It's my life."

"Jesus, Rose." He stalked around the bar toward her, but she didn't back away or so much as flinch.

"Oh, so it's back to Rose now?" She clucked her tongue. "Pity. I was starting to like having you call me by my full name. You make it sound so dirty."

His fingers curled into fists at his sides. He wanted to strangle her. And at the same time, he wanted to scoop her up and tuck her away in his home so nobody could hurt her. "Someone has tried to kill you," he repeated through his teeth. "Twice."

"I know that," she said evenly, but he could hear anger edging into her voice. "I was there."

"Then what the hell is wrong with you?"

Those ice-blue eyes burned with sudden fury. "Nothing is wrong with me, Sheriff. And nothing is wrong with you. We fucked. I enjoyed it. You did, too. End of story."

He growled. "You are the most infuriating woman I've ever met."

"That's what they tell me." She cocked her head to the side. "You know what I think? I think I'm not just a job to you anymore and that pisses you off. You're actually worried about me. You're worried I'm going to get hurt again, aren't you?"

"Dammit, Ambrosia. Don't make my job harder."

"And back to my full name again." She chuckled and glanced down at his pants. "Your job's not the only thing I'm making harder."

She was trying to distract him, and it was working. The woman distracted him just by existing. How the hell was he supposed to keep her safe when he couldn't even keep his eyes off her long enough to scan for danger?

His jaw ached. He really had to stop clenching his teeth around her, or he'd need to visit his dentist. "Regardless of my body's involuntary response to you, I am a law enforcement officer, and I'm going to do whatever it takes to keep you safe."

"And, in return, I'll do whatever it takes to make sure you have a good time." She sauntered closer and trailed her fingers up his chest, toying with his buttons. He shivered, the unexpected touch of her fingers and the scent of her fucking with his head. "So, you see, I think we make a good team."

"I don't know that I agree." He took her hand and removed it from his shirt. He couldn't deny how much she was affecting him. "You're going to get yourself killed one of these days if you don't start taking this shit seriously."

"You really are worried about me. That's sweet."

"It's not sweet. I'm doing my job."

"You did more than your job just now." Her gaze slid back to his crotch. "And you did it really, really well."

"Rose." He caught her hand as she reached for his fly. "Enough."

"Or what?"

"Or I'm going to take you back to my place and fuck you until you can't walk."

She grinned at him. "Promise?"

Ah, hell. There went his mouth again, saying shit before his brain told it not to. "Rose—"

"I don't need you to fix me, Ash. I'm asking you to fuck me. For now. Just for now. Is that too much to ask?"

He stared at her for a long moment, his eyes searching hers. Finally, he let out a ragged sigh. "Fine. But we're not getting involved. I mean it, Rose. If we keep doing this, it's just sex. It's—"

The front window shattered.

Rose turned toward it in surprise. "What?"

"Get down!"

chapter
twenty-five

SHOCK FROZE ROSE to the spot as she realized what that rapid staccato sound was.

Automatic gunfire.

Ash was already moving, shoving her to the ground behind the bar as bullets tore through the window and wall, shredding wood and glass and raining liquor down over their heads. He grunted in pain as they fell, but still covered her body with his own. Something wet and warm spread across her shoulder. She lifted a hand to the spot, but found the blood wasn't coming from her.

"Ash!" She tried to push him off, but he remained steadfastly still, his heavy body pinning hers to the floor.

"Stay down," he growled.

"You're bleeding!"

"I'm aware." He one-handedly wrestled his weapon out of its holster and finally lifted his weight off her as police sirens started up in the distance. He ran to the door, weapon held aloft in his left hand, blood dripping down his right arm at his side. He returned fire and tires screeched on pavement.

Then it all stopped.

Rose swayed to her feet in a daze, her ears ringing, her

heart pounding so hard she wouldn't be surprised if Ash could hear it, too. She took in the destruction around her—wood splinters and broken glass littering the floor, the smell of liquor thick in the air from the broken bottles, bullets embedded in the walls.

Her home.

Her sanctuary.

Ruined by violence.

Again.

Tears blurred her vision, and she tried in vain to blink them back. Why was this happening to her?

"We're clear," Ash said, but she noticed he didn't re-holster his weapon nor move away from his guard stance by the door. "I think I hit one of them."

She watched blood drip from his arm onto the floor.

"You're bleeding," she said again. Was that her voice? It sounded hollow and faint, like she was whispering through a long tube.

He glanced back at her. "Sit down, Rose. You're in shock."

She righted a stool, but one of the legs gave out before she could sit. She stared down as a small metal object dropped out of the wood and rolled across the floor.

A bullet, flattened by its impact with the stool.

Her legs gave out and she sank to the floor. Tears flooded her eyes and spilled over. She couldn't stop them. She wrapped her shaking arms around her middle and bent double as the sobs tore from her.

"Shit," Ash muttered, but stayed put beside the door, gun at the ready. "Hang on, Rose. Hear those sirens? My deputies are coming. They're almost here..."

She heard him continue in a soft, soothing voice, but the words didn't register. She couldn't stop crying. Couldn't catch her breath.

Then he was there, his arms tight around her, pulling her

close. The smell of his blood was almost overpowered by the alcohol soaking their clothes. She wrapped her arms around his waist and pressed her hot face into his chest.

"It's okay," he murmured into her hair. "You're safe now."

He held her tight and let her cry, but he didn't let her collapse completely. He kept her up, supported her, as she poured out all her fear and pain. So much for the tough act she'd been putting on moments before the bullets started flying. She cried until her throat was raw, then cried some more.

When she finally ran out of tears, Ash continued to hold her, stroking a hand up and down her back in reassuring circles. No one had ever supported her like this, been there for her when she was weak. She never realized how much she'd wanted this in her life until now.

It terrified her.

Slowly, she realized they weren't alone. At least four of his deputies were there, guns drawn as they secured the area.

And the therapy group was arriving for their afternoon meeting. She'd forgotten that was today.

One of the deputies held up a hand to stop them, but Ash waved them in. "It's okay, Wright. Let them pass."

"What the hell happened here?" Donovan asked, gingerly stepping over the broken glass. Zak and Pierce were right behind him.

She didn't have the energy to repeat the whole series of events, so she just told them, "Someone shot at the bar."

Pierce grabbed his phone from his back pocket and typed:

> Are you okay?

He held it up for her to read.

She nodded. "Ash is bleeding."

"How bad is it?" Zak asked, looking at his brother-in-law.

"Good question." Ash grimaced as he peeled off his jacket and shirt, revealing a broad chest covered in tight, hard muscles and a smattering of hair the same reddish-brown color of his beard. He held up his arm to examine the wound. "It's just a graze."

"Jesus," Zak said. He leaned over the bar, grabbing a towel from the clean stack she kept on a shelf under there. He wadded it up and pressed it to the wound. A former Army Ranger, he had extensive battlefield medic training and had dealt with all kinds of injuries. "Any lower and you wouldn't be standing here right now."

Ash took the towel from him. "Nah, it went through the door first. By the time it hit me, it didn't have the power to do any real damage."

"Still, you're going to need stitches."

"Fuck that."

"Then at least sit your ass down and let me bandage it before you bleed all over."

Pierce said something in sign language and Zak scowled down at the splatter of blood on the floor. "Yeah, looks like he's already done that. Grab more towels."

"I got 'em." Donovan jumped over the bar and found the stack. He started mopping up the blood while Pierce tapped Rose on the shoulder.

He held out the phone again. It now read:

Are YOU okay?

Numb, she could only nod.

Pierce slid out of his canvas jacket and draped it over her shoulders. She hadn't realized she was cold until the warmth wrapped around her. It smelled like his cologne—a spicy, earthy scent that was calming.

The sweet man. She wished she could communicate with him better. "Thank you."

Ash watched their exchange with a faint scowl while Zak worked on cleaning his wound, then impatiently pulled his shirt back on the moment it was bandaged. He started toward her, but the sight of the blood stains on his shirt made her stomach roll.

"I need to go," she said, voice cracking, and took an unsteady step in the direction of the door.

Ash stopped her, concern written all over his face. "It's not safe out there."

"I can't stay here."

"You're not leaving without me, and I have to stay with my deputies while—"

"I can't stay here!" She was horrified at the hysteria in her voice, but she couldn't dial it back.

Donovan stepped forward, his expression grim. "We'll escort her," he assured Ash, then gentled his voice as he turned to her. "Make sure you get home safely, yeah?"

Except this bar *was* her home. Would she ever feel safe here again? And she couldn't go to Ash's house if he wasn't going to be there. She didn't want to be alone right now.

Zak must have read her mind because he spoke up. "How about you come to the Rescue until Ash is done sheriffing?"

Ash opened his mouth as if to protest, but then must have thought better of it. "Take my Tahoe. It's armored." He rubbed his big hands over her shoulders, down her arms. "Is that okay?"

Rose nodded, grateful for the offer. She grabbed her purse from behind the bar and followed the group out of the building, stepping over broken glass and debris.

The street outside was a chaotic mess, with police cruisers and ambulances blocking the way. She felt like she was in a warzone and guilt and shame washed over her for causing all of this commotion. And that pissed her off. She had nothing to be ashamed about. She hadn't done this. The man— men? —who wanted her dead were responsible.

Were they out there in the gathering crowd, watching their handiwork, checking to see if they had finished the job? She shuddered at the thought and scanned the crowd, looking for anything out of the ordinary. But it was just the townspeople, the men and women she saw every day.

And Connelly Davis.

He stood behind the police barricade, watching everything unfold with a slight frown pulling his dark brows together. When he noticed her watching him, he hitched the strap of his computer bag up on his shoulder and walked away.

Ash and Donovan cleared a path through all the police cruisers and emergency vehicles, while Pierce and Zak flanked her on either side. She was still shaking so hard she felt like the whole world was vibrating.

Zak put his arm around her shoulders. "You okay?"

She gave him a weak smile. "I've never been shot at before."

He laughed as if she'd said something funny, but she wasn't joking. It was unnerving, being a target. She'd never felt so helpless.

"You get used to it," he said.

She stared at him in horror. "I don't want it to happen enough to get used to it."

He inclined his head. "Fair enough." He nodded toward Ash, walking with purpose several steps in front of them. "Don't worry. Ash'll figure out who did this."

She looked up at him, searching his warm brown eyes for any sign of doubt or disbelief, and found nothing but genuine conviction.

They reached the Tahoe and Ash handed Donovan his keys, then pulled open the back door for her. Before she could climb in, he wrapped his good arm around her waist, tugging her gently against his side. He leaned down to kiss the top of her head. "We'll talk when I get home, okay?"

chapter
twenty-six

DEPUTIES FOUND the body of one of the shooters laying in the middle of the street a block away from the Mad Dog. Ash had known he'd hit one of them but hadn't realized his aim had been so deadly. The bullet had ripped open the guy's neck—a wound that most likely spouted like a geyser, which was why his "friends" decided to cut their losses and shove him out of the car.

Ash had seen the make and model of the car—a late nineties Ford Taurus with peeling red paint and extensive rust on the fenders—as well as the first half of the plate. Surveillance cameras in front of The Mad Dog and the bank on the corner would likely give them the other half.

These idiots weren't going to get far, and Ash couldn't wait to get them into his interrogation room.

"Sheriff!"

Ash groaned and turned toward the familiar voice. Alexis Summers shouldered through the crowd of nosy onlookers, her sharp eyes scanning the crime scene, missing nothing behind those stylish glasses. "I've been trying to reach you."

He motioned to the scene with his good arm. "I've been busy."

"I see that." Her blond brows slammed together. "Do you often have drive-by shootings in Steam Valley?"

"No. And I'm not talking to the press. No comment."

"I'm not—" She caught his sleeve as he turned away. He glared down at her hand, and she let go. "I'm sorry. I just wanted to know if you've looked into—"

Jesus, if she said "serial killer" in front of all these people, he would have a riot on his hands. He ducked under the barricade and muscled her away from the crowd. When they were out of earshot of the local gossips, he stopped and faced her.

"Listen. I started to look into it, and you may be on to something."

She opened her mouth, and he held up a hand to stop her.

"But, right now, I have more pressing matters to deal with."

"What's more pressing than a serial—"

He motioned for her to lower her voice.

She glanced around, then finished in a hiss. "A serial killer?"

"A *possible* serial killer," he corrected. "If the same man is responsible, and I'm still not convinced of that, then your research indicated there hasn't been a new victim in at least eight years when he previously took one every six months. So he's either dead, or in prison, or he's moved on, and in that case, as callous as it sounds, he's not my problem until the FBI come knocking on my door."

She scoffed. "Just because I haven't found more recent victims, doesn't mean they're not out there. He goes for women nobody will miss. Women without family connections or local roots."

"Ms. Summers, I understand your concern. I do. But somebody just shot up my town." He waved a hand at the street. "My people are scared. I can't take my very limited manpower away from this to investigate a bunch of cold cases on the off chance they could be connected."

Her stubborn chin hitched up. "Then I'll investigate."

Ash sucked in a breath and strove for patience, but his fucking shoulder hurt, and he was terrified for Rose, and he was just so damn tired. "You said it yourself—if a killer is out there and he's still active, he goes for women without local ties. That's *you*. So my previous threat still stands. I will put you in jail if you try investigating this on your own."

"You can't just ignore it, Sheriff!"

Her raised voice drew several curious stares. He gave the looky-loos his back and walked her farther away from the growing crowd.

"I'm not," he said through his teeth. "I will investigate, but it's not the biggest threat to public safety right now."

She looked toward the barricades and the sheet-covered body on the street beyond, and the mulishness drained from her expression. "I'm sorry. I know you have a lot on your hands."

"I *will* investigate," he repeated. "I started before all this bullshit began, and I will pick it up again as soon as I'm able."

She nodded. "Okay."

Ash got a sinking feeling in his gut as he watched her walk over to a rental car parked on the side street. That acquiescence had come too fast, and she never promised not to look into it herself.

Goddammit. She *was* going to investigate. Nothing he said or did would stop her— short of throwing her in jail, but he'd only be able to keep her for forty-eight hours before he'd have to charge her with a crime or let her go. It'd only slow her down and give him more paperwork to do.

He muttered a curse and turned back to the crime scene just as Jonah Sullivan, his undersheriff, called out, "What the hell, Ash? You were *shot*?"

By the time Ash finally made it to his sister's house that night, it was late. He'd stayed at the crime scene until Jonah forced him to go to the nearest ER and get his shoulder treated, which took hours.

Anna's house was quiet and mostly dark when he let himself in with his key. The place still had that new house smell. He gave himself a moment to miss the old yellow farmhouse they'd grown up in, with its creaky floors and huge wraparound porch. It had been nearly a hundred years old and needed a lot of work, but it had always felt like home, even when he no longer lived there.

This new house was nice enough, he supposed. It was bigger than the farmhouse, with four bedrooms, an office, and an attached two-car garage. It had high ceilings and an open floorplan, and a pretty front porch—not a wraparound—of stone and wood.

But it felt like a stranger's house. He didn't feel his parents here. Dad had never fixed this porch. Mom had never fretted over the paint color of these walls. The realization was like a punch to the gut, knocking all the air out of his lungs. He stopped short in the foyer and fought back a sudden rush of tears. It was like losing them all over again.

He took a deep breath and shook his head, trying to clear it. He couldn't think about that now. He had to focus on the case.

On Rose.

He walked through the house, checking to make sure Anna and her family were asleep. He found her in the master bedroom, snuggled up on the king-sized bed with her adopted daughters, Bella and Poppy. Winston, Anna's Golden Retriever, was curled on the foot of the bed and thumped his tail lazily before rolling to his back and continuing his snooze.

Zak and his dog Ranger were conspicuously absent.

Ash's heart ached for them. Zak needed to get his head out of his ass before he lost the best things he'd ever had.

In the guest room, he found Rose curled up on the bed, sound asleep. Anna's text earlier said she'd made Rose take a sedative, so it wasn't a surprise she was out cold. She had her arms around Dante, who, for a vicious police K9, looked perfectly content with his current role as a body pillow. He wanted to kick Dante out and let Rose use him as a pillow instead, but he was too keyed up to lie down, so he backed out of the room and closed the door.

Was it weird to be jealous of a dog?

Hell yeah, it was weird.

Ash made his way back downstairs to the living room and slumped down on the couch. He rubbed his injured shoulder, grimacing at the pain. He'd refused to take any pain meds at the hospital. Anything stronger than ibuprofen was a slippery slope he had no interest in setting foot on again.

Still, he needed something to numb his senses, something that would help him forget how badly today could've ended.

What if he hadn't been there?

What if he hadn't given in to his desires and shut and locked the door?

Would the shooters have come inside the pub, guns blazing? Rose wouldn't have stood a chance if they had.

The what-ifs had been playing on repeat in his mind in vivid, gory detail all night, and he needed to silence them. He needed just a few hours of peace.

He popped to his feet and went to the kitchen, where he knew Anna had a stash of her favorite tequila. She wasn't much of a drinker, but she loved to indulge in an occasional margarita with her best friend, Sasha, after a hard day's work. And, since Zak was a recovering alcoholic, she'd keep it somewhere he wouldn't think to look...

Ash found a bottle under the sink, hiding in the mop bucket. Ha. Did he know his sister or what? He didn't bother with a lime or salt. He just wanted the burn of the liquor to numb his thoughts and poured some into a glass—then decided to hell with the glass. He sat at the counter and took the shot, followed by a swig straight from the bottle. The tequila burned, but he welcomed the pain. It was better than the pain in his shoulder. He took another swig, relishing how it scorched on the way down, and leaned back on the stool, his mind finally quieting.

At least, until his thoughts drifted back to Rose. The way she'd felt as she'd given into him. The way she'd taken everything he had and begged for more...

"Fuck," he muttered as his body stirred. He took another swig of tequila. He couldn't tell if it was the alcohol warming his body or the hot memories.

He never should've touched her, but he couldn't regret it. If he hadn't been there, if he hadn't locked the door so he could have his way with her without interruption—

The image of her hiding behind the bar, her eyes wide with fear, punched him in the gut all over again. He wanted to protect her, to keep her safe. But how could he do that when he was barely keeping himself together?

The house's silence was interrupted by the front door opening. Ash jolted upright, reaching for his gun before remembering Jonah had taken it as per protocol in an officer-involved shooting.

Zak walked in, looking haggard and defeated. Ranger, as always, was right at his heels.

"Hey," he said as he crossed the living room into the kitchen. "Saw your truck. How's the shoulder?"

"It's fine."

"Stitches?"

"Ten."

"Told ya."

Ash settled back into his seat. "Where were you?"

"Ah." He exhaled hard. "I'm sleeping on a cot in the Rescue's main office. Literally in the doghouse, but..." He shrugged. "I deserve it."

"You weren't drinking, were you?"

"No." He nodded toward the tequila. "But I see you found Anna's stash."

"You're not supposed to know about it."

Zak cracked a smile. "I let her think I don't know she hides it in the mop bucket because she feels guilty for having it. I told her it's fine. Having it in the house won't make me fall off the wagon or anything. Tequila was never my poison of choice."

"No, that was Jameson."

"Exactly. But she could even have that if she wanted, and I still wouldn't touch it." He met Ash's gaze over the island, his dark eyes serious. "I'm not going back there. I go back there, I die. And believe it or not, I'm not ready to die."

Ash's throat tightened. Man, his emotions were all over the place tonight. But he got it, even more than Zak knew. He'd been in the same place once, at that crossroads between life and death, addiction and health.

He lifted the bottle in toast, then took a swig to loosen the knot in his throat. "Glad to hear it."

Zak raised a brow. "You might want to think about slowing down there, man."

Ash snorted. "Now, this is a reversal. You telling me to slow down."

"If you want, I can drag you out of here, cursing the whole time, and dump you into bed." Zak's tone was self-deprecating. "Bring it full circle."

"Nah." He capped the tequila and stood, wobbling only slightly. Despite Zak's reassurances, he decided to take it with him. To his mind, it was better to remove the temptation altogether. He knew he wouldn't be safe alone in a room with an opioid. "I'll walk, thanks."

He almost reached the stairs before Zak called, "You know RWCR has your back, right? Yours and Rose's. She's one of us, and this is starting to feel personal."

"It *is* personal." He paused with one foot on the bottom step and glanced toward the kitchen island. Zak hadn't moved, still stood there backlit by the soft under-cabinet lights. "I want to bring the team in on the investigation. Think we can get everyone here tomorrow for a briefing?"

Zak nodded and pulled his phone from his back pocket. "I'll send out a text now. Ten?" He eyed Ash, then shook his head and started typing. "Nah, noon. You're gonna hate yourself in the morning."

"Appreciate it." His head was already pounding from the tequila. He took another step but then paused again. "Zak?"

"Hm?" he said without looking up from his phone.

"Don't blow it with my sister. I like having a brother-in-law, even if it *is* you." Ash didn't wait for an answer and continued up the steps to Rose's room. The second the door shut behind him, he set the tequila on the dresser, then stripped out of his jeans and crawled onto the bed, pushing Dante out of the way.

"Move it, dog. She's mine."

Dante eyed him, gave a disapproving huff, but finally hopped off the bed. Rose stirred slightly when Ash pulled her into his arms and tucked her against his chest.

"You're safe," he murmured into her hair and ran a

soothing hand up and down her back until she settled again. "Nobody is going to hurt you while I'm around."

But he couldn't protect her forever. He knew that he couldn't always be there to keep her safe. And the thought of losing her was unbearable.

So he had to make sure he got the bastards before they had another shot at her.

chapter
twenty-seven

ROSE GASPED AWAKE and bolted upright in bed, the tendrils of the nightmare losing their grip on her as she surfaced, fading back into the darkness.

Oh, God. Would she ever sleep through the night again?

She reached out, searching for the comforting form of Dante beside her, but discovered his furry body had been replaced with the hard, strong body of a man.

Ash.

He sat up and wrapped an arm around her, dragging her back into the nest of blankets and tucking her against his body. "Shh," he murmured, his breath warm against her neck. "You're okay."

She exhaled, snuggled into his arms, and closed her eyes. She was safe with him. Protected. The tension seeped out of her, the panic slowly subsiding.

His fingers traced soothing circles against her back. "Want to talk about it?"

She shook her head. "Not really. Just a nightmare."

Ash tightened his grip around her. "You don't have to keep it to yourself. I'm here for you, Rose."

She took a deep breath and let it out slowly. "It's always

the same. I'm back in the pub, and they're coming for me. Just these dark, faceless shadows, and I can't escape."

His jaw clenched, the muscles in his arm tensing. "It's not going to happen. I won't let them near you again."

"I know." She turned her head to look at him, the glow of the moon casting his face in shadows. "But what if they come after me when you're not here?"

"They won't," he said, his tone hard with conviction. "I'm glued to your side until we catch them."

She nodded. She believed him, but the fear still lingered.

"Hey." He cupped a hand under her chin and made her look at him. "I will catch them."

"I know." Her breath caught in her throat as Ash's thumb rubbed over her lips and a flame ignited deep in her belly. She shouldn't be feeling this way—not for him—but as much as she wanted to keep hating him, her body betrayed her, responding to his touch in a way that turned blood to liquid fire and made her crave more.

Ash's dark blue eyes flickered with something she couldn't quite place. "You're trembling."

"It's just the nightmare," she said, trying to pull away. But he held her close, his hand sliding down to the small of her back, pulling her even tighter against him.

"Let me help." His voice was rough with desire, and then his lips were on hers.

The kiss was gentle at first, a meeting of mouths that sent shivers down her spine. But his tongue traced the seam of her lips, requesting entrance, and she opened for him, moaning softly as their tongues tangled together in a dance as old as time.

The need between them was palpable, a living thing that filled the room with its intensity.

Ash's hands roamed over her body as if he couldn't get enough of her. He traced the curve of her hip, skimmed up under her T-shirt, over her breasts. He teased her nipples until they hardened into tight little peaks.

She gasped and tangled her fingers in his hair as she kissed him back with equal heat. She knew it was wrong to want him, but she couldn't resist the pull—not when his hands seemed to be everywhere at once, stroking her hair, sliding down her back to grip her hips, pressing her closer until there was no space between them, and she could feel the hard ridge of his erection through his boxers.

He rolled her onto her back, his body a solid weight over hers. She should feel crushed, but she didn't. She was cocooned by him, safe and protected.

His caresses moved up her body. Higher and higher, until his hands clasped her face. He tilted her head to the side to expose her neck, and then he was kissing her there, right below her ear, his teeth scraping against her skin.

"Ash." His name left her on a needy exhale.

"Ambrosia." Her name was like a purr in his throat as his mouth moved lower, finding the pounding pulse point at the base of her neck.

She arched into him, sliding her hands down his back, careful of the bandage on his shoulder. "Oh, I want you."

"Not yet." He sucked a nipple into his mouth through her T-shirt while one hand skated down her side until he reached the waistband of her panties. He dipped inside and she moaned as he brushed over her clit in a feather-light caress. His fingers were rough, his movements sure as he traced the folds of her sex, dipping into her wetness before returning to circle her clit.

Rose fell back against the pillows, her arms flung out on either side of her head in surrender. Ash was in control now, just as he always liked to be, and she had no interest in challenging him.

She rocked her hips against his fingers until her legs trembled and heat seared away the last lingering slime of the nightmare.

But it wasn't enough.

She needed more.

Needed to feel him inside her. Stretching her. Filling her.

"Ash." She slid her hands over his shoulders and down his back then up under his shirt to explore the ridges of his abs. "Please. I want you inside me."

"Not yet." He sat up, dragging her with him, her back pressed against his chest. He pulled her T-shirt over her head, leaving her naked except for her underwear. He palmed her breast in one hand and slipped his other down the front of her panties, tracing a finger between her slick lower lips. "So damn wet already, but I want you weeping for me when I enter you."

He dipped a finger inside her, then added a second. She gasped and arched her back, grinding her ass against the hard ridge of his cock.

Ash growled in her ear and pressed a thumb against her clit. "You like that?"

"Mm."

He rubbed slow circles over the sensitive nub while his fingers continued to thrust in and out of her, slow and steady. Her breathing grew ragged as her orgasm mounted. She whimpered and reached behind her to sink her hand into his soft hair, pressing her face against his neck as the tension coiled tighter and tighter. His beard scratched her cheek as she rode his fingers and it only added to the eroticism of the moment.

And then she shattered, the orgasm ripping through her like a blade, hot and sharp.

Ash held her, still stroking her as she gasped through the last of the spasms.

"Now you're wet enough." His voice was all growl as he turned her to face him. At some point as she was coming apart, he'd freed himself from his boxers and now his cock stretched toward her, long and thick.

She wanted to taste him.

As her body still hummed with pleasure, she scooted down in the bed until she could trace her tongue over his tip and lick away the drops of pre-cum. She glanced up to see Ash's head tipped back, his eyes closed, his throat working. She took him fully into her mouth and he groaned.

"Shit, Rose."

She cupped his balls in one hand and sucked him in long, slow pulls. He was thick and salty and oh so good.

His hand tangled into her hair, and he tugged lightly at the strands. "Aw, fuck. I'm going to come."

"Let me taste you." She sucked harder. His grip on her hair tightened until she had to release him or risk a bald spot.

"No. I'm not finishing like that." He pulled her legs up over his hips and paused for a moment. His eyes were dark, his face taut. "Look down, Ambrosia. Watch how you take me."

Her breath caught on a moan as she watched him slide into her with one hard upward thrust of his hips. She gripped his shoulders and lifted herself off him, mesmerized by the sight of him withdrawing almost to the tip and then slamming back in. "We fit together."

"Yes." He caught her lips in a searing kiss, his tongue plundering her mouth as he fucked her with hard, deep strokes. His thumb found her clit again, and circled in time with his thrusts.

"Oh, God," she gasped.

"Come for me, Rose," he said in a low rumble. "Let me feel that tight little pussy clamp around my cock."

The orgasm ripped through her even harder than the first. She tightened around him until he groaned her name and buried his face in the crook of her neck as he emptied into her.

Ash collapsed back against the pillows, dragging her with

him, his body still buried deep like he didn't want to break the connection. Her heart pounded in her chest, and her breath came in ragged gasps. Her throat ached from crying out, her skin was damp with sweat, and she couldn't remember ever being so sated.

Before, at the pub, he'd insisted this was just sex. They were just fucking, scratching an itch, releasing the tension that hummed between them any time they were alone together.

But she'd been fucked before. What they'd done together in the bar before the shooting—*that* had been fucking.

But this?

This was something else entirely.

chapter
twenty-eight

ASH LAY in bed for a long while after Rose drifted to sleep, listening to her soft, even breathing. Every once in a while, she'd twitch and whimper—even in sleep, she was frightened, and it broke his heart. He soothed a hand over her hair and pressed his lips to her forehead until she settled.

Dante came over to the bed and lay his head on the mattress, watching her with worried brown eyes.

"It's okay, dog," Ash murmured. "She's okay."

Dante huffed. He stared at Rose for a moment longer. Then, deciding she must really be okay, he plodded over to the door and scratched at the frame.

"Gotta go out?" Ash carefully slid his arm out from under Rose. He climbed out of bed and tucked the blanket around her before pulling on his jeans. He opened the door for Dante, then grabbed his T-shirt from the floor and dragged it on over his head as he followed the dog out into the hall.

The house was silent. A glance at his watch told him it wasn't even dawn. Everyone was still in bed. Hell, he should still be in bed, too. He'd managed maybe two hours of sleep, tops.

Ash moved quietly downstairs, his head pounding with

each step—but whether that was from the tequila he'd overindulged in last night or general stress was anyone's guess. Probably a bit of both.

To his surprise, he found the kitchen lights on low. He wasn't the only one up.

Anna sat at the island, a hardcover book open in front of her, though she wasn't reading it. She stared off into space as she sipped on a mug of coffee.

He didn't want to startle her, so he made sure to make more noise on the last few steps. Dante barreled down the stairs and ran past her, disappearing through the dog door into the backyard. Through the kitchen window, he watched Dante greet Anna's dog, Winston.

Anna glanced over and gave a tired smile. "Hi."

"Hey." He nodded toward her mug. "Any more of that?"

"I made a whole pot."

"It's a start." The way he felt now, he'd need gallons of the stuff to make it through the day. He strode over to the coffee maker and got a mug down from the cupboard. When he turned back, steaming mug in hand, he found Anna staring off into space again. "You okay, AJ?"

She shook her head and closed her book. "I think Zak..." She trailed off and her gaze travelled over the island to the empty lowball glass he'd left there last night.

"No," he said and picked up the glass, depositing it in the sink. "That wasn't Zak. I broke into your stash when I got in."

Anna exhaled hard. "I shouldn't have it in the house."

"Anna, I talked to him last night and I don't think he's going to backslide."

"I hope you're right," she said in a hollow voice. "I can't bear to see him go through that again."

"Hey, he's stronger than either of us give him credit for. And if he does slip, he's got us. We'll pull him through, just like last time."

"He said he wanted to leave me." Tears flooded her eyes and his heart clenched. He hated seeing his twin in pain. Her pain always stung like it was his own.

"No, he doesn't want that. He loves you." Ash put down his mug and crossed the kitchen to wrap his arms around her. She leaned into him, her body shaking with sobs. He held her tightly, rubbing her back as she let out all of her emotions.

They were a lot alike, the Rawlings twins. They both bottled everything up until the bottle couldn't hold any more. The difference was, when Anna's bottle broke, she sobbed. When his broke, he broke things.

"I'm scared, Ash," she whispered against his chest when the crying jag passed. "What if I'm not enough this time? I'm so scared of losing him again."

"Hey." He caught her face in his hands and thumbed away her tears. "Listen to me, okay? I've known Zak a long time. He was my best friend for years and I can tell you with one hundred percent certainty, he only said that because he's scared, too. He's terrified of letting you down, which is why he tried pushing you away. It's also how I know he will not drink again, whether or not you have tequila in the house. He's had plenty of chances to leave in the last few weeks, but has he?"

Anna sniffled. "No."

"Exactly. He's still here." He tilted his head in the general direction of the Rescue. "Sleeping out there with the dogs."

After a few minutes, Anna winced, brushing at the damp stains she'd left on his shirt. "Sorry for crying on you."

"Never be sorry for that." He pressed a kiss to her temple. "That's part of my job as your big brother."

She laughed and poked his stomach. "You're only fifteen minutes older."

He let out a wistful sigh. "The best fifteen minutes of my life."

"Liar." She balled her fist and socked him in the stomach, then hugged him. "I love you."

He returned the hug and, for a moment, everything in him settled. "Love you, too, AJ."

The dogs returned, pushing through the doggie door one at a time. Winston nudged his food dish across the floor. Dante just sat in front of his and glowered at them both.

Anna laughed and pulled out of his arms. "The princes are demanding breakfast."

While she went to the pantry and filled both of their bowls with kibble, Ash picked up his mug and took a long drink. He watched the dogs eat, smiling at Winston's wholehearted enthusiasm and Dante's more measured bites.

Damn. That dog really was just like him—grumbly and suspicious and restrained. And Dante liked Rose, protecting her with a fierceness that was reassuring.

Ash breathed out slowly and accepted he'd been defeated by his sister yet again. "Okay."

Anna lifted a brow and picked up her own coffee. "Okay, what?"

She was smirking. She already knew what he was going to say next.

He nodded to the dogs. "Show me what Dante can do."

Feeling eyes on her, Rose slowly opened her own, a smile curving her lips. She expected Ash, but instead found a little girl standing beside the bed in pajamas, eyes sleepy and blond hair a mess.

Oh shit.

Rose reached for the blanket and was relieved to find her

naked body already covered. "Uh, hi, Poppy. How did you get in here?"

Six years old and as pretty as the flower she was named for, Poppy studied her with serious blue eyes. "Are you going to marry Uncle Ash?"

"Uh…" Rose looked around for help, but found she was alone with the girl. Even Dante had abandoned her. "N-no. Why would you think that?"

The girl's brows drew together in confusion. "But you slept with him."

Oh, God. Rose's thoughts stuttered to a halt. How did she even respond to that?

"You only sleep in the same bed with someone when you're going to marry them," Poppy continued sagely. "Like Mom and Dad. Everyone knows that. Well, but sisters don't count. I sleep in Bella's bed all the time. Family doesn't count," she decided with a nod. "But Uncle Ash isn't your family so you must be going to marry him."

"I-I…"

"Poppy!" Seventeen-year-old Bella rushed in and scooped up her sister. "You don't go into people's bedrooms without asking! I'm so sorry," she said to Rose, her light brown skin flushing with embarrassment as she dragged Poppy out and shut the door.

Rose leaned back against the pillows with a relieved laugh.

Ash was going to hate this.

She couldn't wait to tell him about it.

She dressed and wandered down to the kitchen to find a fresh pot of coffee had been brewed and a mug waited on the counter next to the cream and sugar. Somehow, she knew that was Ash's doing. As she poured herself a cup and doctored it, she looked out the back window and spotted him with his sister in the agility yard, working with Dante.

Rose settled into an Adirondack chair on the back deck to

watch the training session. Dante dodged obstacles, traveled over ramps and across see-saws, and ducked into tunnels until he found Ash hiding inside one of them. He gave a vicious bark and lunged as Ash tried to run. Dante clamped his teeth into the thick padding on Ash's arm and dragged him to the ground.

Wow. That was one powerful dog.

When the training ended, Ash and Anna both congratulated the dog, fawning over him until his tail wagged. Then Ash looked up and spotted her. He said something to his sister, gave the dog one more ear scratch, and crossed to the gate that separated the agility area from Zak and Anna's backyard.

"Uncle Ash!" Poppy flew past Rose and raced across the yard, her ponytail swinging. She flung herself into Ash's arms with a shriek of pure joy.

"Popsicle!" He scooped up the girl with his good arm and swung her, making her giggle. The smile that broke across his face would've knocked Rose back a step if she weren't already sitting down. She'd never seen him smile before. She'd seen plenty of smirks and scowls, but not that full blown smile that lit up his eyes and turned him from a stoically handsome man into devastating charmer. He didn't smile like that often enough and it really was a shame for all womenkind.

Anna walked up the porch steps and dropped into one of the chairs. Her smirk was very much like her twin's. "He's handsome when he smiles, isn't he? He doesn't do it enough."

Shit. Had she spoken out loud? "No, he prefers scowling."

"Yeah, he's taciturn and grumpy more often than not." She nodded toward Ash as he swung Poppy upside-down until her blonde hair brushed the grass. Their combined laughter brightened the gloomy morning. "But it's only 'cause he's trying to protect that soft heart of his. He's a good man, Rose."

Rose side-eyed her. "So's your husband, but you're making him sleep out with the dogs."

Anna's smile faded and she took a sip from the mug of coffee waiting on the arm of the chair. "Maybe. But he can be a real jackass, too."

"So can your brother."

Now her smile returned full-blast. "That's true." She lifted her mug and clinked it against Rose's. "Here's to jackass men and the stupid women who still love them."

Rose nearly choked on her coffee. "I don't love Ash. I barely even like him."

"Mm-hm."

"No, really. It's fifty-fifty whether I'm going to punch him or kiss him every time he walks into my bar."

Anna's eyes sparkled. "I'd say that's more sixty-forty for kissing, wouldn't you?"

Now it was her turn to scowl because, dammit, Anna was right. The harder she tried to hang onto her hatred for the man, the less she actually hated him. And how could she dislike a man who made his niece squeal with laughter like that?

"Maybe more like seventy-thirty," she admitted grudgingly.

"It's a start." Anna settled back and watched Ash and Poppy play for a moment. When Zak came out of the Rescue's office and joined them, her eyes went misty. "Zak wanted to leave."

Rose was used to people telling her their secrets. It came with the territory of owning a bar. She shifted in her seat to give the other woman her full attention. "I know."

Anna sniffed and swiped at her eyes. "Oh, right. Sorry, of course you knew. I forgot he went to your place when we had that fight."

"My door's always open. For any of you." Except could she

even leave her door open anymore? Did she even have a door to go back to? She shoved those worries away for later consideration. Right now, it was a relief to focus on Anna's problems rather than her own. "He was pretty torn up."

Anna sucked in a shaking breath. "Yeah, Ash told me. And... it's not all his fault. That fight? When he said he wanted to leave? I pushed him to that. I think... I wanted so badly for him to be okay, that I forgot he isn't. And he probably won't ever be. I made him feel like he had to put on a smile and hide everything, and that's not what I want."

"What do you want?"

"For him to talk to me when he's hurting, like he did when we first got together. For him to lean on me."

"Have you told *him* that?"

"I tried but... I think we're both too raw right now."

Rose reached for her hand. "I knew Zak at his worst. I saw him come into the pub every night and drown himself in alcohol, and so I can tell you he doesn't really want to leave you. If he did, he'd be long gone, not sleeping out in the kennel with the dogs."

Anna laughed softly. "Ash said the exact same thing."

"Ash has his moments of genius."

"Oh, God. Don't let him hear you say that. You'll never hear the end of it."

"We'll keep it between us. Did he also tell you that you'll have to be the one to reach out to Zak?"

Her smile faded. "No, he didn't say that."

"Well, it's true. Because when Zak's spiraling, he doesn't know how to reach for help. He digs deeper into his depression and isolation until he hits rock bottom, and then he keeps right on digging. I watched him do it before from behind the bar. Don't let him do it again."

Anna sighed. "It's exhausting."

"I know it is." Rose thought of the little itch at the back of her brain that she couldn't shake since her abductor pumped her full of heroin. She'd never touch the stuff, but that little itch came with a seductive voice that whispered, *what if...?* And now she understood her patrons better—the ones who came into the bar because they had to, not because they wanted to. Zak also had that itch, but it was accompanied by the depression, anxiety, and night terrors of his PTSD.

"It is for him, too, but you love him, and he loves you, and nobody ever said love was easy." She squeezed Anna's hand before dropping it as the door opened.

Bella poked her head out. "Hey, Mom? Poppy snuck into Rose's room this morning and asked if Rose was going to marry Ash."

"Oh, that girl." Anna made a sound that was half-laugh, half-groan and leaned back in her chair. She smiled across the yard at her younger daughter. "Sorry about that. She has no concept of boundaries or personal space. We're working on it." Then her smile turned sly as she slid a glance in Rose's direction. "It's a good question, though. My brother has been a bachelor long enough. I was going to play matchmaker, but I like you for him better. You keep him on his toes."

Rose felt heat rush into her cheeks and took a long drink from her coffee because she knew she was blushing.

"Oh my God, Mom," Bella groaned and rolled her eyes. "You're just as embarrassing as Poppy. I'm going to Hannah's."

"Be careful," Anna called after her. "Keep your phone on you. Don't do anything I wouldn't do."

Bella scoffed, but it was good-natured. "Oh, c'mon, is that really the best warning you can give me? You got pregnant at my age."

"Luckily, you're smarter than I was."

"And gay. So, no, I won't be getting pregnant." She

stepped out onto the deck to kiss her mom's head. "Love you."

"Love you, too." Anna watched her go, then laughed. "Our Bella is smitten with this new girl in town, Hannah Edwards. It seems to be getting serious. First love." Her gaze traveled back across the yard, where Zak now had Poppy up on his shoulders and was galloping like a horse while the dogs chased him. "There's nothing like it."

"The Scotts are here," Bella called from somewhere deeper in the house and a second later, Donovan Scott burst through the door and scooped Rose up into a rib-crushing hug. Over his shoulder, she saw Ash's smile fade. He crossed the yard and mounted the steps in several long strides.

"Van." His tone was laced with warning.

Donovan ignored him, set her back on her feet, and looked her up and down with narrowed eyes.

"You scared him," Sasha Scott said from behind her husband. "I had to practically tie him down to keep him from going on the hunt to find the shooters."

"Bet he enjoyed that." Rose didn't get the smile from either of them that she'd hoped for. Donovan really did look worried, so she stood on her toes to kiss his cheek. "I'm fine, tough guy. Really."

"Van," Ash said again and stepped between them, a low growl coming from deep in his chest. "Office. Now."

"OKAY," Donovan said as soon as they stepped through the door into Redwood Coast Rescue's new office. At his voice, his dogs, Spirit and Matilda, lifted their heads from their cuddle pile in the corner and gave happy wags. Donovan sometimes left them at the office when he and Sasha had a date night so they wouldn't be lonely.

He smiled at the pair, then swung around and pinned Ash with a scowl. "What the hell was that?"

"Nothing."

"That was not nothing. I gave Rose a hug and you looked like you were plotting my murder."

"I often plot your murder," Zak said and flopped into the squeaky new leather chair behind his desk. Ranger, the golden-eyed demon dog who once tried to take a piece out of Ash's hand, did some doggie yoga stretches in his bed before lumbering over to his person for an ear scratch. Zak complied automatically without missing a conversational beat. "You have a very murderable face, Van."

Donovan pointed at him. "Don't start. I have questions for you next, and hiding behind snark is not going to work." He motioned to the cot in the corner that had very obviously been slept in, then shook his head. "Jesus, when did *I* become the reasonable one?"

Zak held up his hands in surrender. "Yeah, you're right. Let's talk about Ash's issues. He's much more interesting."

Donovan grumbled low in his throat, but focused his attention back on Ash. "So, I repeat, what the fuck was that? Did you think I was sliding in to make a move on Rose?"

Ash let out his breath in a frustrated exhale. "No."

"Good, because in case you forgot..." He held up his left hand and wiggled his ring finger where he wore a plain platinum band. "I'm happily married to the most beautiful woman in the world, and I would never betray Sasha like that. And even if I weren't married, I'm not the kind of asshole who takes advantage of a woman while she's vulnerable."

Was that what he'd done last night? Ash wondered. Had he taken advantage of Rose while she was at her most vulnerable? Because that was the one thing he told himself he wouldn't do.

Fuck.

"Rose is my friend," Donovan continued. "She's been a good friend for years, and she has gone through one trauma after another lately. I'm allowed to comfort her. Unless she says otherwise, I'm allowed to hug her."

Disgusted with himself, Ash crossed his arms over his chest and returned Donovan's glare. "I don't know what it was. Sorry," he added grudgingly.

"You don't know?" The question dripped with doubt.

"Yeah, I said I don't know, okay? I don't fucking know what's wrong with me." Unable to stand still any longer, he started to pace the length of the room. "The thought of another man's hands on her—even a happily married man's— makes my blood boil. And the idea of someone hurting her again makes me lose my goddamn mind."

Donovan and Zak shared a long look.

"He's got it," Donovan said, all serious like a doctor giving a terminal diagnosis.

"Yep," Zak agreed. "Told ya he's more interesting. I believe we're witnessing the fall of Lost County's most eligible bachelor, Sheriff Ash Rawlings."

Donovan nodded. "We should have popcorn for this show. Better yet, sell tickets."

"There's gonna be a lot of unhappy single ladies in the county when they find out."

Ash stopped pacing and glowered at the two of them. "What are you two jackasses going on about?"

Donovan grinned. It was all teeth with just an edge of mean. "You, my man, are in love with Rose."

He scoffed. "That's ridiculous. I don't do love. I don't have time."

Zak let out a low whistle. "You are so full of shit I'm surprised you're not choking on it. Every time she so much as breathes in your direction, you go all soft and gooey."

"Bullshit."

"Yep, like a marshmallow." Donovan nodded again. What was he, a bobble head? "It's time to admit it, dude. You're in deep. You might as well start picking out china patterns and kids' names now."

A muscle in his cheek twitched. His jaw ached from how tightly he was gritting his teeth. How could they be so certain that he was in love with Rose? Sure, he was worried about her safety, and the sex was the best he'd ever had, but love?

No. That was a whole other level. One he had no interest in going to.

He tried to come up with a witty retort, but his mind was blank. All he could think about was the way her hair smelled like something dark and spicy and floral all at once and how the gentle curve of her body fit so perfectly against his as he held her close.

Kids' names?

Fuck.

Donovan and Zak erupted into raucous laughter.

"Look at his face." Donovan gasped and bent double, clutching his ribs as tears streamed from his eyes.

"Like he's chewing glass." Zak snorted, which set them off again until they were practically rolling on the floor. The dogs thought they were playing and joined in with a chorus of happy barks. Spirit jumped around the room like her feet were spring-loaded while Matilda let out a howl.

"Wait, what did we miss?" Sawyer asked from the doorway as he and Zelda stepped through. Pierce was right behind them with his dog, Raszta, who looked like the love child of a bear and a mop. The dogs all sniffed each other and wagged in greeting.

"Apparently, Ash is falling in love with Rose," Zak said with barely contained glee.

Ash tried to deny it again, but the teasing had planted a seed of doubt in his mind. Maybe there was something there, something more than just physical attraction. But he wasn't ready to admit it yet, not even to himself.

Sawyer raised an eyebrow. "Why is this news?"

Ash whirled on him. "What?"

He shrugged. "I'm a blind man, and even I can see you're head over heels for her."

Pierce nodded and signed, *"It's obvious."*

Ash let out a frustrated growl. "You want to hear this briefing or not?"

"Typical Ash," Zak sighed.

"All work and no play makes Ash a dull boy," Donovan agreed. "And you used to be the instigator of all our mischief. What happened?"

"I grew up," Ash said through his teeth. "Something you two dipshits have yet to do."

Zak and Donovan looked at each other again, then shrugged.

"Meh," Zak said.

"Growing up is overrated," Donovan added, but waved toward the whiteboards at the front of the room. "But I want Rose to be safe, so let's hear it. Who do we have to kill?"

"We're not killing anyone." Ash walked over and opened the file he'd brought in with him. He taped a photo of a skinny kid with spiky blond hair on the whiteboard, then turned to face the group.

The dogs all settled in beside their people, looking for all the world like they were paying attention to the briefing, too. He found himself wishing Dante was at his side—after seeing what the German Shepherd was capable of, he had nothing but respect for the animal—but was glad the dog seemed intent on protecting Rose and was sticking close to her.

"This is Dale Shields," he told the room. "He's the suspect we found dead after yesterday's shootout. When Mike Conti showed Rose his picture last night, she confirmed he was one of the men who first attacked her three weeks ago at the Mad Dog. Shields was an active member of the Golden State Nationalists and has been known to run with the Erickson brothers, Gethin and Isaiah. We suspect they were the other shooters yesterday, and Gethin is likely the second attacker from three weeks ago, though Rose couldn't positively identify him." He pinned two more photos up next to Shields. Gethin Erickson was a tall man with hard, dark eyes, a shaved head, and a bristly sprig of a goatee sprouting from his chin.

Donovan whistled. "Tell me you're a neo-Nazi without telling me you're a neo-Nazi."

"His brother looks like an accountant," Pierce signed.

Ash stepped back and studied the photo. Isaiah Erickson did look like an accountant, complete with a bland haircut and square, black frame glasses. He was slightly smaller than his younger brother, but no less mean. Either one of them could have been the man Ash confronted at the old gas station on Route 10.

"Do we think this is race-based?" Donovan asked. "Is GSN attacking Rose because her mom's family is of Hispanic and Native American ancestry?"

"It's possible. That is their M.O.," Ash said, but then shook his head. "It doesn't sit right with me, though. Rose passes for white, so unless they know her family tree, she's not the most obvious target in the community. If their motive was purely race-based, why wouldn't they attack the Salazars and the Arrow Tree Brewery or Ajani Wilson and her art gallery or the Williams family and their restaurant? But Rose is the only one they're focusing on."

"Like it's personal," Pierce signed.

"Seems that way. Motive aside, we need to keep in mind that both of the Ericksons are extremely dangerous, but Gethin is the more volatile of the two. He'll be the one wanting to go down in a blaze of glory and become a martyr for the cause. We can't give him that opportunity." He waited to make sure he had everyone's full attention. "This will not become another Waco or Ruby Ridge."

"How do we take them down without it turning into a bloodbath?" Sawyer asked. "They'll be armed to the teeth."

"Go in fast and quiet with a small team," Zak said and looked at Ash for confirmation. "That's why you want us in on it. For back-up because we've been trained in military tactics."

"Exactly," Ash said. "I don't have the manpower and my deputies don't have your level of training. And—" He stopped short.

Donovan's eyes narrowed. "You don't know who you can trust."

He hated to admit it, but it was true. There were still

deputies in his department who were loyal to Tennison. He needed to clean house, but he couldn't do that until this was over. "The only guys I trust implicitly are Jonah Sullivan and Walter Wright. And of course Mike Conti, which is why he's guarding Rose today."

His biggest fear was that once GSN realized what was happening at their compound, they would send people after Rose in retaliation.

"Aw, Ash." A slow grin spread across Zak's face and for the first time in weeks, he sounded more like his usual sarcastic self. "Are you deputizing us again?"

Ash bit the inside of his cheek to stop the smile. "For the duration of this investigation."

"At this rate, you might as well just give us badges," Donovan said.

"Not a fucking chance."

Sawyer raised his hand. "Uh, not to point out the obvious, but..." He pointed to his face. "Blind."

"Ish," Zak muttered. "You can see movement."

"Yeah, but I still wouldn't trust my faulty eye-brain connection in the middle of a raid. So, unless you want to dig a bullet or two out of me—"

"Tempting."

He ignored Zak. "What can I do to help?"

Ash nodded. He'd already considered it and had a plan. "I hear you're good on a computer."

A smile ticked up the corner of Sawyer's mouth. "I have my moments of brilliance."

"*More than brilliance,*" Pierce signed. "*He turns the screen reader speed up so fast, it sounds like another language.*"

Sawyer turned toward him and focused on his moving hands, then grinned. "Coding is another language, my man. But, yeah," he said to Ash. "I'm good. Not as fast as I used to be when I could see, but I still get the job done."

"Good," Ash said. "I need as much information as you can dig up on Chester Montgomery-Duran and Harmony Galasso. And any connection to GSN, Dale Shields, and the Erickson brothers. We're arresting them for yesterday's shooting, but my gut tells me this is all somehow tied to Harmony's murder. I just need proof."

"Got it."

"Do it all above-board. Nothing illegal. And you can forward everything you find to Cal Holden. He's defending Pete Galasso now, and plans to file an appeal to get his conviction overturned."

Sawyer nodded. "Glad to help."

Ash returned his attention to the rest of the group. "And while he's doing that, Zak, Donovan and I will approach the GSN compound with the arrest warrant. I want Spirit sniffing for explosives and Ranger..." His gaze dropped to the yellow-eyed dog. "I want him looking like he's going to rip off important body parts if we let him off leash."

Zak reached down and rubbed Ranger's radar dish ear. "You hear that, mutt? You get to play bad cop to Ash's good cop."

Ranger's tail wagged.

"You, too, Zak," Ash said. "I want you to scare the shit out of them."

Zak's grin was full of menace. "Oh, I plan on it."

"Pierce, I need you and Raszta to hang back with my deputies on the road and make sure we don't have any squirters. Anyone tries to make a run for it, let the mop dog do what he does best and herd them back."

Pierce always had a poker face, but now his expression was downright deadly. *And watch your deputies, too?*

"You got it. I know people talk around you thinking you can't hear them. I want to know what they're saying behind my back. I want to know who I can trust in my department."

Pierce nodded.

"One more thing," Ash said and faced his brother-in-law. "Zak, I need you to put me in touch with Tucker Quentin."

Zak choked on his coffee and set the mug down on his desk with a thunk. "What makes you think I know how?"

"You know guys who work for him, right? The team that rescued you from Afghanistan?"

"I mean, I haven't stayed in touch with any of them. I didn't want the reminder." Zak ran a hand back and forth over his short hair, then sighed. "My buddy Greer probably knows how to reach them. He's the one that sent them after me. Or, hell, he might even know Quentin personally. I could call him, but he's gonna want to know why?"

"Fair enough," Ash said. "I need a sit-down with Chet Montgomery-Duran, and I've had no luck getting through the layers around him."

"And you think Quentin can get you in?"

"I'm assuming billionaires run in the same circles."

"You know what they say about assuming…"

Ash spread his hands. "At this point, I'm desperate enough to look like an ass."

Zak shrugged. "All right. I'll see what I can do."

AS THE BRIEFING WRAPPED UP, Ash pulled down the photos and returned them to the file. "I have to go brief the deputies I've selected for this. We'll meet you at that old gas station on Route 10 where I found Rose, and head up the mountain from there."

And now that he thought about it, it made sense that GSN would stash Rose there, the perfect halfway point between town and their compound. It also made sense that they'd threaten him, his family, and Redwood Coast Rescue. Tennison had a very hands-off approach to the mountain people, which Ash suspected was the reason for the disproportionate amount of crime in such a rural region.

Which reminded him...

He hung back as the others filed out, then slid his cell phone from his pocket.

She answered on the first ring. "Sheriff."

"Ms. Summers."

"I didn't expect to hear from you," Alexis said. "Are you finally looking into the possibility of the Shadow Stalker being more than an urban legend?"

He smothered the spike of annoyance. "It's on my to-do list."

"Uh-huh." A pause. "So why are you calling?"

"There's another case you might be interested in podcasting about. It's right up your alley—sex, billionaires, Neo-Nazis."

"Okay," she said slowly. "You've piqued my interest."

"Have you ever heard of Harmony Galasso?"

"No."

"She was murdered thirteen years ago, and her husband was convicted, sentenced to life in prison. You should look into it."

"Why? It sounds pretty straight-forward."

"Because he was convicted without a body." He waited, letting that sink in before he hit her with his ace in the hole—the thing he knew she wouldn't be able to resist. "And we just identified the Double R Fire Jane Doe as Harmony Galasso."

Alexis sucked in a sharp breath. "You're kidding."

"I don't kid."

"Yeah, I've heard that about you, Sheriff." A longer pause, heavy with suspicion. "Are you telling me about this just to keep me from investigating the Shadow Stalker?"

"Yes," he admitted. "But also because I believe Pete Galasso is sitting in jail for a murder he didn't commit and any publicity he can get will help him get an appeal. You can contact his lawyer, Callum Holden, for more information."

"I'll do that. Thanks for the tip." It sounded like she was typing something in the background, and he hoped that meant she was already looking into the case.

"Good." He started to hang up. Paused. "And Alexis? You didn't hear any of this from me."

"I'm sorry, Sheriff," she said, all sweetness. "Hear what?"

He grunted a laugh. "Yeah, let's keep it that way."

Ash stepped out into the hall to find Zak leaning against

the wall and Donovan standing there with his arms crossed over his chest.

Donovan's deep scowl said he'd overheard the conversation and disapproved. "Why are you making deals with the devil?"

Ash pocketed his phone and started for the door. "She's not the devil."

Zak pushed away from the wall and followed, hooking a thumb over his shoulder at Donovan. "Uh, are you forgetting she had the whole fucking country ready to lynch Van for a murder he didn't commit?"

"Which is why I'm giving her a chance to redeem herself." Ash stopped walking and turned to face them both. "Van, you know what Pete Galasso's been living with. You lived it, too. The only difference is he actually got convicted and has lost over a decade of his life. And, fine, Ms. Summers may be the devil, but she's the devil I know, and using her to get the word out about Pete's wrongful conviction can only help his case."

Donovan's mouth was open to argue, but he snapped it closed without making a sound.

"I fucked up thirteen years ago by going with what Tennison said and not listening to my gut. I destroyed Rose's life. Now I'm trying to fix it, and I'll use any weapon in my arsenal to do so. Including Alexis Summers and her podcast." He met Donovan's gaze. "So if you have a problem with that, bow out now."

"No," Donovan said after a tense moment and sucked in a deep breath. He exhaled through his nose, then shook his head. "No, I get it. If Sasha were in Rose's position, I'd do the same."

Ash glanced around Donovan to Zak. "We good?"

Zak held up his hands. "If Van's good with it, I've got nothing to say."

"That'd be a first."

Zak's lips quirked and he elbowed Donovan. "Hey, he's not just falling in love. He's already gone splat at the bottom of that cliff."

Ash growled, turned on his heel and marched down the hall, shoving open the door that led outside. He ignored Donovan and Zak's laughter. He wanted to go get his dog and his woman and take them home where they'd be safe.

And that thought brought him to an abrupt halt like he'd hit a brick wall.

When had Dante become his dog?

And Rose definitely wasn't his woman.

He gave his head a shake to dislodge the idea and strode into the misty rain of the afternoon. Rose stood by the gate that connected the RWCR facility to Zak and Anna's back-yard. She looked exhausted and beautiful in her navy coat and black leggings, the rain making her black hair cling to the pale curve of her cheek. The bruises there were fading, but still too noticeable for his liking, and his heart lurched with something that he refused to name.

And that pissed him off.

He didn't want to be in love with her.

It would complicate things, make it harder for him to do his job. He didn't have the time or energy for a relationship. And yet here he was, standing in the rain and staring at her like an idiot, feeling something he wished he could deny.

Anna and Rose glanced over at his approach.

"Hey," Anna said, her brows drawing together with concern. "Is everything okay?"

He nodded stiffly and forced himself to look away from Rose before he said something stupid. "Yeah."

"Then why are you pissed off?"

He didn't answer his sister's question, and instead turned to Rose. "I'm taking you home," he said, voice gruff. "Mike will be there to guard you, and we're taking Dante with us."

Anna gave him a strange look, but didn't say anything.

Rose frowned. "Are you going after GSN?"

"Not until I take you home and make sure you're safe."

Rose's expression softened. "Okay," she said. "Let's go."

They made their way through the yard and house and all the way to his truck in silence, with Dante trailing them. Ash left her side long enough to load the dog into the back of the truck, then slid behind the wheel. She already had the heater blasting to ward off the cold March air.

It was the first time they'd been alone together all morning, without the buffer of family and friends, and as he pulled out of the circular drive in front of Zak and Anna's house, the silence between them hummed with tension. His knuckles were white on the steering wheel. He tried to focus on the logistics of the upcoming raid, but it was hard to focus when he could feel Rose's presence next to him, could smell her natural perfume mingling with the rain.

"Thank you for last night," Rose said finally, her voice quiet. "I was in shock still, I think. I needed the distraction."

Distraction?

Okay, if she wanted to call fucking each other into exhaustion a simple "distraction," he could roll with that.

Ash grunted in response, not trusting himself to say anything more. He didn't know what was wrong with him. He'd never felt this before—this need to protect someone with everything he had. Not even with Anna, and he was notoriously overprotective of his twin. But this was something more. Something deeper, primal.

And he didn't know how to deal with it.

They drove the rest of the way to his house in silence, and he was relieved to find Mike Conti already waiting when they arrived. He needed the buffer of another person.

"Sheriff," Mike said and touched the brim of his hat in greeting. He'd opted to go with his full uniform instead of jeans and a T-shirt today, which Ash appreciated. It made this feel more official. Because the idea of leaving Rose alone with a man—even a happily married man like Mike—rubbed him the wrong way.

He nodded back. "Deputy Conti."

"Hi, Mike," Rose said. "I'm sorry you're sidelined for the big raid, but I'm glad you'll be here with me."

Ash told himself not to grit his teeth at the warmth in her tone when she spoke to the man. It didn't mean anything. She was just being friendly.

Mike shrugged. "I'd be lying if I said I wasn't a bit disappointed, but my wife's happy I'll be safely out of the line of fire. She made cookies." He hitched his chin toward the house. "As did most of the other deputies' wives. Some casseroles, too. You won't be running out of food for a while. The whole force is just sick over what happened at the Mad Dog yesterday. They all wanted to pitch in."

Rose all but melted and wrapped her arms around the deputy for a quick hug. "Aw, that's sweet. Thank you."

Once again, Ash found his throat closing up. What was wrong with him? He didn't do emotion. But he always thought of his deputies as just that—his deputies. Now he realized they were as much his family as Anna and Zak and the girls. And maybe he should have more trust in them. "Thanks, Mike."

"No problem. Now go kick some scummy skinhead ass for me."

"That I can do." Ash circled to the back of his truck, and opened the door to let the dog out. Dante poked his head out as soon as the hatch opened and gave a slight wag.

Ash took his face in his hands and looked him in the eyes. "You better not eat the rest of my furniture. Or the cat. I like the cat."

Dante huffed and Ash couldn't help the smile that

twitched on his lips. The dog looked so annoyed by the restrictions.

"You keep her safe, okay? I'm trusting you with—" He stopped himself because he'd been about to say, "the woman I love." Which was ridiculous. That was Zak and the guys getting into his head. He finished, "I'm trusting you with her."

Something like determination flickered in Dante's eyes. Those were cop's eyes, hard and flat. He'd seen that look often enough in the mirror.

"Yeah, good dog." He gave Dante's ear a scratch then let him jump out. Dante bounded towards the house, nose to the ground, tail straight up like a warning flag.

Already on the job.

Very good dog.

When Ash closed the truck's hatch, he found Rose standing right there within arm's reach.

"Ash." She caught his hand. "You'll be careful?"

He met her gaze, his heart wrestling with something big he didn't dare name. "I'm always careful," he said finally.

Rose gave him a small smile. "Yeah, well, you say that, but you weren't yesterday. You got shot, and I don't want you coming back to me with more bullet holes. I... I care about you. A lot."

He sucked in a sharp breath. "I thought you hated me."

"It's a fine line between hate and love." Holding his gaze, she leaned in and pressed a gentle kiss to his lips. It was over before he fully realized what she was doing, but the warmth that radiated through him at the contact was undeniable.

She laughed softly. "And I know it's crazy, but I crossed over that line sometime in the last few weeks." Her fingers trailed over his lips then stroked his beard. "I just didn't realize it until now."

He wanted to close his eyes and lean into her touch, but he couldn't. If he let himself, he wouldn't want to leave her, and he had work to do. Work that would, hopefully, end with her attackers behind bars.

Then, maybe, he could explore which side of that line he still stood on.

"Be safe, Ash," she whispered. Her grip tightened on his hand, and he realized that she was scared. Scared for him, for RWCR, for the other deputies, for herself. And that only added fuel to his need to protect her.

"I will," he said, forcing the words out through his tight throat. "I promise."

The feeling of her touch lingered long after she stepped back, and he climbed into his truck. As he pulled out of the driveway and made sure the gate to his property was closed, he stole a glance in the rearview mirror.

She'd retreated to the house, but still lingered in the doorway, watching him leave.

"Go inside, Rose."

As if she'd heard his plea, she shut the door.

He let go a relieved breath. She was safe. Mike and Dante would make sure of it. Now he had to make sure she stayed that way.

He pulled out onto the quiet road and tried to switch his brain over to cop mode. He couldn't let his feelings for her cloud his judgment, not when the stakes were so high. But that was easier said than done. He couldn't shake the feeling that he was heading toward something dangerous—but whether that was the upcoming raid or the thing between him and Rose, he didn't know.

Either way, he was in deep trouble.

thirty-one

THE SIGN POSTED at the front gate of the Erickson home warned, TRESPASSERS WILL BE SHOT, and looked as if it had been used for target practice. Ash grabbed a pair of bolt cutters from his trunk and snipped the chain holding the gate closed.

"Charming," Zak said when he slid back in behind the wheel of his Tahoe. "Really leaning into the hillbilly stereotype."

"It's not an empty threat." He shifted the truck into gear and lifted his foot off the break, edging through the gate. Behind him, two deputy cars followed, while two others blocked off the road. "They will shoot first, ask questions later."

"Then they better be damn good." Zak drew his gun and rested it on his good knee. "They take a shot at me or my dog, that's the only one they're getting."

Ash eyed the gun. "You're not gonna go all cowboy on me, are you?"

"I didn't survive Afghanistan by being a cowboy."

No, but he had been taken prisoner by the Taliban because

he'd strayed from his original mission. It was cruel to point that out, so Ash kept his mouth shut and focused on the road.

The narrow dirt driveway beyond the gate wound deeper under the canopy of the soaring redwoods and the landscape seemed to grow colder and more desolate.

"Don't like this driveway," Zak muttered. "It's a fatal funnel."

A cliff dropped off the mountain to one side of the road and the other was a steep uphill climb. No doubt GSN had chosen this location to hole up for this very reason.

Ash cracked his window. Rather than the typical hushed sounds of the forest, the thump of a heavy bass beat vibrated through the air.

They were close.

When they cleared a tight bend, several trailers came into view and one old cabin that had seen its best days back during the Gold Rush.

Ash stopped the truck in front of the cabin and stepped out. This high up on the mountain the air was cold and damp, heavy with mist, and his breath clouded as he waited for everyone to fan out into position around him.

Donovan led Spirit near GSN's vehicles and along the sides of the barns and trailers, searching for explosives.

Zak and Ranger took up position several paces behind him.

"Ranger," Zak said softly. "Mean face."

The dog widened his stance and his lips peeled back in a fair imitation of Cujo.

This was the moment of truth, and Ash steeled himself for what was to come. He reached into his pocket and took out the envelope that contained the arrest warrant, then stepped up onto the groaning porch and pounded a fist on the door.

The music abruptly cut off.

He pounded again.

Moments passed, and he dropped his free hand to his gun.

A gruff voice called, "Who the fuck's out there?"

"Sheriff's Office. I have a search warrant for the property." He decided to let them discover the arrest warrants on their own. He didn't want to give them any excuses to shoot.

The voice inside fell silent for a few seconds, and then the door swung open with a loud creak. The smell of pot and cigarette smoke wafted out, only slightly masking the chemical stench of harder drugs.

The man who stepped out wasn't either of the Ericksons and Ash hadn't ever seen him around town. He was short and stocky with a shaved head. Bands of tattoos wrapped his thick arms and a swastika stood proudly on the side of his neck. He regarded Ash with cold, hard eyes, then his gaze shifted to Zak and Ranger and his shoulders visibly tightened.

"You got no jurisdiction here, Sheriff."

"Last I checked, you're in my county." He shoved the search warrant at the guy's chest and tried to muscle through the door, but the skinhead wasn't moving.

His mouth twisted into a cruel smile as he dropped the paperwork without looking at it. "Whatever you're looking for, you ain't gonna find it here."

That was probably the truth. He wouldn't be surprised if GSN had cameras all along their driveway and had seen the convoy of Sheriff's Department vehicles coming.

Ash pushed harder against the door, but the man didn't budge. "I suggest you step aside before I make you."

The guy's hand twitched towards his waistband.

Ash stepped back, drew his own weapon, and aimed it at the man's chest. "Hands where I can see them."

The skinhead hesitated, then slowly raised his hands in surrender. But he was still smiling, and the flash of yellowed teeth sent a skitter of fear down Ash's spine.

"Ash," Zak said under his breath and Ranger growled a warning.

He risked a quick glance back. Men had poured out of the trailers and surrounded Zak, Ranger, and his deputies. The only reason they hadn't closed in was Ranger straining on the end of his lead, all but foaming at the mouth.

"We'll give you one chance," the skinhead said. "Leave now, or you won't leave at all."

Ash cursed under his breath.

This was a trap.

And he had walked right into it.

The skinhead moved suddenly, grabbing a gun from his waistband. He had it only halfway out when Ash pulled the trigger. The shot echoed through the forest and the man crumpled to the ground, clutching his chest.

The gunfire was all the signal that GSN needed. They swarmed, and the world exploded into chaos.

Ash dove off the porch, ducking behind a nearby woodpile as bullets whizzed past him. The sound of Ranger barking and Zak shouting orders filled his ears.

This was a battle he wasn't sure they could win, and guilt tightened his chest. He had made a fatal mistake in underestimating GSN's numbers.

Had he led his friends to slaughter?

No. He couldn't afford to think like that, couldn't let his emotions freeze him up. He had to come out on top, or else this homegrown terrorist group would only become bolder and more dangerous. They'd already shot up town once. There was no telling what they'd do next if he lost this fight.

He took a deep breath and peeked around the woodpile, scanning the area for any sign of the enemy. He spotted a group of GSN members huddled behind a stack of hay bales, reloading their weapons.

Ash aimed his gun and opened fire, picking off several of

the skinheads before they could react. Many of them were wearing body armor, and the shots only incapacitated them.

Zak shouted something unintelligible, and Ash turned to see him sprinting towards one of the trailers. He could tell from the way Zak was moving that he was injured, and that only made Ash more determined to finish this fight as quickly as possible.

He began to advance, firing his weapon as he went. The gunfire was deafening, and he could barely hear himself think. But he had to keep moving, keep fighting, or else he was dead. And so were his friends.

Movement at the edge of his vision caught his eye and he turned just in time to see a man charging towards him with a machete. He pulled the trigger. No hesitation. The man fell to the ground and didn't get back up. He hadn't been wearing body armor.

But there were more of them, too many to count. They were coming at him from all directions now, and Ash knew he was in trouble. He was just about to make a break for it when a hand grabbed his shoulder and pulled him down to the ground behind a rusted out Chevy Impala on cinder blocks.

It was Zak, his face streaked with blood and sweat. "You're bleeding."

Ash glanced down at himself. Blood soaked through his shirt behind his bullet proof vest. "Must have popped the stitches." He eyed Zak. "So are you."

"Bullet grazed my thigh." Zak propped himself up on the car and ran his hands over Ranger. The dog flinched at every pop of gunfire. "This is fucked."

"I thought they'd hole up in a standoff, not outright attack. I underestimated their stupidity."

"Yeah, well, I think we're the stupid ones right now. Your fucking deputies scattered like rodents when the shooting started." Reassured that his dog was okay, Zak checked his weapon. "How are you on ammo?"

Ash checked his gun, found it empty, and reloaded. "Don't have enough."

"Yeah, same. Shit."

"Have you seen Donovan?"

Zak's expression was grim. "No."

Ash cursed under his breath. "We have to find him before—"

A deafening wave of sound crashed through the trees, followed by an explosion that rocked the mountainside. Ash and Zak hit the ground on their bellies, covering their heads as a rain of debris showered over them. Ranger barked and hunkered underneath the car, his tail tucked between his legs.

"Found him," Zak said.

Ash shook his head. The world had gone muffled save for the ringing in his ears. But as his hearing cleared, he realized it really had gone quiet.

GSN had stopped shooting.

He peeked around the car. Flames consumed what was left of the main cabin and at least four bodies of GSN members littered the ground. One of them was on fire and, given that he wasn't moving or screaming in pain, he was probably meeting his idol in hell right about now. The remaining survivors had apparently made a run for it.

With any luck, Pierce and the deputies left behind on the road would round them up.

"Fuck," Ash said softly and holstered his gun as his gaze snagged on the tan and green uniform on one of the bodies.

Donovan stepped out from behind the cover of a trailer with Spirit trotting happily at his heels. His grin was malicious as he studied his handiwork. "Nice."

Ash straightened and helped Zak to his feet.

"Jesus, Van," Zak hissed, limping a little as he put weight on his non-metal leg. "Trying to blow us off the map?"

Donovan shrugged. "Worked, didn't it? They stopped shooting."

Ash walked over to his deputy and knelt, gently rolling him over. His heart sank when he saw the man's blank eyes staring up at the sky.

Chief Deputy Walter Wright.

One of the only people in his department he trusted.

Wright's gun lay inches from his hand. He'd died from a bullet to the head, but judging by two bodies next to him, he'd taken his murderers with him.

"Fuck," Ash said again and swiped at his burning eyes.

"He was a good man," Donovan said softly.

"Yeah, he was." Ash pushed to his feet. "I need to call the state police for backup. Hell, maybe the FBI, too." He turned toward the deputies slowly emerging from their hiding spots. Anger burned a hole through his gut. These assholes ran and hid while Wright stood his ground and gave his life because of it. "Someone cover Wright's body and secure the perimeter. We have a long night ahead of us."

Ten dead, including Gethin Erickson.

Six wounded, including Zak. Ash made him go to the hospital, then called Anna to ensure she didn't hear the news through Steam Valley's grapevine. She thanked him profusely and he had no doubt she rushed to the hospital to be at Zak's side.

They'd be okay. If he had any doubts before about it, he

now knew for sure they'd pull through this rough patch in their relationship.

Pierce and the deputies had managed to round up three runners on the road, one of whom was Isaiah Erickson. He was immediately arrested and taken to the county jail, where he was fingerprinted and booked on a host of charges.

Three hours after the shootout, Ash walked into an interrogation room at the prison and sat down across from the man who had tried to kill Rose multiple times. He was boiling with rage by that point, but somehow managed to keep his tone cool.

"Why Rose Galasso? Why did you, your brother, and Dale Shields shoot up her pub yesterday?"

Isaiah's lip curled into a sneer. "You killed my brother. Why the fuck would I answer your questions?"

Ash sighed. Of course it couldn't be easy. "No, your bone-headed friend, Jackson Duvall, killed Gethin when he decided to pull a gun on a law enforcement officer. Duvall's dead, too, in case you're wondering."

"You had no right to be there."

"I had a warrant. That gave me the right." He laid out the pictures taken of the Mad Dog after the drive-by and of Rose's injuries after her abduction. "It was you out at the old gas station that day, wasn't it?" Now that he was face-to-face with the man, he was sure of it. "What was the plan there, huh? Shoot her up with heroin until she overdosed? Make her look like a drug addict so the sheriff wouldn't look too closely at her death?"

Isaiah crossed his arms over his chest, making his chains rattle, but said nothing in response.

"Well, I have a news flash for you. I'm not Jerry Tennison." He leaned over the table and stared into the man's eyes. "I look closely at every-fucking-thing. By tomorrow, I will know everything there is to know about you. I will know everyone you've ever spoken to or fucked or made deals with, and I will use it to bury you for hurting Rose and killing one of my best deputies."

Isaiah scoffed. "I'm not afraid of prison."

"You should be. I hear rats don't survive long behind bars."

"I'm not a rat."

"Doesn't matter. If I whisper the idea in the right ear and have enough circumstantial evidence to back it up..." He trailed off.

"Lawyer," Isaiah said, and his mask cracked—only slightly, but Ash saw the fear underneath.

It was enough.

For now.

He gathered up the photos and walked out without another word. Donovan and Pierce waited for him in the hallway, along with Cal Holden.

He groaned when he spotted the lawyer. "Jesus, Holden. Don't tell me you're that asshole's lawyer."

"Nah. Told ya, I don't defend skinheads."

"So, what, you just hang out at prisons all night for fun?"

Cal grinned and tilted his head toward Donovan. "Van called me. He thought you might get something pertinent to the Galasso case."

Ash shook his head. "Not tonight. We need to let Erickson stew for a while, then he might talk. *Might* being the operative word. He's pissed enough about his brother, he could decide to clam up entirely."

"He'll talk. He's a rat," Cal said without a shred of doubt in his voice. "Been around enough of them to know. But how did *you* know GSN had one?"

Ash dragged a hand over his face. He was exhausted to the bone and his brain was starting to feel sluggish. He needed about a week of sleep to feel remotely human again. "ATF called me an hour ago. They're pissed I fucked up an ongoing investigation for them and heavily implied they have an informant among my prisoners. I took a stab in the dark. The other guys we have are all either burned out drug addicts or just plain not smart enough to make that kind of deal with the feds. Process of elimination pointed me to Isaiah."

Cal nodded. "If he's talked before, you can all but guarantee he'll talk again if he thinks it will save his neck. Whoever his lawyer is, they will also see the value in a deal."

"Good. But not tonight," Ash repeated around a yawn. "No more work tonight. Let's all go home."

"Wow," Donovan said and whistled. "Ash wants to stop working— and look!" He spread his hands. "The world hasn't ended."

"Fuck you, Van."

He grinned. "I'm sure my sexy wife will as soon as I get home."

In the parking lot, they all went their separate ways to their vehicles, but Pierce hung back. Ash stopped walking and studied the man. He watched Donovan and Cal go, then his hands started moving.

"You wanted to know about your deputies?"

Ash was still learning sign language and it took him a moment to process the question. "Yeah. What did you overhear?"

"The ones you left with me are mostly okay." Pierce signed slowly so Ash could follow, but then pulled out his phone and started to type.

> But I'd get rid of Matt Howell and Vince
> Houston if I were you. They were bitching
> about how you fired Jenkins and think you
> should leave Tennison's cases alone.

Ash wasn't surprised. "They're part of the old guard. All

three of them—Jenkins, Houston, and Howell—were hired by Tennison long before I joined the department."

They're worried about what you'll find if you keep digging. I got the feeling they've done some corrupt shit, too. Ross Black is also iffy. He never said anything outright against you, but he was agreeing with everything Howell and Houston said. You definitely have a dirty house, Sheriff.

"I know." He just hadn't realized how filthy it was until tonight. He'd already canned all of the deputies that ran from the firefight, but he knew he'd be handing out more pink slips soon. "And I plan to do a thorough spring cleaning as soon as things calm down around here."

chapter
thirty-two

ROSE FELT the bed dip and sighed in relief as Ash's arms slid around her waist. "Is it over?"

He grunted a reply, curled around her and buried his face in her hair.

"Ash." She tried to roll over to face him, but he held her tighter. Her heart squeezed with a mixture of fear and worry. "What's wrong? Are you okay?"

"A good deputy died today." His voice was muffled by her hair. "Maybe one of the only good ones I had. I lost control of the situation and he paid for it with his life."

She tried to roll over again and, this time, he let her. His eyes, when he opened them, were wet with tears.

"Oh, Ash. I'm so sorry." She stroked her fingers over his beard. "But you shouldn't blame yourself."

"I lost control—"

She silenced him with a finger against his lips. "You can't be in control of all things all the time."

He kissed the pad of her finger, then pulled it from his lips and laced their hands together. "I have to be. When I lose control, bad things happen to the people I care about."

He couldn't truly believe that.

She sat up on her knees and scowled at him. "Oh, c'mon." When he only stared back, his stormy blue eyes serious, she blinked in shock. "Really? I never expected that kind of magical thinking from you."

A muscle ticked in his jaw. "It's not magical. It's true." He also sat up and stared sightlessly at the wall over her shoulder. "I'm not— I'm not a good man, Rose."

She doubted that. Bad men didn't worry about whether they were good or not. But it was true that he was nothing like she thought. She'd always thought of him as kind of shallow, with a one-track mind and a monochrome view of the world. But he was so much more complex than she'd given him credit for, with a darkness in him that she couldn't quite comprehend. She had always been drawn to danger, and maybe that was why she found him so attractive. That darkness was exhilarating and terrifying at the same time.

She took his hand in hers. His skin was rough, calloused from years of hard work. She traced his knuckles with her fingers, trying to soothe him.

"I'm not afraid of your darkness, Ash," she said softly. "I want to understand it."

He turned back to her, his eyes blazing with intensity. "You don't know what you're asking for."

"You said that to me once before, and I liked what I got." When he didn't respond, she leaned in and kissed him on the lips. "I want to see all of you, the good and the bad."

Ash hesitated, then pulled his hand away and swung his legs over the edge of the bed. He combed both hands through his hair then locked them behind his neck and leaned forward with a groan that sounded a lot like pain.

But not a physical pain.

Rose waited, steeling herself for whatever he said next. Because she knew he would tell her—he was going to give her a peek behind his shields, and she didn't want to react the wrong way when he did.

"I was out of control as a kid," he said after several long minutes of silence. "Partied all the time, drank too much, did any drugs I could get my hands on. I was aimless, had zero ambition. Figured I didn't have to put in any effort because my future was already decided for me. I had a massive trust fund and, someday, Rawlings Ranch would be mine, too. I didn't give a fuck and had no intention of changing."

He took off his shirt and she noted the new bandage on his shoulder with spots of blood seeping through. She wanted to ask about it, but kept her mouth shut. There would be time for questions later. Right now, he needed to talk.

"But there was this girl," he said and balled up his shirt like he was trying to strangle it. "Amanda. Mandi. She was gorgeous. Smart. And she loved me despite the fact I was an entitled shithead. She was going places, you know? Had that go-getter attitude and the will to make her dreams happen. She was accepted to school in San Francisco, wanted to be a pediatrician and treat kids with cancer. How selfless is that? I still wonder what she saw in me."

Probably the same thing I see, Rose thought, but still didn't speak.

"I was such a loser." His abrupt laugh was full of bitterness. "I didn't think so at the time, but looking back— Jesus. I was constantly goading Zak and Donovan into stupid things, getting them into trouble, never realizing that they didn't have the shield of the Rawlings last name and legacy to hide behind. Zak got it easier because his family was well-respected, but Donovan..." He shook his head. "Would he have been accused of murder if not for all the shit I made him do over the years? I put him on Jerry Tennison's radar and Tennison couldn't get me or Zak, so..." He trailed off, shrugged. "He went after Donovan at the first opportunity."

"What happened to Mandi?" Rose asked when he stopped speaking, realizing he was working his way around the story rather than through it.

Ash took a deep breath and finally met her gaze. "I killed her."

"What?" she breathed. She'd been expecting him to say something else, something less horrifying. But the reality of his confession hit her like a bucket of ice-cold water. Nothing could have prepared her for it.

"I killed her." His face was a mask of pain and sorrow. "She would come home between semesters to be with me. We'd party all summer, then she'd go back to school. I got her hooked on Oxy and when she went back to school, she couldn't afford the pills anymore, so she turned to heroin. She lost her scholarship, ended up homeless. Her parents went down to the city to find her and bring her home, get her help... but all they did was bring her back to me and the pills. I kept taking her out to parties, feeding her more drugs. I thought her parents were being overprotective and ridiculous and I didn't see the problem right up until the night I couldn't wake her up. She kept asking for more and more pills and I kept giving them to her. She died in my arms."

Tears streamed down his face as he spoke, his voice trembling with each word, and her heart ached for him.

"I'm so sorry," she whispered, reaching out to take his hand once more. "That's a heavy burden to carry."

Ash shook his head and yanked his hand away. "I don't deserve your sympathy. I made a choice that ruined her life, and it killed her. When I realized what I'd done, I got clean and joined the Sheriff's Department. You called me a hypocrite once. I am. The worst kind."

Rose didn't know what to say. She couldn't imagine the regret and self-hatred he carried every day. "That's why you know what withdrawal feels like."

"Hell. Pure hell." He winced. "I get why Mandi couldn't do it. I wouldn't have been able to either if I wasn't so determined to make her death mean something. She was supposed to help people. Kids. I took that from the world, so I wanted to make sure I gave something back. I couldn't go to med school. I didn't have the grades or the patience. But I could be a cop and maybe protect people like I was supposed to protect her." He pulled his badge off his hip and tossed it aside. It landed on the bed and bounced onto the floor. "But no matter how many people I help or lives I save, I'm still a fucking monster underneath who doesn't deserve this town's respect or trust. Maybe that's why my deputies are all turning on me. They sense it in me."

"No," Rose said firmly. "You're not a monster. You made a mistake as a kid. A terrible one, but that doesn't make you a monster. You're still a good person, Ash. I know it."

He looked at her, surprise obvious in his bloodshot eyes. "How can you say that? I ruined your life, too. I helped tear your family apart when I *knew* what we were doing wasn't right. And I didn't speak up. You should hate me."

She winced. Couldn't stop it. For years, she had thought that way. He'd arrested her dad for her mom's murder, so it was his fault she ended up an orphan. It was his fault she no longer had a family. She'd held on to that flame of anger for years and fanned it into hatred every time she saw him, without ever really analyzing it.

Was it Ash's fault her mom was murdered?

Was it his fault her dad had been so wrapped up in shady dealings at the bar that he looked guilty?

Was it his fault her mom had multiple affairs and her parents' marriage was falling apart?

No, no, and no.

Ash hadn't been there for any of that. He'd only stepped into her life after everything had already crashed down around her. She'd blamed him because it was easier than blaming Pete or Harmony.

She sucked in a breath and let it out slowly. It was time to grow up. "You were just barely an adult yourself, in a new job, doing what you were told." And, she realized now, probably still reeling from the grief of Mandi's death. "I don't hate you, Ash. I don't think I ever really did. I was angry and hurt and looking for someone to blame. You were the easiest target."

Ash stared at her for a long moment, then closed his eyes as if in relief.

Rose squeezed his hand, trying to convey all of her complicated feelings in that one gesture. "But now I see you. I see the man who has dedicated his life to helping others, who has saved countless lives and made a difference in this world. I see the man who is working himself to exhaustion trying to make up for his mistakes. That's the kind of man I want to be with, Ash. One who is flawed, but who strives to be better. One who knows what it's like to fall and pick himself back up again."

He opened his eyes and looked at her, tears still spiking his lashes. Then, slowly, he leaned in and kissed her. It was a raw kiss full of emotion—pain and need, longing and regret. She felt all of it, and she responded with equal passion. She wrapped her arms around him, tangling her fingers in the short hair at the back of his neck, and pulled him closer.

Ash deepened the kiss, his tongue seeking entrance to her mouth. She eagerly obliged, tasting the earthy flavor of his lips, the saltiness of his tears. She wanted to soothe away his pain as he had done for her the night before.

But he broke away, tucked a strand of hair behind her ear, and stared at her with reverence. "I don't deserve you, Ambrosia."

"Stop saying that," she said. "You made mistakes as a teenager, but that doesn't mean you don't deserve to be loved.

You deserve love and happiness just like anyone else. And you didn't kill Mandi. You didn't force her to take the pills, right? She made that choice herself. You didn't follow her to school and force the heroin on her, either. Those were her decisions."

"But if I hadn't—"

"She would've been introduced to drugs while in school. I mean, San Francisco? You really think she wouldn't have tried drugs while there? C'mon."

His eyes widened. "That's not—"

"Shut up, Ash." She held up a hand, stopping him. She wanted to make sure he heard this next part loud and clear. "You have this idealized, angelic version of Mandi in your head —and I'm sure she was amazing, but there also had to be something a little broken in her to push her toward the drugs to begin with. And even if you hadn't come along, that broken bit would've surfaced eventually."

He opened his mouth, but again, she stopped him, pressing a finger to his lips. "I'm not saying that to diminish her memory. I'm saying it to help you see that you're not solely responsible for what happened. You were a part of it, yes, but it wasn't all on you. She probably would have found her way to the drugs with or without your help, so you can't keep blaming yourself. And now I get why you try to control every-thing and everyone around you, but shit happens, Ash. You can't control life. If you keep trying, you'll drive yourself crazy and push everyone you love away."

Ash stared at her for a long moment, then took her hand away from his mouth and cupped it to his cheek, leaning in. The gesture reminded her of her cat, when Fanta sought comfort.

"How did you get to be so wise?" he murmured.

She gave a self-deprecating laugh. "I wouldn't go that far, but I'm starting to see my own mistakes a bit more clearly and I have so many regrets, too. Look at how I blamed you for my parents' fuck-ups for years. But I forgave you, so it's time to forgive yourself and move on."

He looked at her, his eyes searching hers. "You've forgiven me?"

"How could I not?" She smiled softly. "So now it's your turn."

"I don't know how."

"You let Mandi's memory be a source of strength, not a cause of pain, and you keep being the amazing cop that you are." She retrieved his badge from the floor, pressing it into his hand, closing his fingers over it. "Keep helping people. Keep making a difference. And..." Her heart pounded as she stepped closer and wound her arms around his neck. "You let me love you. Because I do, Ash. Somehow, you made me fall out of hate with you and into love."

chapter
thirty-three

ASH SUCKED IN A SHARP BREATH.

She couldn't mean that.

But the look in her eyes told him she did.

It was pure adoration, love, trust—everything he had never allowed himself to feel for a woman, every huge, terrifying emotion growing inside his chest. All of it reflected back at him in her gaze.

He could have this. He could have her.

He was so unworthy of her love, but he could try to be.

"I—" He closed his eyes and took a deep breath, willing himself to be brave, but the L word caught in his throat. "I want to make you happy."

Rose leaned back to look at him. "You do?"

He nodded, his heart racing. "It scares the hell out of me, but I know that I want to be with you. I want to be the man you deserve."

Tears glistened in her eyes as she took his face in her hands and pressed her forehead to his. "You already are."

Ash felt something shift in his chest when she kissed him. Maybe it was the guilt that had been crushing him for so long finally beginning to lift. Or maybe it was the realization that he could love and be loved despite his past mistakes. Whatever it was, it made him feel lighter, freer. He pulled her close, savoring her soft curves.

Rose responded eagerly and he surged to his feet, shifting their positions, laying her down on the mattress. He explored her body with his hands and mouth until he found her already bare under her nightshirt, already wet for him. He shouldered her thighs apart and dove his hands under her ass, rising her to meet his lips. He wanted to taste her, lap her up until she came, screaming his name...

But she resisted.

She pulled on his hair until he was forced to look up.

"No," she whispered. "Not your mouth. I want your cock inside me, now."

His hips rocked forward of their own volition, pinching his aching cock against the bed. Who was he to say no to that?

Ash took a deep breath to steady himself, but the intoxicating scent of her filled his nose, and made him giddy. His restraint crumbled. He ripped his boots and pants off and pushed her thighs apart again with his hips. She was more than wet. She was soaked, all but sobbing for him. He positioned himself and she whimpered as he dragged his tip back and forth along her slit.

"Ash." His name was nothing but a sexy plea on her lips.

He slipped into her wet, tight sheath and held there, trembling, his fingers clamped around her hips as he struggled for control. The head of his cock was buried so deep inside her, she pulled at him with each ragged breath she took. He wanted nothing more than to pound into her until he found release, but if he didn't slow down, it wouldn't last. He wanted to savor this.

He rocked back and shuddered at the sensation of her body sucking on him, trying to hold him. He slid almost out of her and then ground back in until his balls slapped against the sexy curve of her butt. Over and over, he worked himself in and out of her, watching the play of emotions on her face.

She reached down and clutched his ass, pulling him deeper. "More. Fuck me harder."

His balls tightened in anticipation and heat gathered along his spine. His control was slipping. He wasn't going to last, so he clamped his hands around her hips and began to piston into her.

She let out a gasping cry. "Ash! More."

Yes. That was exactly what he wanted, too. Harder and faster, until the bed creaked and the headboard thunked on the wall. She trembled and pushed back against him, meeting him thrust for thrust, the muscles of her pussy clenching tighter around his cock every time he pulled out. He was so close to the sharp edge of his own climax—too fucking close.

He reached out to grab a handful of her hair, giving it a harsh tug. "Are you going to come for me, Ambrosia? Are you going to come on my cock like a good girl?"

She moaned. "Yes. Ash, please."

"No, you're not. Not yet." He released her hair and pulled out of her, watching her writhe on the bed as if in pain.

"Come back," she whimpered.

"No." He grinned and settled between her thighs, spreading her legs wide and reaching under her. He found her clit and began to roll it between his fingers, pushing down on it with his palm to give her a little extra pressure. She gasped and her hips jerked, but he held her in place. He leaned down and licked her hard little nub, and she went rigid.

She came apart with a scream.

Her body shook and her pussy throbbed around his fingers as he continued to press down on her. As soon as she settled, he lifted his head and pulled her back up to a sitting position. He hooked a hand behind her neck and brought her in for a kiss, making her taste her sweet juice and the salty muskiness of their combined sex.

She wrapped her arms around his neck and held him tight, her lips moving eagerly with his.

"Ash, please," she murmured between kisses.

He grinned. "Please what?"

She squirmed and, still quivering with aftershocks, rubbed her wetness against his throbbing shaft.

It almost killed him, but he pulled back. "You don't already want more, do you?"

Her eyes flashed. "I want all of you."

"My greedy little Rose. With petals so soft…" He stroked one hand between her legs, swirling his fingers through her wetness, while the thumb of his other hand brushed back and forth over her lower lip. She sucked the digit into her mouth, and a dark mischief glinted in her eyes moments before she bit down.

Hard.

His cock kicked against the bed in response, and he growled. "But with so many thorns. I adore that about you." He rolled over, shifting their positions so that she was on top. "Ride me. Let me watch you."

She dropped onto his length without protest, taking him deep, all the way to the root. Letting out a sexy little moan, she began to move, grinding her clit against his pelvis with each downstroke, ass flexing with each lift. He lifted himself enough to swirl his tongue around one nipple, sucking it in the way he knew drove her wild. Then he turned his attention to the other one and relished the feel of her next orgasm building deep inside her. She whimpered and ground down on him, her breath coming in short gasps.

No. He didn't want it to be over yet.

He picked her off him and shifted positions again, dragging her up to her hands and knees so he could take her from behind. Her cry as he drove in deep tightened all of her muscles and nearly pushed him into his own orgasm.

"Ash..." She all but sobbed his name and her arms trembled. "I can't... I can't..."

"I'm here, Ambrosia. Right here with you. Let's fall together." He banded an arm around her waist and kept his strokes strong and deep, pushing on through the blazing pain in his shoulder. He wanted to feel it, use it to push himself over the edge. He was so close that he would come the moment she did.

He ground his teeth together and tried to hold on, but when she let out a breathless scream, oblivion rushed over him with the force of a hurricane. As the pleasure wracked his body, he leaned in and bit the back of her neck. She let out another little cry and a primal satisfaction filled his chest.

He'd left his mark.

She was his.

He released her neck and buried his face in the crook of her shoulder, whispering her name into her skin. She collapsed onto the bed, sated and sweaty. His arms felt like noodles, and he eased himself down, careful not to crush her with his weight as he rolled to his side and dragged her limp body with him.

He chuckled. "Are you still alive?"

She exhaled a dreamy breath. "Barely." She laid a hand on his chest, and he covered it with his own.

Rose fell asleep fast, but he didn't mind. He couldn't remember the last time he was this content. His shoulder ached and he knew he should move, but he didn't want to wake her. He wanted to hold her like this—his heart beating against her palm, all of his senses filled with her—until the end of time.

His eyes drooped and he felt himself drifting.

No.

Wait.

He had one thing left to do to ensure she felt completely safe again.

Prying his eyes open, he groped for his phone on the nightstand.

chapter
thirty-four

THE NEXT MORNING, as Ash guided the Tahoe into the parking lot in front of the Mad Dog, Rose's face lit up just as he hoped it would.

All of Redwood Coast Rescue was there—Zak and Anna sweeping up the broken glass; Sawyer and Veronica painting the new door the same bright, deep red as the old; Donovan and Sasha hanging the new sign; and Pierce and Cal filling in bullet holes in the brick wall with mortar.

"What...?" Rose jumped out of the car and pressed her hands over her mouth as tears overflowed her eyes. "What are you guys doing?"

"You're early," Zak grumbled and limped a little as he straightened with a dustpan full of glass in his hand. He dumped it in the trashcan beside him. "You were supposed to bring her by after we finished."

Ash shrugged. "She was impatient to get here and assess the damage."

Rose whirled on him. "You knew about this?"

"It was his idea," Anna said and stopped sweeping when Zak slid an arm around her. She leaned into him, and he pressed a kiss to her temple.

They were okay again.

They would *always* be okay, Ash realized and his relief at the sight of them together morphed into wonder. No matter what life threw at them, what arguments they had, what sorrows befell them, Zak and Anna would always figure it out. They'd survive. They'd thrive.

Together.

He glanced over at Rose. Could he have that with her?

His sister grinned at him, a knowing twinkle in her eyes. Of course she knew exactly what he was thinking—she always knew. It was the curse of twindom.

He ignored Anna and lightly touched the nearly faded bruise on Rose's cheek. "I didn't want you to be reminded of what happened. I wanted it erased, so you could start fresh."

"Ash!" She squealed his name and flung herself into his arms, wrapping her legs around his waist and kissing him repeatedly on his lips, nose, eyelids, forehead.

Okay, this reaction was even better than he'd hoped.

He laughed and let her rain her love down on him, soaking it all in, enjoying every second of it until someone cleared their throat. He let Rose slide down his body until her feet touched the ground, but kept an arm around her as they faced their friends.

"So," Cal said after a long moment and wiggled a finger in the air between them. "You two...?"

"Yes," Ash said. The word came out more forceful than he'd intended, but he wanted to make damn sure the panty-dropping playboy knew she was off-limits now.

Cal grinned. "I saw that coming. Anyone else see that coming?"

"We all did," Donovan and Zak said at the same time.

"Even me," Sawyer added.

"Oh, ignore them." Sasha stepped forward and looped her

arm through Rose's. "Come see what we did inside. I hope you like it."

"We had to move a few things around..." Anna took her other arm and, together, the two women guided her toward the pub's door. She smiled over her shoulder at Ash, shining as bright as a sunbeam with happiness, lighting up the foggy, gray day.

Donovan snorted. "Okay, wipe that goofy look off your face and get your ass over here. I need help with this plywood."

Ash shook his head slightly. He did have a goofy look on his face. He could feel it. He crossed to the sheet of plywood leaning along the wall of the wheelchair ramp. "Didn't you call the glass guys?"

"Yeah, but you wanted a custom window with the Mad Dog logo on it. That's going to take some time. Until then, we have plywood or plastic. And plywood is safer."

Ash would never argue with anything that made Rose safer. It was already going to be hard enough letting her come back to work. He picked up one side of the plywood and helped wrestle it up the ramp to the window. He opened his mouth to ask Veronica—since she was the closest person with sight—if they had the whole window covered, but she wasn't paying attention to them. She stared across the street and the color drained out of her already pale face.

Ash turned to see what had frightened her and scowled when he spotted Connelly Davis standing there, watching them.

Veronica's reaction coupled with the fact the writer conveniently disappeared right before the drive-by was enough to set off all of Ash's warning alarms. He dropped the sheet of plywood.

"Hey!" Donovan fumbled the other side. "Ash, what the fuck?"

Ash ignored him and strode across the road. "Who are you?"

To his credit, Connelly didn't flinch back even though Ash had several inches on him. Unperturbed, he met Ash's gaze. "I already told you, Sheriff."

"Bullshit. You expect me to believe you're some hotshot bestselling author who just blew into town to finish a book?"

"Would you like to call my agent? I can give you his number."

Ash let the snarky question slide. "And you just happened to show up while all this shit"—he motioned back toward the bar—"is happening in my town?"

"That's exactly right. I don't know what all this shit is and I'm questioning my choice of vacation spots."

"Vacation? I thought you were finishing a book?"

That finally broke through his facade of calm. Just a bit, but Ash saw the flash of uncertainty in his eyes as his gaze strayed back to Veronica.

Ash stepped into his line of sight again and crowded him, backing him into the brick wall of the hair salon. "Who are you really and why are you here? And you better think long and hard about your answer, because if you have *anything* to do with these attacks on Rose—"

"I don't." Connelly exhaled in defeat and dug his wallet out of his laptop case. He handed Ash a Washington State driver's license that listed his name, Connelly James Davis, and gave his address as Seattle. "I *am* an author, and I *am* finishing a book, but I could do that anywhere. I came here for Veronica. Vee," he called to her, and his voice changed, softened. "Tell the trigger-happy sheriff you know me."

Ash looked over at her. "Do you know him?"

"We grew up together." She still looked like she'd seen a ghost, but now seemed resigned about it. She pulled her sleeves over her hands before crossing her arms defensively. "What are you doing here, Connelly?"

He broke away from Ash's grip and started toward her, but stopped several feet away when Zak and Donovan blocked his path. He glowered at the two men, but quickly turned his attention back to Veronica. "Your dad's worried about you. *I'm* worried about you. We let you run away and hide, but we want you to come home."

She shook her head. "I am home."

"Vee." He tried to get closer, but again Zak and Donovan blocked his path and, this time, Cal joined them. Pierce and Sawyer flanked Veronica, like they planned to whisk her to safety if given the signal.

Connelly growled in annoyance. "Who the fuck are these guys?"

"Leave," she said so softly it was almost inaudible. "Please."

"You heard her," Donovan said.

"Bye," Zak added.

Connelly glared at them for several seconds, but then looked at Veronica. Tears tracked silently down her cheeks. He held his hands up and backed away. "It's time to stop hiding now, Vee. I'm not letting you disappear again." He turned and shot a narrow-eyed glare at Ash before walking away.

"I knew this was a bad idea," Veronica said and hurried away in the opposite direction of Connelly.

Nobody moved for a moment, until Zak's phone rang, and he stepped away to answer it.

Donovan frowned at Veronica's retreating back. Her head was down, shoulders hunched. "Is this something we need to be worried about?"

"Not sure yet." Ash watched as Connelly tossed the computer bag into the backseat of a sleek BMW X7 and slid behind the wheel. Anyone could fake a driver's license. He'd run a background check as soon as he was back in the office, to make sure the author was who he claimed to be.

"One problem at a time," Zak said, ending his call and coming back to the group. "Ash, you got your meeting, but you need to be in LA this afternoon."

Ash's heart clenched with dread as he looked toward the open door of the Mad Dog. Things had been going so well that, for a few hours, he'd forgotten Rose still wasn't safe.

But, hopefully, after this meeting, she would be.

LA was a ten hour drive. Even if he jumped in the car now, he wouldn't make it. He pulled out his phone and navigated to his favorite travel app. "I'll see if I can book a flight."

"No need," Zak said. "Quentin is sending a plane."

Donovan whistled. "Can you imagine having that kind of money? Just snap your fingers and send a plane anywhere in the world? Shit."

Ash hesitated.

"Hey." Zak grasped his shoulder. "Go. We'll make sure she gets home safe."

Ash started toward his truck. "If I'm not back tonight, have Mike Conti stay at my house with her."

"We'll handle it. Go and finish this."

chapter
thirty-five

ASH DROVE HOME and packed a duffle bag, then changed into his uniform before going to the airport. He didn't know exactly what waited for him in LA, and wanted to look as official as possible.

The private plane was small, a cushy eight-seater. It was surreal stepping off the jet in LA and having a car and driver waiting for him right there by the hangar. He watched the city pass in the golden light of the setting sun. He'd only been here a couple of times—once doing the tourist thing with his parents and Anna when they were kids, and once for a LEO conference.

How was this city, with its endless concrete, golden sun, and tropical palms, in the same state as the mountains and huge trees in his cool, mist-shrouded county? The two places looked like they belonged on different planets.

He much preferred his version of California.

The driver left him at the entrance of a hotel that looked to be having some kind of black-tie gala. He'd never felt so out of place anywhere in his life.

A tall blond man waited in the lobby, chatting with a group of guests in glittering gowns and tuxedos.

Tucker Quentin.

Ash would recognize him anywhere. During Quentin's short-lived movie career as a heartthrob in the early 2000s, he'd starred in a couple of Ash's favorite horror movies. He'd always played the dumb blond jock who died in the most ironically hideous way.

He was older now, of course—had to be nearing forty—and carried himself like a man who was comfortable in his own skin. He was surprisingly muscular with wide, heavy shoulders, but his tailored dark gray tux downplayed that fact.

Quentin spotted him, excused himself from his group of admirers, and strode over, holding out a hand. His smile was straight and perfectly white, made for Hollywood.

"You must be Sheriff Rawlings."

Ash accepted the handshake. "Mr. Quentin. I appreciate your help in this matter."

"Please, call me Tuc. It's not a problem." He held out an arm, indicating they should walk. "Any friend of Zak's is a friend of mine. How is he?"

They stepped into an empty room, and his demeanor shifted, almost like he dropped the mask of civility. Underneath, Ash glimpsed a warrior—same as Zak or Donovan. While he'd known Quentin's many businesses included private military contractors, he hadn't expected Quentin to be one himself.

"Okay, no bullshit. How is Zak really?" Tuc asked again, his tone less cultured and more direct. He shook his head and crossed to the bar along one wall. "I still regret we didn't get him out of there before he lost his leg."

"He's okay."

Quentin arched a brow. "Last I heard, he was drinking himself to death." He held up a decanter of golden liquid. "Drink?"

"No, thanks. I'm technically on duty."

"So am I." He eyed the decanter, swirling the liquid inside. "Truth be told, I'd rather be up to my ass in mud with my men, hunting bad guys, but duty called and I'm here schmoozing as the billionaire philanthropist instead. But fuck it. I need to be drunk to get through these galas nowadays." He nodded and poured himself a healthy glass, then motioned with it to the arrangement of leather furniture in the corner. "Have a seat, Sheriff. Your interview subject will be here shortly."

"You can call me Ash." He chose a chair and sank into it. "Duran's coming here?"

"Luckily, I didn't have to pull any strings at all. He had already RSVP'd to this thing, so I just had my people arrange a meeting." Tuc lounged back in the other chair and balanced his glass on his knee. "So Zak's really okay?"

"Yeah. There have been some bumps in the road, but for the most part, he's doing great. He's not drinking anymore. He married my sister, and they adopted two girls. He's running a team of tactical K9s and their handlers now."

Tuc sat back and closed his eyes, exhaling softly. "Thanks, I needed to hear that. So often what my men and I do ends badly. We had one that just—" He stopped. Shook his head and took a long drink. "Anyway, it's good to hear a happy ending for once."

Ash studied the man. Tucker Quentin was nothing like he'd expected. Under the polish, he looked tired, beaten down by the horrors of the world. He could use his obscene amounts of money to insulate himself from those horrors, but instead, he walked into them and tried to fix them.

And in doing so, he'd helped rescue Zak.

Ash's respect for the guy ratcheted up several notches. "I know my sister would want me to thank you for going over there and digging Zak out of that hellhole. You brought him home and gave her a second chance at her first love. And you gave me one of my oldest friends back. Even if he came home a little busted, it was better than him not coming home at all. So thank you."

A smile ticked up the corner of Tuc's mouth. Not the Hollywood smile, but a real one. "I imagine neither one of us hear that enough in our lines of work."

Ash chuckled. "That's the truth."

"I'll be sure to tell my men. It will mean as much to them as it does to me." He took another drink. "Why do you want to talk to Chet Duran?"

Since Tuc had been so straightforward with him, Ash decided not to mince words. "I suspect he's funding a neo-Nazi group in my county. And potentially behind multiple attacks on a local businesswoman."

Tuc studied his glass, considering. "Huh."

Something in his tone tweaked Ash's cop instincts. "You know him, right? What's your read?"

"Know is a strong word," Tuc said after a moment and finished his drink. "We're acquaintances. He shows up to my galas to up his social cred. I sometimes go to his if I'm not busy and it's for a good cause. The Montgomery-Duran family are everything I hate about this part of my life—selfish, entitled, and massive suck-ups to anyone they think can pull them up another rung on the social ladder. Chet's never had to work a day in his life. He suckles the teat of his parents' empires and thinks he's somehow superior because of it. But the operation you're describing? That's ambitious. I think he's too lazy to pull something like that off."

Ash thought it through. "He could just be the wallet. The money behind the attacks."

"He could." Tuc's phone gave a discreet buzz, and he pulled it out of his jacket pocket, checked the screen. "Looks like we're about to find out. He's here."

Ash stood up as the door opened and revealed Chet

Duran. He was in his fifties and of average height, but still in good shape, with the honed body of a much younger man. Probably one of the perks of being an heir to a fitness empire. He wore a perfectly tailored tux, and his streaky blond hair was slicked back, giving him an air of confidence that bordered on arrogance. He walked in, his shoulders squared, and his eyes darting around the room, assessing everything and everyone.

"Mr. Duran," Tuc said, standing up and walking over to him. "Thank you for coming."

"Quentin. Always happy to support a good cause." Chet nodded, his eyes flickering over to Ash, and then back to Tuc. "What's this meeting about?"

Tuc gestured to Ash. "This is Sheriff Ash Rawlings of Lost County up north. He has some questions for you regarding the recent attacks in his jurisdiction."

"Attacks?" Chet's lips twisted into a smirk. "Where even is Lost County? I've never heard of it."

Ash stepped forward and kept his voice low and measured as he said, "We have reason to believe you may be funding a domestic terrorist group called the Golden State Nationalists."

The smirk remained on his lips, but his eyes gave him away. He was panicking. "I'm sorry, Sheriff, but I have no idea what you're talking about."

"Cut the crap, Duran," Ash said. "We've linked your financial transactions to the group."

"What?" Under the outrage, he seemed genuinely puzzled. "I honestly have no idea what you're talking about, Sheriff. I'm a philanthropist. I donate to many causes, but I would never support anything as despicable as white supremacy."

Tuc spoke up. "Chet, I've known you for a while now, and I have to say, I'm disappointed to learn about these accusations. I might have to reconsider some of my business dealings with your family."

Chet scowled, his fists clenching at his sides. "I'm not involved with this. I don't know who this sheriff thinks he is, but—"

"What do you know about the recent attacks on a woman named Rose Galasso?" Ash interrupted.

"Galasso?" Chet's indignation vanished and in its place was an expression of absolute devastation. "I-I need to sit down." His legs wobbled as he walked over and sank into one of the chairs. He dragged a hand over his face. "That's a name I never thought I'd hear again."

Ash dropped into the chair opposite him. "How do you know it?"

"I..." He glanced at Tuc. "I had an affair with a woman by that name. Harmony Galasso. It was...thirteen or fourteen years ago."

Finally they were getting somewhere. "How did you meet Harmony?"

"At a bar in San Francisco. She was beautiful. It was—" His voice caught. "For me, it was love at first sight. I'd never experienced anything like that before. I didn't care that she was married."

"Are you aware that Harmony Galasso was murdered?"

"Yes," Chet said softly. "Her husband found out about our affair and killed her for it. I heard about it on the news a week after it happened. I was out of the country at the time, if you want to check. Italy. I didn't know why Harmony wasn't answering my calls until I got back to the States and saw the news."

Ash nodded, taking in the new information. The man was actually heartbroken. It was written all over his face. "I'm sorry for your loss, but we have reason to believe that Rose Galasso, Harmony's daughter, is being targeted because of you and your connection to GSN."

Chet shook his head. "I told you, I've never had anything

to do with neo-Nazis. I'm not that kind of man. Some of my best friends are black. If they got money from me, it was under false pretenses. The only person I've given money to up there is Harmony's daughter. I set up an account so Rose would be taken care of. I know that's what Harmony would've wanted." He pushed out of his chair. "We're done here."

After Chet stormed out, Ash sat back in his seat and frowned in thought. Rose had never mentioned Duran or the money he'd supposedly sent her, and she would have if she thought it was somehow tied to the attacks.

Tuc walked over to pour himself another drink, then leaned against the bar and took a sip from his topped-off glass. "Do you think he's telling the truth?"

"I don't know. None of it is adding up." Ash scrubbed his hands over his face then pushed to his feet. "But I gotta get back."

"My jet's still waiting for you at the airport." Tuc held out a hand. "It was good meeting you, Ash."

"Likewise." He accepted the handshake. "I have to say, you're not what I expected."

Tuc chuckled. "Yeah, I get that a lot."

ROSE SAT in the middle of Ash's bed with Connelly Davis' new book open on her lap. Dante snoozed at her side and Fanta was curled up on her legs, purring softly. Dad wanted her to read the book before she gave it to him so they could discuss it, but she was having trouble concentrating on the words.

She picked up her phone, but sighed when she didn't see any notifications. Ash should be landing soon. He'd called almost an hour ago to let her know he was back on the plane and on his way home, but he wouldn't say more, and she was itching to know what he'd learned.

She just wanted this to be over. She wanted her pub back. Her life.

Finally, she gave up on the book and marked her page with the inner flap of the dust jacket. Dante lifted his head and looked at her as she picked up the cat and scooted off the huge bed.

"Let's go see what Mike's doing." Still holding Fanta, enjoying the deep rumbles of his purr, she walked out into the living room.

At first glance, everything seemed normal—the two chairs,

the missing couch, Ash's ever-growing stack of files on the coffee table.

Except Mike wasn't there.

She opened her mouth to call out, but then heard the front door creak slightly as it opened.

This wasn't right. Nobody should be here, and Mike had no reason to go outside.

Heart in her throat, she silently backtracked to the guest room and shut the door behind her. She set Fanta down, then crossed to the nightstand where she'd hidden her gun that first night here. She grabbed the ammo and loaded it in easy, practiced movements. Her dad was a hippie, all about peace and love—but Pete Galasso had also refused to let his daughter grow up at the base of Murder Mountain without learning how to handle a gun.

She clicked off the safety and eased out into the hallway.

Voices. She couldn't make out what they were saying, but they were both men.

"Mike?"

The voices stopped.

"Is everything okay?" she asked from the hallway, then moved without making a sound across the living room toward the foyer where Mike and the other man were.

"Everything's fine," Mike called. "It's just another deputy stopping in to check on us."

Liar. His voice was strained, raspy and uneven with nervousness.

It wasn't over.

After everything Ash had sacrificed to keep her safe, she was still in danger—and that danger had finally come for her.

A wave of exhaustion washed through her. For a split-second, she thought about laying down her weapon and just letting whatever was about to happen, happen. But then she thought of Ash coming home and finding her body in his living room. Or, worse, never finding her at all. It would destroy him. He'd work himself to death looking for answers.

No. She couldn't let that happen. She wasn't giving up.

She sucked in a breath and let it out in a calming whoosh before swinging into the foyer with the gun raised.

Mike stood there with the door wide open. A shadow loomed out on the porch.

Cold air seeped inside and swirled around them, raising goosebumps on her skin. Or maybe that was just her fear. "What are you doing?"

Mike glanced back at her with guilt written all over his face. "I'm so sorry," he said softly. "I like you, Rose. I do, but I need the money. I have gambling debts. If I don't pay them off, I'll lose everything."

Her heart bungeed to her stomach and back up into her throat, but she was proud that the gun didn't wobble in her hand. "What money? I don't have any money."

"He says you do." Mike opened the door wider, letting the shadow on the porch come inside.

The first thing she registered was the gun.

The man had a gun.

And... she knew him.

He wore a black mask with the GSN skull printed on it, but it didn't matter. She'd recognize that beard anywhere.

She knew him.

She'd trusted him.

She'd trusted them both.

"Oh my God," she breathed.

A dog-shaped bullet streaked past her, Dante snarling as he charged her attackers. Mike grabbed for his service weapon as Dante flew toward him, teeth bared.

He was going to kill the dog. He was going to—

Rose didn't think.

She pulled the trigger.

The shot echoed in the small space, leaving her ears ringing. For a heartbeat, nobody moved.

Then Mike staggered back, his eyes impossibly wide in shock as blood bubbled from his mouth. He sank down the wall, leaving a streak of blood behind him. He died before he hit the floor.

Dante, realizing Mike was no longer a threat, changed course and went for the other man, but he was ready for it. He already had his weapon aimed.

She held up a hand. "No, wait—"

And the gun went off.

The bullet hit Dante in the chest, and he fell to the ground with a thud.

"No!" With tears streaming down her face, she swung her gun toward the man, but she was moving too slow. He was ready for it and grabbed her arm, twisting until the gun fell out of her hand. He kicked it away and pressed his own weapon to her temple.

"I'm sorry, Rosie," he said, his familiar voice muffled by the mask. "I really am."

"Then why are you doing this?"

"I didn't want to." He almost sounded regretful. "But you have something that belongs to me."

She gritted her teeth, hating the way her body trembled with fear. "What's that?"

"The pub."

THE JET HAD JUST LANDED when Ash's phone rang.

"Rawlings," he answered without looking at the ID.

"You need to get back here," Zak said, his voice tight, urgency radiating from every word. "Now."

A chill scraped down his spine. "What happened?"

"Mike Conti's dead."

The dread morphed into a hot sizzle of panic. "Where's Rose?"

"Gone."

"What do you mean, gone?"

"Hang on." There was suddenly a lot of noise on Zak's end—barking, shuffling, voices.

Ash held his breath and prayed. He grabbed his bag and ran to the front of the plane, pacing the aisle as it finished coasting to a stop.

Gone.

Not dead.

Zak wouldn't have minced words if she were dead, too.

He hoped.

God, please, not dead.

He exited the jet as soon as the flight attendant opened the door, jumping onto the stairs before the ground crew had them locked in place. He clambered down them and broke into a run across the tarmac.

By the time Zak returned to the phone, he was out of the small regional airport and racing across the short-term lot to his Tahoe.

"It looks like Mike was in on it," Zak said. "Your security system recorded the whole thing. A man in a black GSN mask knocked on the door and Mike let him in."

"Fuck, fuck, fuck! I trusted that bastard."

Were any of his deputies trustworthy? Pierce had told him he needed to clean house, but he was starting to think he needed to burn the whole house down and start again.

"Yeah, well, he got a bullet in his heart for his efforts," Zak said. "Rose shot him."

Ash staggered to a halt. "She... *what*?" He hadn't even known she had a gun.

"She shot Mike to protect Dante. When we find her, remind me to tell her she's a badass." There was another pause, some muffled voices and shuffling in the background, then he came back to the line. "I'm mobilizing RWCR. Donovan, Spirit, Pierce, and Raszta are searching in town, starting at the pub. Anna and I are headed into the woods around your house with Ranger and Winston. Sawyer's coordinating at base. I'll lose signal on the mountain, so you'll want to contact him, and he can radio me. How far out are you?"

If RWCR was mobilizing, then they believed Rose was still alive.

Ash dove into the driver's seat of his truck, tossed his bag in the back, and cranked the engine. It was usually a forty-minute drive from the airport to Steam Valley. He flipped on his siren and peeled out of the lot. "I'll be there in twenty and I'll get deputies there to help with the search. Where is Dante?"

Zak's voice was grim. "The masked asshole shot him before he took off with Rose."

A vise clamped around Ash's windpipe. "Is the dog...?" He couldn't finish the sentence.

Zak understood anyway. "We don't know. Your security camera showed him getting up after they left and wandering out into the woods."

"Zak." His voice broke. "Find her. Find them both."

"We're on it, brother. Get here."

Less than twenty minutes later, he pulled up to Redwood Coast Rescue as a cold rain drizzled from the dark sky.

Sawyer was in the new command center in front of a computer setup that was like something out of a spy movie. Zelda waited patiently between his feet, watching his every move. Despite his blindness, he navigated between the computers effortlessly and juggled the many various elements of the search so that it ran like clockwork.

The biggest screen on the wall showed a map of the area sectioned into blocks. Some were filled in green, some yellow, but most were red.

"Sawyer," Ash called so as not to startle him. He shook rain off his jacket. "What's the situation?"

Sawyer glanced toward his voice and held up a finger. He tapped his earpiece and told someone to move on to search grid 1C, then pulled the earbud out, letting it dangle over his shoulder. "We've searched the woods, but so far the dogs haven't found her scent and the people haven't found any signs of her. We're expanding the grid now."

"What about Dante?"

"Zak and Ranger picked up his scent from your house and tracked him through the woods to Bear Gulch Road, then lost him."

Ash cursed under his breath. "Bear Gulch Road? That goes up the mountain."

And it was where Harmony's body had been found. That couldn't be a coincidence.

"Which is why we're expanding the search grid." Sawyer grabbed the earbud and shoved it back into his ear, replying to someone on the radio before typing a command on his braille keyboard. A section of the map changed from red to green.

Ash stepped over to study the map. "What does all this mean?"

"Green is searched and cleared," Sawyer said. "Yellow means searched but with potential hits. Red is unsearched."

There was a lot of red on that map. "Fuck."

Where was she?

"We will find Rose," Sawyer said without a hint of doubt. But Ash heard what he wouldn't say—that she might not be alive when they did.

Jesus, his chest hurt. He rubbed a hand over his heart.

He wanted to go out to every one of those red squares himself. He wanted to rip the county apart, rock by rock, tree by tree, until she was safe in his arms again. But he wasn't trained in search and rescue—at least, not like the guys of Redwood Coast Rescue. He had to trust them to do what they were good at.

He'd help more by doing what he was good at—being a cop.

Ash spun away from the map. "Keep me updated."

"Where are you going?" Sawyer called after him.

"The prison."

"Why Rose?"

Isaiah Erickson's lip curled into a sneer. "Didn't that dumbass Crusher already tell you? It was Duran's order."

"Yeah, except that's a lie. I flew to LA and spoke with Chet Duran. He doesn't know you or GSN. So who is giving you orders to kill Rose?"

Isaiah stayed mulishly silent. He wasn't talking.

This was a waste of time.

Ash strode out of the room and paced the hallway outside. There had to be a way to get Erickson to talk. Just had to find the right strings to pull, buttons to push, but he needed more information first. He grabbed his phone and saw several missed calls from Sawyer.

Heart drumming painfully, he tapped Sawyer's name and raised the phone to his ear. "Did you find her?"

"No. Shit, I didn't think—sorry."

He refused to feel disappointment. They *would* find her. "It's fine. What did you need?"

"You ran out of here before I could tell you what I found while you guys were getting shot up yesterday. The money connection between Duran and GSN? It doesn't flow in a straight line. Which you gotta expect, especially if he doesn't want anyone tying it back to him. But here's the weird part—it went from a personal account with Rose's name on it into a business account for the Mad Dog Pub."

Ash stopped pacing. "What?"

"Yeah, really weird, right? This account had millions of dollars in it until yesterday. Almost ten. I started thinking if Rose knew about that money, would she be living in a shabby apartment above her hole-in-the-wall bar and driving a nine-year-old car that breaks down if you sneeze at it? Doubtful. So I kept digging. Duran deposited the money in larger amounts to Rose's account, then smaller amounts were transferred out into the business until that first account was empty, then even smaller amounts went out to the Erickson brothers and GSN.

But the GSN transfers are new. The money has been going into this funnel since Harmony's murder, but the transfers out to GSN only started recently."

Jesus. Duran hadn't been lying about sending money to help care for Rose. "How recently?"

"Uh... about five years ago."

So the transfers to GSN started when Rose turned twenty-one and took over the Mad Dog. Another piece clicked into place, but Ash still couldn't see the whole picture yet. "Sawyer, who controlled the pub in the eight years between when Pete was arrested and Rose came of age to run it?"

"Good question. Hang on."

Ash heard the clicking of a keyboard in the background, then silence. It stretched for a long time, and he bounced on the balls of his feet with impatience. "Sawyer?"

Finally, he came back. "Looks like the pub transferred to Rose's aunt, but Rainbow didn't have much to do with the day-to-day operations."

"So who did?"

"Uh... yeah, she hired the chef to manage it. Marcel Dupont." Sawyer went silent, then whistled. "And guess who has a lengthy criminal record and family ties to GSN? The Ericksons are his fucking cousins."

And there was the string he had to pull. "Where's the money now? Still in the pub's account?"

"Far as I can tell, it was all transferred offshore yesterday."

And *that* was the button to push to get Isaiah talking. "Send everything you found to my email." He rattled it off.

"Done," Sawyer said.

"I owe you one." Ash hung up and shoved back into the interrogation room. He sank into the chair across from Isaiah and leaned back like he didn't have a care in the world. "Did you know Duran sent nearly ten million dollars to help take care of Rose after her mother's murder? He's a smarmy, entitled piece of shit, but I have to say this for him, he really did love Harmony."

Isaiah's eyes narrowed, but he still didn't speak.

"Your cousin told you it was less, didn't he? He told you he was giving GSN everything because he only wanted the bar when you killed Rose."

"That's not—" Isaiah bit off what he'd been about to say and shook his head.

"Not true?" Ash finished for him and took out his phone to access his email. He pulled up the relevant documents and set the phone on the table so Isaiah could see the screen. "See, I have the paper trail to prove it. In reality, Marcel was pocketing all that money for himself. He needed Rose dead to hide his theft because with me looking into her mother's murder again, that bank account was sure to come to light. Isn't it convenient for him that you're in here facing a life sentence, your brother is dead, and so are most of your GSN friends? It's almost like he knew you'd fail in your attempts to kill Rose and I'd catch you, put you away. Solves a big problem for him, doesn't it? Now he doesn't have to share the money."

Isaiah clenched his teeth so hard, Ash could hear the man's molars grinding.

"And there's only one thing standing in his way of millions: Rose herself. He didn't actually expect you'd succeed, so he must've had a plan to end this. How would he do it? Where would he take her?"

Isaiah's gaze dropped to the phone again. "I want a deal."

"She'll be dead before your lawyer can get here, and if she dies, your information becomes worthless. You won't get a deal."

Isaiah sat back and crossed his arms. "Then I'm not talking."

"You're willing to rot away in prison—probably in solitary because your life will be in danger when the other prisoners figure out you've been snitching to the feds—while Marcel gets to disappear with millions to some tropical country without an extradition treaty?" Ash nodded and picked up his phone, straightening away from the table. "That's one way to handle this. Me, personally, I'd be pissed. Family or not, I'd want revenge. But..." He shrugged and turned to the door. "I guess you're a better person than I am."

His hand was on the knob when Isaiah spoke up. "Wait."

Ash glanced back.

Isaiah was grinding his teeth again. After several beats of silence, he said, "Make him pay and I'll tell you everything."

chapter
thirty-eight

IT WAS MARCEL.

Rose couldn't believe it, but now that she was faced with the truth, all the pieces fell into place. He left early the night of the first attack, stating that business was too slow for him to stick around. He left again right before the drive-by, citing the same reason.

He'd known what was about to happen both times.

Even in the hospital, when he and Rainbow had visited her, he'd been the one to suggest she take a walk in the hospital's garden. He'd sent that thug after her. It was pure luck Ash had stopped by when he did, or else she would've been there alone and weak and unable to defend herself.

Easy pickings.

But his thugs had failed all three times, so now he was here to finish it himself.

After leaving Ash's, he drove her up the mountain and stopped in front of a tiny A-frame. They were up high enough that snow formed big pillows around the cute house. The place looked so innocuous, like hundreds of other vacation rentals in the area, but dread twisted her stomach into knots.

If she went in there, she'd never come out again.

Rose kicked at him as he reached into the backseat to drag her out, and managed to land a solid blow to his stomach. Marcel grunted. He backed up, but only long enough to pull his gun.

He motioned toward the house with the barrel. "Out."

She stilled and held up her hands. "Please, don't do this. We're friends. You're like an uncle to me."

His expression was full of disgust and... was that hatred? It contorted his face into something unrecognizable. How had she not seen it in him before?

Again, he motioned with the gun. "Get inside."

She decided to comply. At least for now. She was still only in her nightshirt and a pair of cotton pants. She didn't have a coat or shoes and would freeze if she tried to run.

The house was one small room with an overhead loft. While it looked like a cute vacation rental on the outside, inside was dirty and smelled musty. The carpet was threadbare and faded and the furniture looked older than she was. A large, tattered flag, bearing the unmistakable symbols of neo-Nazi ideology, hung prominently over the fireplace.

It didn't make sense.

Marcel was dating her aunt, who was part Mexican and part Native American. How could he love Rainbow and also be a member of GSN?

He shoved her to the floor and her head bounced off the wood planks as she landed. She saw stars. Every instinct screamed she should run, but he'd only catch her again if she tried. Her best bet was to stay calm and make him think she was unconscious. He obviously wasn't ready to kill her yet—if he'd wanted her dead, he would've shot her right there in Ash's foyer when he shot Dante, but he seemed to be waiting for something or someone first.

Playing possum gave her time to think. Plan. Maybe she

could even buy enough time for Ash to find her, because she had no doubt he would.

Marcel stood over her. His breathing was heavy, and she could feel his eyes scanning her body. She had to fight the urge to flinch away from his touch as he lifted her chin.

His thumb brushed over the nearly faded bruise on her cheekbone. "Those idiot cousins of mine did a number on you. I'm sorry for that. They weren't supposed to torture you." He actually sounded regretful, which made her stomach twist.

She opened her eyes and stared straight into his. "If you're so sorry, why are you doing this to me?"

"You took the bar from me."

She blinked in shock. That was what all this was about? He said it so matter-of-factly, like it was a perfectly reasonable explanation for trying to kill someone. "It was never yours, Marcel. I know my aunt made that clear when she hired you. You were a placeholder until I could legally run it."

"Your aunt," he spat the words like they were distasteful. "She never intended for you to live long enough to take over the pub. Or inherit your money."

No, she couldn't believe that. Rainbow loved her. Had raised her like a daughter. Her aunt would never do something so insidious. "You're full of shit."

"Oh, Rosie." He gave a bitter laugh. "Why do you think you were sick all through your teenage years? She was poisoning you. You have no idea who Rainbow is or what she's capable of."

A chill blasted through her. She sat up and her head spun. She thought for a moment she'd be sick, but nothing came up.

Something creaked and groaned at the front of the cabin, like footsteps crossing the old porch. Marcel whipped around toward the noise, and she took full advantage of his distraction. She bolted for the door, grabbed the handle, pulled it open—

Marcel caught her by the hair, dragging her backward until her scalp screamed, and tears popped to her eyes. He pressed the barrel of his gun to her temple.

Oh, God. This was it. He was going to kill her.

Rose sucked in a breath and held it, waiting for the bullet. Except it didn't come.

Marcel made a strangled sound—a choked-off scream? — and dropped her. For several precious seconds, she lay on the floor, stunned, unable to process what she was seeing. A furry black animal had barreled through the door and clamped onto Marcel's arm with big teeth. His gun clattered to the ground, and he screamed as he tried to punch the—

Dog?

Yes, dog.

Dante!

The amazing canine had somehow followed them up the mountain with a bullet wound and was still trying to protect her.

Rose's brain finally came back online, and she stumbled to her feet. She reached for the gun, but Marcel saw her going for it and kicked it. It slid deeper into the house, away from the front door.

Dante's eyes locked on her. He still hadn't released his bite and blood dripped from his muzzle to the floor. She swore she could hear his voice telling her to run.

Which was stupid.

He was a dog.

Maybe that was her own voice.

Maybe she should listen.

She didn't want to leave him, but realized Dante was in a better position to defend himself than she was. Her bare feet slipped on the cold wood planks of the floor as she scrambled outside. She gasped at the blast of frigid air and stumbled to a halt in the ankle-deep snow.

Shit.

She'd forgotten about the snow.

Even if she followed the road down, she'd freeze to death before she made it below the snow line.

She looked back at the cabin as something crashed inside. Her chances were slim in the forest, but better than staying. Staying was an automatic death sentence.

She ran. The woods were intimidatingly dark. And quiet. And cold.

"Rose!" Marcel's voice boomed through the trees behind her. "Stop!"

She didn't stop and, a moment later, a gunshot tore through the silence.

No!

Dante.

Her heart ached and a sob slipped from her throat. She ran until she couldn't feel her feet anymore and every sawing breath sent ice chips into her lungs. Only then did she slow to a walk, her teeth chattering and her body shaking. She pulled her arms inside the T-shirt, hugging her chest, trying to preserve as much body heat as possible, but it was no use. The cold gnawed at her bones as snowflakes danced in front of her eyes, swirling around her head like a halo of glowing white stars.

She could barely see through the darkness, but she had to keep moving downhill, one step in front of the other, or else she would freeze to death. She stumbled forward, her legs heavy with cold and fatigue, plunging into the snowdrifts as though walking through an ocean of pudding. Her toes burned with each footfall as they dragged across the ground.

But she had to keep moving.

One step.

And the next.

And the next.

All the way down the mountain until the snow was gone and she found help.

Until she found Ash.

She imagined his arms closing around her, holding her tight, his warmth radiating through her until she wasn't cold anymore. She pictured him scowling at her as he scooped her up and carried her to safety—her grumpy, uptight, workaholic sheriff. The man who scowled more than smiled, but also unapologetically played pretend with his niece. The man whose smile put the sun to shame when it finally did make an appearance, and whose rare laughs made her belly flutter. The man she'd spent half her life hating and wanted to spend the rest of her life loving.

Oh, how she wanted to see him again.

The forest was eerily silent, and it seemed like every tree was closing in on her, threatening to swallow her whole.

But then, suddenly, it wasn't silent.

A car engine?

She lifted her head and squinted against the headlights spearing through the darkness.

Ash?

Hope surged, sending a fresh blast of adrenaline through her. She ran towards the vehicle, waving her numb arms, her legs screaming in protest with every step. She knew it probably wasn't Ash, but at this point, she didn't care who was behind the wheel.

All she knew was that it was her salvation.

The truck slowed, then stopped as her legs finally gave out and she crumpled to the snow in the middle of the road.

The driver's side door popped open. "Rose?"

She let out a sob at the familiar voice. "Auntie."

But Rainbow didn't move out from behind the car door. "Fuck."

Rose's heart turned to lead in her chest. "Auntie?"

"Goddammit. That fucking man can't do anything right." Rainbow slammed the car door shut and reached into the bed of her truck, pulling out a shotgun.

"Auntie, what's going on?" Her voice came out in barely a whisper, small and child-like.

Rainbow didn't answer. She simply strode towards Rose, shotgun in hand, her expression grim. She stopped two feet away and raised the gun, pointing it directly at Rose's face.

"I'm sorry, baby."

Rose sat rooted to the spot, reeling with disbelief. Her beloved aunt. The woman who had raised her and soothed away her nightmares in the awful months after her mom's death and her father's arrest. The woman who had taught her to make a mean cocktail and bake an award-winning pie. Shown her how to knit and garden and fish. Taught her to love and laugh at a time she thought she'd do neither again.

The woman who had loved Rose since she was a baby and had patiently endured all her teenage antics. The woman who always said she would do anything in the world for her...

That same woman was now pointing a gun at her face.

THE GUN SHOOK in Rainbow's hand. "It wasn't supposed to be like this. Harmony just wouldn't listen to reason. She took you for granted. She took Pete for granted. I was trying to help you. Trying to save you."

And, suddenly, everything made sickening sense.

Rose dropped her hands. "You killed Mom. Your own sister!"

Rainbow cursed under her breath and lowered the gun, her ever-present bangles sliding down her wrist. Rose used to find comfort in that sound, but now all it made her think of was bones clicking together and she shivered harder.

Rainbow knelt down, her eyes softening as she took in Rose's disheveled appearance. "Oh, baby. You're so cold. Come on, let's get you into the truck and warmed up and I'll explain everything."

Rose pushed her hands away. "I'm not going anywhere with you."

"Please. I don't want to hurt you. That was all Marcel's doing. He got greedy and stupid. But I love you. I loved your dad. I swear, everything I did was for you."

Rainbow reached out to touch her arm and Rose flinched away. "How can you say that? You killed my mom. You let Dad go to prison."

Rainbow's face hardened, her lips flattening into a thin line. "That wasn't supposed to happen, but Tennison..." She trailed off, shook her head. "Please, let's just get in the truck and I promise you'll understand— "

The sound of another engine rumbled in the air.

Rainbow's complexion paled and she scrambled back to her feet, swinging the gun toward the incoming vehicle.

Rose looked up to see a familiar Tahoe barrel toward them. It pulled over in a cloud of snow, and Ash stepped out. As more sheriff deputies clogged the road behind him, he strode toward them, gun drawn. His expression darkened as his gaze went from the shotgun to Rose trembling on the ground.

"Rainbow," he said gruffly. "Put down the gun and lace your hands behind your head."

Rainbow's eyes darted between Ash and Rose. "Sheriff, please," she said, her voice choked with emotion. "You don't understand."

He didn't lower his weapon. "I understand perfectly. You killed your own sister out of jealousy, and you were going to kill Rose, too, for money."

"That's not—" She grabbed Rose's shirt and hauled her to her feet, pointing the shotgun at Ash. "No, you don't understand. I was trying to protect her! I didn't want her to end up like my bitch of a sister. Harmony was selfish and entitled and used people until she got what she wanted from them, then she threw them away like trash. She didn't deserve a daughter. She didn't deserve Pete. I loved him so much and not only did she steal him away from me, she gave him the one thing I couldn't—a daughter. I loved our little Ambrosia Wildflower from the moment I saw her and knew I'd do anything to protect her."

Rose felt strangely calm. Maybe she was going into shock, but the whole thing was like a movie scene—something playing out on a screen in front of her, rather than actually happening to her.

"Auntie, you're holding a gun on me. This doesn't feel like protection. This doesn't feel like love."

"I'm sorry. I'm so sorry." Rainbow sniffled. "This isn't what I want."

"What do you want?" Ash edged a slow step forward.

"I want her to understand this was all for her."

"Then tell me what happened," Rose said.

"You don't want to know the details."

"But I do. Help me understand. What did you do to my mom?"

"I dreamed about it for years," Rainbow said after a pensive second. "The perfect murder."

Rose shut her eyes and pictured her mom—the soft black waves of Harmony's hair, the freckles across her nose, the smile that crinkled that nose and made her eyes squint. She'd been a free-spirit, as wild and untamable as the forest surrounding their home. Harmony had danced barefoot in the rain and sang songs to the moon and wove dandelions into Rose's hair and gave the best hugs.

God, she missed her mother.

"I lured Harmony to my farm," Rainbow continued, oblivious to the memories. "It was easy. She was so angry at Pete. He was in the bedroom, sleeping off another night of drinking, so I offered for her to come stay at my place. Once she was there, I slipped a fatal dose of fentanyl in her favorite dandelion tea. Marcel—he worked for me back then, before he went down to the city and made a name for himself as a chef. He helped me bury her body deep in the woods where nobody would ever find her. I figured everyone would think she finally ran off with her rich lover like she always threatened to do.

"But then everything went wrong. Pete was arrested. And then convicted. And I couldn't tell the truth without implicating myself, so I took you in and tried to shield you from it." Her arm squeezed tighter around Rose's waist. "But Marcel knew about the money, and he wanted the pub."

"I don't understand," Rose said and shook her head. "I don't have any money."

"But you do, baby. Harmony's lover sent it. Jesus, she had that rich fool wrapped around her little finger. You weren't even his kid and he still sent you millions."

Rose noticed Ash had slid another step closer. His eyes met hers and through the swirl of snow, she saw the fear and worry. She also read his thoughts loud and clear: keep her talking.

"But Marcel could've taken the money," she said. "I wouldn't have known."

"The problem was Harmony's body," Ash said. "Rainbow knew I'd investigate. She knew I'd find the money and it would lead me to Marcel, and then to her."

"That's not what happened." Rainbow backed up a step and dragged Rose with her. "Stop moving!"

"Why did you encourage me to give my DNA?" Rose asked, drawing her aunt's attention away from Ash. "You knew it was mom. You knew she'd be identified when I did."

Emotions flickered across Rainbow's face. Sorrow. Regret. "I had hoped Pete would finally be cleared. I never meant for him to be arrested. I thought he'd get out and maybe we could pick up where we left off before Harmony."

Rose nodded as if that made perfect sense. "And Marcel didn't like that. He saw his golden goose slipping away and decided to kill me and steal the money." She turned and fully faced her aunt. Rainbow swung the gun from Ash to her and back. She hated the fresh flood of tears blurring her vision, but this hurt. Every word of the confession was like a knife twisting deeper into her heart. "Did you know his plan?"

"Not at first," Rainbow admitted. "Not the first time. But he convinced me..." She trailed off and her hand shook harder.

Rose fleetingly thought she should be worried that the hand holding the gun was trembling, but she was too cold, too numb. "He convinced you it was the only way to get away with mom's murder. Kill me, steal the money, and run. You were going to let him kill me. I loved you like a mother, and you tried to have me killed." She let the tears in her eyes fall. "He said you poisoned me when I moved in with you. Is that true?"

"I-I... no. That was a mistake. He convinced me to do it." Rainbow stared at her with big, unblinking eyes, then looked down at the gun. "Oh my God. What am I doing?" She opened her hand and let the weapon fall to the snow. "I'm sorry, baby. I'm sorry. I'm so sorry."

Ash and his deputies swarmed forward, and he kicked the shotgun away. "Rainbow Rodriguez, you're under arrest for the murder of Harmony Galasso and conspiracy to commit murder."

Tears streamed down Rainbow's face while Ash handcuffed her.

Rose watched in numb silence as he led her aunt away, handing Rainbow off to one of his deputies. Her legs gave out suddenly, but Ash was right there, catching her in his arms, holding her close.

"You're safe now," he murmured, rubbing her back soothingly. "I'm so sorry I wasn't here. I'm—" He shoved her behind him at the rustle of sound in the bushes to the right of the road. He raised his gun, then lowered it when Dante limped out. The dog's black muzzle was blood-stained, and he had a fresh wound on his back hip, but he was alive.

He. Was. Alive.

And that was when Rose lost it. The tears exploded from her until she was gasping. Ash held her through it, his arms banded around her.

Finally, the sobbing fit slowed to hiccups and he pressed a kiss to her forehead. "Are you okay?"

She nodded. Her tears had frozen to her face, but she felt lighter. "I'm just so cold."

Ash pulled off his jacket and draped it around her shoulders before scooping her up and carrying her to his Tahoe. His jacket smelled like him, she thought and nestled into the warm fleece lining. The scent was clean and comforting, mingling with the bitterly cold mountain air.

As Ash settled her into the passenger seat then helped Dante into the back, Rose closed her eyes and leaned her head back, the events of the past few hours replaying in her mind. She still couldn't quite believe her aunt had been capable of such heinous acts. The betrayal cut deep, leaving her raw, aching. Would she ever be able to trust anyone again?

But then she felt Ash's hand close around hers, warm and steady.

Him.

She could trust him. She hadn't always known it, but it had always been true.

She opened her eyes and looked over at him, taking in the strong lines of his face, the grim set of his mouth. Her sheriff. "I love you."

He barely glanced at her as he turned the Tahoe around and weaved it through the cluster of police cars. "You gave me fifty gray hairs tonight."

"I know."

His hands tightened on the steering wheel until it creaked a protest. "No, you don't." He sounded pissed. "I don't love easily or gently or—fuck, I don't know. Sweetly."

She thought of their time in bed together and the memories warmed her more than the blasting heater that he'd turned up to surface-of-the-sun hot. "I'm very aware of that fact, Ash."

"I'm possessive as fuck and jealous and—Goddammit." He pulled the truck to the side of the road, shoved it into park. He fanned his fingers into her hair and sealed his mouth to hers in a hard, breath-stealing kiss. It was urgent and hungry and demanding, and Rose melted into it, losing herself in the sweet taste of his desire, his tangy desperation, his bitter fear. He pulled her tightly to him as if he was afraid to let her go.

And, finally, for the first time since this nightmare started, she felt completely safe.

They broke apart, both gasping for air, and Ash rested his forehead against hers. "I don't know what I'd do if I lost you," he whispered, his voice rough with emotion.

"You won't lose me," she promised and stroked a hand over his beard. "Take me home and love me in your possessive, jealous, unsweet way."

He kissed her again, soft this time despite his claims that he wasn't gentle, then carefully set her back in the passenger seat. He shifted, adjusting the bulge at the front of his pants before pulling the truck back out onto the road.

"No."

She straightened. "Excuse me?"

"You heard me. You and Dante are both going to the hospital. No arguments," he added when she opened her mouth to do just that.

"I take it back. I might hate you again."

Ash's scowl twitched into a smile. "I'll risk your hatred if that's what it takes to get you checked by a doctor."

"Yep. Definitely hate you." She slumped in the seat and frowned until Dante poked his head forward and nuzzled her cheek with his wet nose. She gave him a pat. "Oh, not you, handsome. I could never hate you. You're the best doggie in the world, unlike your daddy, who is the absolute worst because he insists on being reasonable instead of taking me home and fucking me senseless. I hate him so much."

Ash's low laugh warmed her belly. "I hate you, too, Rose."

chapter
forty

THE NEXT WEEK was spent in a whirlwind of police interviews with every alphabet soup agency in the states and at least one from Canada.

Marcel had been busy in his off-time from the pub with everything from illegal gambling to drug smuggling.

Ash had dropped Dante at Sasha Scott's clinic to be treated for two gunshot wounds, then settled Rose in at the hospital to be treated for frostbite. As soon as he was certain she was safe and sound with all of Redwood Coast Rescue standing guard, he returned to the mountain. His deputies found Marcel's body at a cabin owned by GSN, dead from a self-inflicted gunshot to the head. That was the shot Rose had described hearing as she ran away. Marcel had known the jig was up and decided to end it.

Ash couldn't say he was sorry Marcel was dead, but he hated that the bastard had escaped justice.

Rainbow was another story. She wouldn't escape. She confessed to everything again at the station, on record, detailing how she'd killed her sister out of jealousy—though she still insisted it was out of love for Pete and Rose. But when

Ash pointed out the inconsistencies in her story, she changed her tune and started crying victim. It was all Marcel's plan from the beginning. He abused her. She was afraid of him and did what he wanted—including poisoning Rose as a teenager —out of fear for her own safety.

Whether or not that story would fly in court was anyone's guess.

The moment Cal Holden had her confession in hand, he worked his lawyer magic and within days, a judge overturned Pete's conviction and exonerated him of all crimes. After thirteen years behind bars, Pete Galasso was a free man.

As long as he lived, Ash would never forget the absolute joy on Rose's face as she flung herself into her father's arms with no glass or chains between them. Rose sobbed and hugged her dad like she never wanted to let him go. Pete cried, too. Even the judge looked misty-eyed. Ash, standing at the back of the courthouse, slipped outside before anyone could see his tears—but he wasn't stealthy enough.

Cal followed him out. "Do my eyes deceive me, or did the big, gruff sheriff shed a tear?"

Ash scowled at him. "Shouldn't you be inside celebrating with your client?"

"Not my win. I barely did anything." He lifted a shoulder and glanced back at the courtroom doors. "Besides, Pete and Rose deserve this time together."

Which was the exact same reason Ash had slipped away. His scowl only deepened. "You know, you make it very difficult to dislike you."

"What can I say? It's a superpower."

"I'll still try."

Cal's grin was quick and full of amusement. "Knock yourself out, big guy. I'll just make you like me more."

They walked outside together in silence, but then Cal

paused on the sidewalk and eyed the growing crowd of reporters gathering in the parking lot.

"Better go share the good news," Ash said and headed toward his Tahoe.

A faint line of worry formed between Cal's blond brows, and he caught Ash's arm. "Wait. That podcaster you sent to me—"

"You better not be about to thank me. She wasn't a gift. She was a means to an end."

"Oh, come on. Give me some credit. I don't fuck every woman I talk to." He dropped his hand from Ash's sleeve and looked at the reporters again. "I haven't heard from her."

Ash shrugged. "Sounds like she ghosted you. I get that must be a new experience, but I can assure you it happens to all of us mortal men at least once in our lives."

"Sarcasm doesn't suit you, Sheriff."

The guy was actually concerned. Ash saw it written all over his face, which had a little alarm bell dinging at the back of his mind. For all of Cal's faults, he wasn't usually an alarmist. If he was worried about Alexis Summers, he had a reason.

Ash fully faced him again. "When did you last speak to her?"

"Two days ago. I told her about Pete's hearing, and she wanted me to pull some strings, get her a seat in the courtroom despite the media ban. With Pete's permission, I pulled those strings, because I believe in what Alexis is trying to accomplish with her podcast. But she didn't show today. After the judge gave his ruling, I texted her the outcome." He held out his phone so Ash could see the red undeliverable bubble around the unsent text. "Her phone's not just off—it's been disconnected."

"So she forgot to pay her bill."

Cal arched a brow, his expression dubious. "You've met

the woman, right? She lives on her phone. That's not something she'd forget. Listen, I'm not telling you how to do your job, but I have an excellent nose for trouble, and something about this situation stinks."

"Alright, I'll put out an APB and have my guys check in with her contacts. Maybe she's just off the grid for a bit."

Cal nodded, but the tension in his shoulders didn't ease. "Thanks, Sheriff. I just... can't shake this bad feeling. Nothing short of an apocalypse-level disaster would've stopped her from being here."

"I'll look into it," Ash said and clapped Cal on the shoulder before continuing to his Tahoe.

As he drove away from the courthouse, he glanced in the rearview mirror, saw Cal still in the same spot, and a sense of unease settled over him.

Alexis Summers was a pain in the ass, but she didn't deserve to have something happen to her.

He'd told her not to go poking around. What if she'd found proof that the Shadow Stalker was more than an urban legend? What if she'd discovered something that made her the target of a serial killer?

Goddammit. Now he had to go through every case she'd researched with a fine-tooth comb. Even if just to make sure her disappearance wasn't somehow connected.

By the time he made it home, it was late. Much later than he'd anticipated. Dante was probably eating his remaining chairs.

Since Dante's wounds both proved not to be life-threatening, he'd been bringing the dog to work with him every day, but with the court hearing, he'd opted to leave Dante home today. As he pulled into his driveway, he promised himself he'd spend time with the dog tomorrow, come hell or high water. Dante deserved that much from him.

He gathered the box of old case files from his backseat and

made it halfway to his front door before his exhausted brain registered the person sitting there.

Rose.

"Jesus." He nearly fumbled the box in surprise. "Why aren't you with your dad?"

"I was, but he fell asleep on my couch. I think it's the first decent sleep he's had since Mom died, so I left him to it." She nodded to the box. "Another case?"

For some reason, the question strummed on his nerves. "Crime never stops."

"No, I guess it doesn't. So, what is it this time?"

Again, the question, and the tone she'd asked it in, needled him. Was she doing that on purpose? He ground his teeth. "The podcaster, Alexis Summers, has disappeared. Her family hasn't heard from her, and she's missed her last two check-ins with her boss at the network she works for. Her sister just flew in from New York to report her missing officially."

"I'm very sorry to hear that." She stood and brushed off the back of her jeans, then looked pointedly at his front door. "Are you going to invite me in? It's cold out here."

He frowned. "You should go home. Get some rest. You've had a long day. Spend time with your dad."

"I love Dad, and I can't even put into words how happy I am that he's free... but he's not the one I want to spend time with." She took the box from his arms and set it on the ground, then stepped forward and ran her hands up over his chest. "You've been using work to avoid me. Avoid this conversation."

His heart thumped and not just because of her hands creeping under his shirt, her fingers tracing the waistband of his jeans. She was right, and they both knew it. He'd been using work as a shield since he drove her off that mountainside a week ago. "I'm not avoiding it. I just thought—"

She pressed a finger to his lips. "Stop thinking." She

dragged that finger over his chin, down his neck, and flattened her hand over his heart. She had to feel it beating like a war drum, but gave no indication. "And just tell me what's in here. Do you want me?"

"I..."

"It's a simple question, Sheriff," she said, her voice low and husky. "You either want me, or you don't. You can't have half of me."

She'd given him that ultimatum once before, and they'd ended up fucking on the bar at the Mad Dog. The hot memory tightened his stomach and his cock stirred.

"You know I want you, but we can't... You shouldn't want..." His thoughts splintered as her fingers dipped inside the front of his jeans and brushed lightly over his lengthening erection. "Aw, fuck." He caught her hand before he lost all reason and moistened his suddenly dry lips. "Rose, it's more complicated for us than—"

"Complicated?" She scoffed and removed her hand from his pants, which allowed him to suck in a full breath again. The oxygen helped restart his stuttering brain, and he extracted himself from her embrace, stepping back from her reach.

"You know it is. There's a large age gap between us. A lot of bad history and, recently, nothing but danger and trauma. The way you feel now could just be a product of that. We need to slow it down and—"

Her eyes flashed with indignation. "That's such a cop-out, Ash."

He spread his hands in a helpless gesture. "I'm just trying to be reasonable here."

"Well, I don't do reasonable. I don't do slow." She poked his chest. "With me, either you're all in, or you're not. And if you're not, then you need to let me go."

Fuck no.

The thought was immediate and visceral. The mere idea of letting her go, letting some other man have her, twisted his stomach and made him physically ill.

And, he realized, that should tell him everything he needed to know about his feelings for her. They weren't reasonable, and he didn't care.

Ash's jaw tightened, and he stepped closer to her, crowding into her space, snaking a hand around her waist and dragging her against him until their bodies melded from chest to knee.

"I'm all in, Rose. Every damn part of me. I can't let you go because I'd lose my fucking mind and shoot any other man who touched you like I want to right now."

She gasped softly and pressed against him. "Then show me."

He cupped the back of her head and brought his lips down on hers. It wasn't a gentle kiss, but a mashing of lips and teeth and tongues. It was a brand. A claim.

Her hands went to the front of his jeans, and she gave a quick tug, snapping the button free. Before he could react, she'd pulled down the zipper and slipped her hand inside. Her fingers closed around him, tight and hot, and he groaned as she began to stroke him, slow and steady.

He slipped his hand down the back of her jeans, under her panties, and cupped her ass. His fingers found her, and she was already wet.

"Inside. Now." He stepped back out of her reach and lifted her until she had no choice but to circle his hips with her legs. He carried her toward the front door and fumbled with the key when she bit his earlobe. She laughed against his neck.

Swearing under his breath, he tried to shove the key into the lock again with a trembling hand and finally got it in, twisting it hard enough to bend the metal. He all but kicked the door open, carried her inside, and turned, pinning her against the door as it closed. The need was clawing at him now. His skin was on fire.

She was laughing, gasping, as he pulled her shirt over her head and dropped it to the floor. He kissed her again, but then he needed to see her, needed to be sure she was here and whole. It was all he'd wanted to do this entire week, all he'd denied himself because he was so damn scared her feelings would fade with the adrenaline of the last few weeks. He couldn't lose her, so he'd convinced himself it was easier if he kept his shields up and didn't let her any closer.

Of course, this was Rose. His strong, fierce, sharp-tongued Ambrosia. She wasn't going to let him hide behind those shields, and he loved her for it.

Jesus, he loved her.

He dragged his mouth down the column of her throat, over the curve of her shoulder and past the edge of her bra.

Rose gasped again and her head fell back against the door as her fingers fisted in his hair. She pulled him tighter against her and he obliged, latching onto her nipple through the lace. He rolled it in his mouth until she moaned and arched against him.

He reached back and undid her bra, freeing her gorgeous breasts, then bent to take the hardened nub of her nipple into his mouth again. Her fingers tightened in his hair, her nails digging into his scalp.

He couldn't get enough of her. His hands were everywhere, sliding to her hips, then her thighs, pushing her jeans down so he could get to her panties. He was frantic, his hands shaking as he skimmed the material off her legs.

She gasped when he pressed his face against her cleft, inhaling deeply. He parted her with his fingers and pushed his tongue inside, groaning at the sweet taste of her.

"Ash, please." She tangled her fingers in his hair, drawing him closer.

He slid his tongue down her seam, then pushed it inside her. So sweet and wet. Her juices dripped down his chin while she made little mewling sounds that prickled over his skin like a caress. He slid two fingers inside her and thrust in and out, matching the rhythm of his tongue against her clit.

She threw her head back, and her body bowed toward him. "Oh, God, it's so good."

He was relentless, kissing, licking, sucking until her knees buckled. He grabbed her ass, and her fingers were still tangled in his hair, holding him against her. She was moaning, begging, pleading, and he was ready to give her anything she wanted.

Anything she needed.

He sucked her clit hard between his lips and she came with a sharp cry, her nails digging into his scalp and her hips jerking against his mouth. He held her there at the peak, prolonging her pleasure until she was gasping for air. He loved making her come. Wanted to make her come over and over again until she couldn't walk out of this house.

As she eased down from the orgasm, he stroked her thighs with his hands and lapped gently at her slit with his tongue, soothing her.

"Please, Ash." Her voice came out soft and breathy. "I need you inside me."

He needed it, too, more than he needed his next breath. He dragged his mouth up her body, detouring to trace the rose tattoo on her ribs with his tongue, then he took her other nipple between his lips and sucked just as he had with the first.

She arched into him, her hand flitting down his abs to his zipper and yanking it down with a rough jerk. "Your clothes. Take them off."

He shoved his jeans down to his thighs, then stood back to watch as she kicked her panties and jeans the rest of the way off. She was totally naked and the most beautiful woman he'd ever seen. He stepped closer, backing her against the door once again, and she reached for him, locking her arms around his neck.

She tugged at his lower lip with her teeth. "I love you."

His heart stopped for a second. It wasn't the first time she'd said the words, but it was the first time he'd really heard them. The first time he really believed them. They sank into him and lit up every dark corner of his soul. He'd never loved anyone—at least, never like this. It was deep and fierce and burned him from the inside out.

He said nothing—couldn't form words around the knot in his throat—so he caught her hips and lifted her onto his aching cock. He'd just have to show her how he felt with his body.

Rose cried out, her head falling back against the door. Her inner muscles clenched him like a fist.

So fucking hot.

He lifted her and pulled out, dragging his tip over her sensitive clit. She whimpered and lowered her head to watch the joining of their bodies. Once he was fully seated in her again, he raised her chin with a hooked finger and claimed her mouth. He was starving for her—for her taste, her scent, her skin.

All of her.

He began to move. She was tight, so tight, and she fit him perfectly. He couldn't get deep enough, couldn't be close enough. She clawed at his shoulders and cried out as he thrust into her harder, again and again.

"You're mine, Ambrosia." His voice was a near growl. "Mine. No one else's. Say it."

"Yours." She arched her back and circled her hips, her fingernails digging into his shoulders. "Only yours."

"Mine," he repeated, and he meant it in a way he'd never meant anything before. "Only mine, because I love you and I'm not letting you go. I fucking love you."

"Ash," she gasped, and he felt her walls clench around him. "Oh, God, Ash. I'm coming again."

"Yes." He slid his hand between them and found her clit, rubbing it with his thumb until a shudder rattled through her. "Come for me, my love. Come hard."

He took her mouth, kissing her fiercely, swallowing her scream as her muscles rippled around him and sucked his own orgasm from him. He thrust into her one last time, burying himself as deep as he could, and let go.

As her orgasm faded, he pulled out and lifted her from the door, then carried her through the silent house. Dante lifted his head, and if dogs could scowl, he would absolutely be scowling now.

Hang on, Ash mentally told the dog as he carried Rose down the hall to his room and laid her on the bed. She was breathing hard, her chest rising and falling. Her cheeks were flushed, and her eyes glittered.

He leaned over and kissed her forehead. "I have to let the dog out. Don't go anywhere."

She sighed and stretched. "Wasn't planning on it. Even if my legs weren't noodles right now, you're stuck with me." She tilted her head to the side and gave him a look he could only describe as sly. "After all, haven't you heard the news?"

He frowned. "What news?"

She laughed, and he stepped back to eye her suspiciously because that was a scheming kind of laugh. "Rose... what did you do?"

"I didn't do anything, I swear. But you should really try to be more in the know, Sheriff. Maybe start hanging out at the pub more often. You'll hear all the juicy gossip then."

He shook his head. He was still fuzzy from the mind-shattering orgasm and his brain wasn't keeping up. "What are you talking about?"

She blinked innocently. "Why, Sheriff, I'm talking about your fiancée."

The air left his lungs in a whoosh. "I don't have a fiancée."

"Well, according to the town grapevine, Ash Rawlings and Rose Galasso just got engaged." Her tone was mockingly serious as that damn smirk played on her lips. "Congratulations to us."

He shook his head again.

Opened his mouth.

Closed it.

Opened.

Closed.

"The look on your face." Rose fell back against the pillows, laughing so hard she wheezed, and tears leaked from her eyes. "It's like you're... you're..." She couldn't seem to come up with the right word.

"Chewing glass?" he suggested and felt the corner of his lip twitch with a smile.

"Yes. That's exactly it."

"Jesus." He walked from the room and called to the dog, letting Dante out into the backyard to do his business.

Ash waited and stared out over the yard. Beyond his property line, down in the valley below, Steam Valley twinkled in the moonlight.

That fucking town with its busybodies and gossip mongers. Now he'd have to go back to work tomorrow and correct everyone. Because no doubt the entire town was already buzzing with the rumor.

Unless you don't correct them...

No. That was ridiculous.

He'd bet his badge the rumor started with Janine, his secretary. The woman was scarily efficient, but she was also a hopeless gossip. And if there wasn't any juicy gossip to spread, she was not above creating some.

Fuck.

She must have overheard Anna telling him it was okay if—

Dante woofed. He had already trotted back inside and now sat in the kitchen, eyeing Ash like he was crazy for standing naked in the cold.

Ash pulled the door shut and looked down at the dog for a long moment, considering. "Anna did say it was okay."

Dante cocked his head.

"Do you think she'd say yes?"

Dante turned his head in the other direction, his ears perked.

Ash strode to the coat closet in his foyer and eased open the door, tugging on the string to turn on the overhead bulb. The bankers box on the top shelf was all he and Anna had left of their parents after the wildfire destroyed their family farmhouse last fall. A handful of photos, some old ranch documents, Dad's favorite 49ers ball cap, and...

He pulled out the ring box. The blue velvet had worn thin over the generations. He flipped it open and stared down at the engagement ring—rose gold with diamonds and pearls clustered around a central garnet. It was old, but still glittered and sparked, even under the weak light of the closet. It had belonged to his paternal grandmother before Dad gave it to Mom. And before that, his paternal great-grandmother had worn it. He didn't know how far back it went, or when the first Rawlings man gave it to the woman he loved.

He closed the box and looked at Dante, who had followed him to the foyer. "Anna gave her approval."

Dante pushed his nose against Ash's hand—the one holding the box—as if saying, "Go for it."

Ash shut off the closet light and closed the door.

Then, ring box in hand, he walked back to the bedroom to continue the long-held Rawlings tradition, giving the ring to the woman he loved.

epilogue

ALEXIS SUMMERS HAD NEVER BEEN SO cold in her life.

The man—no, he wasn't a man. Monster. Demon. Evil incarnate—had snatched her in broad daylight as she climbed out of her car at her hotel. She didn't know how many days ago. She'd initially tried to keep a tally, using the clock on her fitness tracker to scratch the days into the wall, but the tracker had died, and her concrete prison didn't have windows to give her any indication whether it was night or day. So she sat there in the cold, damp dark of her cell, shivering uncontrollably, wishing she had never come to this godforsaken corner of the world.

God, she'd been so stupid.

So smug.

Thinking she was so smart.

Thinking she was invincible because her honey-blond hair and public persona meant she wasn't the Shadow Stalker's type.

But she was wrong.

Oh, so wrong.

He didn't have a type.

And he didn't have a soul.
Because he wasn't human.

In shadows so deep, the Stalker hides.
Fear his presence, where moonlight dies.

Alexis had always thought of herself as a strong and independent woman, but that was before she had been taken by this monster. He had beaten her, tortured her, and violated her in ways she couldn't even bring herself to think about. She was a broken shell of her former self, with no hope and no way out. She didn't even have the energy to cry anymore, and just passed the hours numbly, gazing into the darkness, wishing it would swallow her up.

For the first few days of her captivity, as the cold first settled into her bones and made her ache all over, she tried to conjure up memories of warmth and light to keep her spirits up. She thought of the cozy fireplace in her childhood home, the hot summer sun on her skin during beach vacations, the warm embrace of her sister. But she could never hold onto the memories long, each thought quickly replaced by the reality of her situation.

Beware his bunker, hidden and dark,
Where he preys on souls, leaving his mark.

The Stalker came to visit her every day. He never spoke, and always wore a balaclava, never showing his face.

But his eyes...

She'd see his eyes every time she closed hers for the rest of her life. Those cold, black eyes always watched her with feverish intensity as he violated her.

Again and again and again.

Alexis tried to fight him at first, but he was too strong.

Then she tried to avoid him, huddling in the corner of her cell whenever he came near. It never worked. He always got what he wanted. And soon, he'd want her dead just like Maria Socktish and the thirty-two other woman he'd destroyed.

It was only a matter of time before she became his next victim.

On the last day, after The Stalker finished with her, he left her cell unlocked, the door hanging open. She could see a hallway beyond, and dust floating in the faint orange rays of a setting sun. She didn't move, didn't dare to hope that he was letting her go.

It was a trap.

A trick.

He had to be out there, waiting to punish her if she tried to leave.

Footsteps echoed down the corridor and her heart began to race. She thought she could see a shadow moving through the darkness, skirting around the dusty light beams. Fear gripped her chest, and she began to shiver again, her breath coming in short, sharp gasps.

The Stalker stepped into view. He was carrying a hunting rifle on his shoulder and threw a small bundle into her cell. It landed with a loud thunk. She cowered back.

"Dress."

She blinked at him. It was the first word he'd ever said to her. She edged closer to the bundle and realized it was a winter coat, snow overalls, and boots. She didn't even care that they were bloodstained and scrambled into them, wrapping the coat tightly around her shoulders.

The Stalker stepped back from the door and held out an arm, inviting her into the hall.

And, suddenly, the rest of the nursery rhyme came back to her with startling clarity:

In woods so still, his hunt begins,
Fear his presence, where moonlight thins.
One by one, his tally grows,
For in the shadows, his secret shows.

She backed into the wall. "No. Please..."
He raised the gun and pointed it at her head. "Run."

Will Alexis become the subject of her own podcast?

Find out in the next Redwood Coast Rescue book,
SEARCHING FOR REDEMPTION.

also by tonya burrows

Redwood Coast Rescue

Searching for Rescue

Searching for Risk

Northern Rescue

Northern Escape

Northern Deception

Northern Salvation

HORNET

SEAL of Honor

Honor Reclaimed

Broken Honor

Code of Honor

Reckless Honor

Honor Avenged

HORNET: Class Alpha

Fragmented Loyalty

Wilde Security

Wilde Nights in Paradise

Wilde for Her

Wilde at Heart

Running Wilde

Too Wilde to Tame